"Why?" The husky vibration rattled along her spine, spreading warm fingers up her neck, and puddling somewhere near the base of her brain.

"Because . . . This is just a game to you. I've played enough in my lifetime to know the difference."

He straightened away from her, pulled the towel from around his neck, and rubbed his hair for a good long stretch.

When he was finally through, he said, "I have to think about what you're asking. I've never had that kind of relationship, you know?"

Amanda sucked in a breath. What was he talking about now? Did he think she'd been asking him to make a commitment of some sort?

"What . . . What?" She was inarticulate again.

"You want me to be your man. Yours exclusively?"

Amanda was almost wild with desperation. "No . . . No, that's not what I meant at all. I was saying that . . . That this . . . This thing between us is not serious. So to talk of love and that sort of thing is crazy. I mean especially since it's all fake anyway."

He took her hand and pressed her palm to his chest. "Feel." The thudding was so intense that the vibrations sent a ripple of tremors through her.

"Is that real?" he asked.

She sucked in her bottom lip, then let it back out. "It's just biology."

He leaned down to kiss her softly on the mouth. "And this?"

Tears of need pricked the backs of her eyes. "Chemistry," she muttered and stood on tiptoe to kiss his mouth again.

BOOK YOUR PLACE ON OUR WEBSITE AND MAKE THE READING CONNECTION!

We've created a customized website just for our very special readers, where you can get the inside scoop on everything that's going on with Zebra, Pinnacle and Kensington books.

When you come online, you'll have the exciting opportunity to:

- View covers of upcoming books
- Read sample chapters
- Learn about our future publishing schedule (listed by publication month *and author*)
- Find out when your favorite authors will be visiting a city near you
- Search for and order backlist books from our online catalog
- Check out author bios and background information
- Send e-mail to your favorite authors
- Meet the Kensington staff online
- Join us in weekly chats with authors, readers and other guests
- Get writing guidelines
- AND MUCH MORE!

**Visit our website at
http://www.zebrabooks.com**

SWEET TEMPTATION

NIQUI STANHOPE

ARABESQUE
★BET
BOOKS

BET Publications, LLC
http://www.bet.com

ARABESQUE BOOKS are published by

BET Publications, LLC
c/o BET BOOKS
One BET Plaza
1900 W Place NE
Washington, DC 20018-1211

All Kensington Titles, Imprints, and Distributed Lines are available at special quantity discounts for bulk purchases for sales promotion, premiums, fund-raising, and educational or institutional use. Special book excerpts or customized printings can also be created to fit specific needs. For details, write or phone the office of the Kensington special sales manager: Kensington Publishing Corp., 850 Third Avenue, New York, NY 10022, attn: Special Sales Department, Phone: 1-800-221-2647.

First Printing: November 2001
10 9 8 7 6 5 4 3 2 1

Printed in the United States of America

To my parents and to my brothers, who are the real Champagne men. Also for Allison, Holly, Linda, and Mayleen. Thanks for being such great friends! Especially for my niece Abina. Your enthusiastic reading and suggestions helped make this book. Special thanks to Jim Brickman. Your beautiful music helped me write this book.

Dear Readers:

Nicholas Champagne invites you to the wedding of his brother Gavin Pagne. It's taken him four long years to get Gavin and Summer together, and now that he's finally done it, he intends to see them married in a lavish and elegant ceremony on the island of Jamaica. So sit back, if you will, and enjoy the extravagant nuptials, for Gavin and Summer also have a surprise or two in store for Nicholas. . . .

Enjoy!

Niqui Stanhope

PROLOGUE

Ocho Rios, Jamaica

Nicholas Champagne hid the bunch of speckled red roses behind him before lifting a hand to knock on the closed door.

"Summer? It's Nick."

He had raised his hand to knock again when the door sprang back and he found himself looking into a pair of dancing golden eyes. Nicholas grinned down at her. She was simply stunning. Her hair was swept into a sleek chignon atop her head, and tiny jet-black ringlets fell softly to her shoulders, forming a silken cloud around the diamond-studded tiara perched neatly on her head. Her gown—another matter entirely—was the kind of dress that would surely send his brother's blood pressure through the roof. It was a wonderful blend of silk and satin; a beautiful tapestry of lace and fine baby pearls that wrapped itself around her in the most incredible way. True, it had cost a hefty sum, but it was his special gift to his brother.

Summer twirled before him now, her eyes brimming with laughter.

"Well . . .aren't you going to say something? What do you think? Will Gavin like it?"

Nicholas nodded. "This is it. This is definitely it. Turn again for me?" And she obliged him, spinning so that the hemline of the dress danced around her.

"You'd better remember to name your firstborn after me, my girl," he said. Then, as if as an afterthought, he removed the bouquet of roses from behind him. "These are for you too."

Summer accepted the scarlet blossoms with trembling fingers. She thanked him, her voice thick and scratchy, all the while promising herself that she would not cry. She would not. Nicky Champagne was a wonder, an absolute darling of a man. Second only to her fiancé, Gavin, of course. Had she been blessed with a brother, she would have wanted him to be exactly like the man standing before her. From the first moment they met, they had gotten along famously. He had been her champion. Her partner-in-crime, and now, he would be her brother-in-law.

Summer took a deep breath. "Nicky, don't you dare make me cry. Not now."

Nicholas pinched the side of her cheek. "Not ever." He stepped into the spacious hotel suite, closed the door behind him, and asked with a devilish lift of his brow:"

"So, are you ready for this?"

Not surprisingly, that very question was being asked of Gavin Pagne on the opposite end of the same hotel. He stood before a long mirror, in shirt-sleeves and pants, his fingers fumbling valiantly at his neckline as he somehow managed to twist the black bow tie about his neck into the most horrible mess. He swore thickly beneath his breath for the umpteenth time, and grunted at Harry Britton.

"No, I am not ready. Can anyone tell me what in

the name of heaven is the matter with this blasted necktie?"

He ripped it from his neck yet again, and glared at Harry. "Where is Nicholas?"

Harry did his utmost to maintain an appropriately serious countenance.

"Gone over to see Summer," he said with glinting eyes. "Mr. Stevens is on his way up, too, by the way. I think he intends to have the talk with you."

Gavin turned from the mirror for a moment. "The talk?"

Harry nodded. "You know. *The* . . . talk."

"Good God Almighty, that's all I need right now. Stall him for a few minutes while I sort out this"— and he gestured at the crumpled tie on the bed— "this . . . confusion of cloth."

Harry chuckled softly as he closed the door and left Gavin Pagne to wage his dubious battle. *Weddings*—thank God he would never be faced with a similar situation. Both he and Nick Champagne had vowed years before never to cross that particular bridge. They were both unapologetic bachelors, and neither one had any intention of ever changing that.

"Young man."

Harry turned to face the older man who now approached. There was a look of purpose about him, which reminded Harry quite a bit of his own dear father, who was, even now, probably knee-deep in some political skirmish in Guyana.

"Yes, sir?"

"Where is my future son-in-law? I would like a word with him."

Harry took a breath, and lied. "Actually, sir . . ."

And his brain flashed like lightning through the possibilities. "Gavin is . . .still in the shower, I believe."

Henry Stevens nodded. "I'll wait."

Harry gestured to another door a short distance down the corridor. "In here, if you'd like. Mik and Rob should be almost dressed and ready."

Harry waited for Henry Stevens to catch up before setting off for the suite at the other end of the corridor. Silence stretched between them as they walked, and Harry racked his brains for something to say.

"You know," he finally said, "Gavin is one of the best guys around. He raised Nicholas, Mik, and Rob singlehandedly, and built Champagne Industries into the giant it is today."

Henry Stevens gave a nod of approval. He knew all about Gavin Pagne. Summer had been singing his praises quite consistently for the past four years. After meeting him, Henry had to admit that he was quite an impressive man. A very impressive man. Still, it was hard for a father to give up his only daughter. He had always known that one day she would marry, and start a family of her own, but how was it that the years had passed so very quickly? Wasn't it just yesterday that he had walked her so very carefully to school? Stood at the gate and waved to her until she was in the building? And what about when she had fallen and bruised a knee? Wasn't it he whom she had come to? He had dried her tears, made everything better. Now, someone else would do that. It was hard for a father to see his daughter married. He was happy, but he was sad, too. But it was good sorrow. When he and her mother were gone, Summer would have someone there who would always take care of her. He recognized strength of character when he saw it. And Gavin Pagne had that certain quality about him that great men carried with ease. It was a depth of spirit, an intangible generosity that was completely impossible to define.

The door ahead of them was thrown open suddenly, and a tall, curly-haired teenager on the verge of adulthood appeared.

"Harry . . . where de rass is that Nicky?" The words were out and hanging there in the air before the boy could properly restrain himself.

"Watch your language, bwoy." Harry grinned, responding in the Jamaican patois that was second nature to him.

Rob's eyes glinted with suppressed humor. Harry was Guyanese, and it was always amusing to hear him speak Jamaican patois.

"Sorry, sir," Rob said to Mr. Stevens, "but we have a situation here."

Sounds of struggle, accompanied by glass-breaking shrieks, were now clearly audible.

"What's . . . ? Harry began; then the realization settled over him. "Amber."

Rob nodded. "Amber. She says she wants to go naked."

"Oh, God," Harry said. He was definitely not up to doing battle with a headstrong four-year-old. His sister Alana would know what to do. She had two very strong-willed toddlers of her own, but she was now over at the ceremonial cake house with the mother of the bride and the other bridesmaids. How in the name of heaven did you get a child into a long and very intricate gown that she didn't want to wear, without rending the entire thing to shreds?

As they entered, they could hear Mik's pleading voice.

"Come on, sweetheart . . . just one arm . . . don't you want to look pretty today?" The question was almost drowned out by a volley of screeches that left no doubt as to the child's feelings on the matter.

Mik looked up. "This is useless. We'll have to get Gavin in here."

Henry Stevens took the gown from Mik, and gave him a little pat on the shoulder. "Let me have a try."

He perched himself on one of the long couches in the suite. "Come here, little girl." The four-year-old blinked at him, took a huge breath, and then hollered for all she was worth.

Henry Stevens raised a finger. "Stop that noise right now," he said in a tone of voice that brooked no argument. For a moment, memory of another time, another little girl flashed before his eyes. His first daughter, Catherine, had been quite a handful, too. But she had mellowed with age, and had become a very sweet-tempered girl. It was funny how he still missed her, after all these years. She would've been a grown-up young lady now, had she lived; had she not been abducted. Hazy reflection clouded his eyes. Weddings always brought back memories; Memories that were better off dead and gone.

His vision cleared slowly and he refocused on the little girl. She had paused in mid-bellow, and was now giving him a very dubious look.

"I'm not going to give in, so you'd better let me put on the dress," he said. Amber eyed the stern-looking man seated before her with the beginnings of a reluctant respect. Only Uncle Gavin spoke to her in this manner. But this was not Uncle Gavin.

"Don't want to wear it," she said, stomping her little foot.

Henry Stevens leaned forward. "Well, you're going to, little girl. Lift your arms." He held the dress above her head, and obligingly, one little arm went up.

"Both of them."

Within seconds the dress was on, and the screaming session was officially over. Harry scraped a hand through his hair. "I am never having kids."

Henry Stevens chuckled. "You've just got to know how to talk to them. Children respond very well once they understand who's in charge."

"Who's in charge?" a deep male voice asked from somewhere near the door.

"Dada," the little girl shrieked, as she sped across the room to be scooped into Nicholas's arms. He held her aloft for a moment, taking great care not to muss her shimmering turquoise gown. Then he kissed her soundly on both cheeks, and put her down to stand before him.

"How pretty you look," he said. And his comment produced a chubby-cheeked smile that was the feminine equivalent of his own.

"You wouldn't believe the racket she was making just a few seconds ago," Harry said. "Your daughter definitely has a mind of her own."

Nicholas came fully into the room. "She is a Champagne."

"Well," Henry Stevens said, standing, "I want to say a few words to the bridegroom before the ceremony . . . and I guess you men would like to finish dressing. How's Summer doing?" he asked, turning in the doorway.

Nicholas smiled. "A bit teary-eyed, but she'll be fine."

ONE

It was the middle of May, and the skies were a smooth azure blue. It was a beautiful day for a wedding. Soft white clouds scudded slowly by, caught up in some graceful cosmic dance as old as time itself. A fragrant breeze rolled softly in off the ocean, stirring the coconut palms to a chorus of gentle whispering. There was an infinite peace about, a soul-stirring quiet. It was almost as though God in his heaven had decreed that this day be perfect, and it was so.

Into this great magnificence came the procession of the cakes. The bridesmaids—Alana, Racquel, Morganna, Christine, Mayleen, and Neisha—walked gracefully, in perfect harmony, perfect synch, hips swaying, cakes balanced on silver trays atop their heads, as demanded by Jamaican tradition. They were gorgeous in their gauzy turquoise finery, and it was a spectacular procession. Everyone knew what it meant, too. Someone was to be married. So the children ran behind, taking great care not to get in the way as the women wound their way across the expansive property.

From a distant window, four pairs of eyes watched. Nicholas was the first to break the silence. He noticed the emotion in his big brother's eyes, and knew instinctively that Gavin needed him to say something, anything to fill the silence.

"I wonder if Summer will see this on her end of the hotel."

Gavin turned from the window, and his eyes locked with those of his younger brother. "Thank you," he said, and his voice was thick, husky. "She is everything I've needed for so long and thought I would never find."

Nicholas shook his head, a suggestion of tears in his eyes. "We love you," he said. "Thank *you* for putting your life on hold and for taking care of us"—his voice broke—"all these many years. You took us from the streets of L.A. and brought us here to a new life. You've been like our father, our brother, our friend."

Gavin swallowed hard as he looked from one to the next. *His boys.* They were all of a similar height now, but Nicholas, at six feet three, was the tallest, and without question, the best-looking. Four years before, he had been merely handsome. Now, he was a darkly beautiful Adonis with curly black hair that had a tendency to hang low at the collar, and an athletic body that had filled out in a manner that was completely pleasing to the female eye. Long gone was the skinny angularity of young adulthood. He was now a powerfully built man who attracted women in droves.

And, Mik, his youngest brother, how wonderfully he had grown. He carried the mantle of blossoming maturity so very well. In just a year he would be a fully qualified physician. Not his kid brother anymore. And his cousin Rob, whom he had raised from the time he was a babe in swaddling clothes—although still a work in progress, the boy was very much on his way. Time had passed so very quickly. But they were all grown now. An entire generation of Champagne men had made it.

Gavin cleared his throat once, then again. "Nicky . . . you, Mik, Rob—you're my life. I'm so proud of the men you've all become." And his characteristically strong voice became a whisper. Without regard to masculine reserve, Nicholas, Mik, and Rob embraced him. They stood with their arms wrapped about one another until there was a knock at the door. Harry Britton, Damian Collins, and Sean Kirkpatrick entered.

"What is this? What is this?" Harry said, his eyes flicking over the huddled men. "Something's going on. . . . I can tell."

Damian grinned. "Please don't tell us the wedding's off, Gavin. Alana will kill you."

Sean nodded. "And Summer will finish off any pieces of you left over."

Gavin gave a hoarse chuckle. "They would. There'd be a price on my head, that's for sure."

Harry wrapped an arm about Gavin's shoulders, and coaxed in a stage whisper, "You know, there's still time to change your mind about this marriage thing. We could smuggle you off to Guyana. Hide you . . . maybe somewhere deep in the Essequibo territory. What do you say? Want to make a run for it?"

The suggestion caused a great chorus of guffaws all around. "You'll be the next one to go down, Harry," Nicholas said, slapping his friend on the back.

Harry's eyebrows lifted. "Care to make a little wager on that?"

"I'll get in on that action," Damian said as he fished around in his pocket for his wallet. "Alana

would love to see her baby brother married off."
And he pantomimed a noose being tightened about
his neck.

Mik slapped his wager on the shiny surface of the
center table. "I'm going to have to go with Nicky,"
he said.

Rob pumped a fist in the air and chanted:
"Nicky . . . Nicky." Laughter filled the suite. Soon
there were dollar bills in every hand as outrageous
wagers were made against Harry Britton.

Harry nodded. "Uhm-hmm. OK . . . OK . . . it's
like that?"

Nicholas grinned. "That's the way it is, my friend.
You know you can't beat me in a fair fight."

Harry slung an arm about Nicholas's shoulders
and exchanged a sly look with Gavin. "As they say,
there's always a first time."

An hour later, the groomsmen, dressed in tailored
black tuxedos with elegant tails, stood on the stairs
outside the lovely old church. Despite its massive
size, the rangy wooden structure still somehow managed to retain its quaint Old World charm. The
stained-glass windows had been polished to sparkling just a day before. And garlands of white hibis-
cuses with white rose centers snaked around the
metal banisters leading up to the grand double
doors. In the background, the foaming blue of the
Caribbean Sea was so sharp that it almost hurt the
eyes to gaze upon its smooth undulating beauty.

Inside, the vaulted ceilings, with their intricately
carved artistry, soared to dizzying heights, making
the tiny flickering tea candles, which covered almost
every available surface except the center aisle, appear even more like clusters of delicate fireflies.

Several hundred guests now waited, and in the very first row, dressed nicely in a sedate but tastefully selected gown of blue organza, was Ester Champagne, the woman who had borne, but not raised, Gavin, Mik, and Nicholas. She sat primly with her legs crossed and hands nicely folded in her lap. Beside her, also dressed appropriately for the occasion, was her nurse, Mrs. Robbins, a very capable woman, well experienced in the care of psychiatric patients.

Ester Champagne was not violent by any means, but she had the unfortunate habit of saying and doing the most wildly inappropriate things at the worst possible times. So, given the importance of the occasion, Gavin had requested that the nurse sit beside his mother in the event such an impulse came upon her during the ceremony. But, to Mrs. Robbins's relief, thus far, her charge seemed happy enough to sit and observe the proceedings as they unfolded, asking only an occasional question. Ester appeared neither especially excited nor upset, just generally interested in the day's happenings.

"When will it begin?" she asked now, sliding a sidelong glance at the nurse.

Mrs. Robbins picked up the cream-colored program with the nicely twisted gold tassel, and thumbed down to the appropriate point. "Soon," she promised. "It'll be the caroling of the bells first; then the groomsmen will come in. Then Gavin."

Ester nodded her approval, and then inquired, "Just how ugly is the girl he's marrying?"

Mrs. Robbins took a steadying breath. Things had been going so very well. "Summer's not ugly at all. Don't you remember her? She's the very talented young lady who designed the interior of your cottage on the beach."

"Yes." Ester nodded. "The girl with the yellow

cat eyes. I'm saying it again, and I don't care who gets upset by it, but, . . . there's something wrong with that girl. Last week she tried to poison me with a dish of egg custard. It was truly the worst thing I have ever tasted."

"I'm sure Summer was only trying to be friendly to you," Mrs. Robbins said with great patience.

Ester snorted loudly, causing a few heads to turn in her direction. "You didn't taste that mush she made. You weren't forced to spend several hours in the bathroom."

Mrs. Robbins lowered her voice. "Would you like to take your medication a bit early today, Ester?" She felt around in her bag. "I've the pretty pink pills you like."

Ester shook her head resolutely. "No pills. Not now."

They were saved from further discussion of the matter by the melodious pealing of a succession of silvery-sounding chimes that seemed to whisper and sing in the same breath. The bells filled the air so suddenly, so sweetly, that the entire gathering was instantly hushed. Then came the deeper chimes, in a seamless blend with the lighter tones, pealing brightly and filling the church with a tapestry of wondrous sound.

On perfect cue, the church doors opened, admitting a procession of smartly tuxedoed pageboys. They walked in a slow, very exact formation, tossing red and white rose petals before them as they went. A few paces behind were the flower girls, dressed in flowing gowns of pink and white. Each little girl carried a bouquet of white roses, with a solitary red rose in the center.

The pageboys paused halfway to the altar, stood motionless as each little girl gave her bouquet to a family member strategically placed at the lip of each pew. Then, with rehearsed perfection, the girls glided to their partners, and together each couple continued to the altar.

Ester Champagne pressed both hands to her lips, then whispered to her nurse, "Oh, they're darling . . . just darling. Look at them. Have you ever seen anything like it?" Mrs. Robbins, who had been thinking the exact thing, nodded and shushed her patient at the same time.

The chiming of the bells had changed now. The ringing was more urgent, more clamorous. The bells no longer whispered and sang; they demanded everyone's attention for miles around. And the people came. It did not matter that they had not received a personal invitation; Gavin had announced that anyone who cared to attend was welcome at his nuptials. The winding road leading to the church was now lined on both sides with a crush of people, each person strained this way and that, hoping to be the first to see the bride all decked out in her wedding finery.

In the bride's suite, just two miles away, Mavis Stevens adjusted the intricate headdress atop her daughter's head. She straightened the long lacy back, and then reached around to fluff the veil. When she was satisfied that everything was just so, she stepped back a pace to admire. Her daughter was an absolute wonder, she admitted. So perfectly shaped, so tall and slim. She had grown into a stunning yet completely good-hearted woman, and it made Mavis proud, so very, very proud to look at her now. Tears pooled in her eyes, and Mavis Stevens grabbed for a tissue.

Summer peered at her mother through the

gauze. "Mom . . . you crying?" And she fiddled with the front of the veil in a futile attempt to lift it.

Her mother sniffled bravely, then ordered in a voice that made Summer's hands fall away immediately, "Don't touch that veil . . . don't touch *that.*"

"But you're crying." In all of her years, Summer had never seen her mother in tears.

"I'm fine. Just fine. I was remembering you as a little girl. You were such a sweet little thing. How did you grow up so quickly? It seems like only yesterday, only yesterday. Now, you're getting married. You're to have a husband of your own. A family."

Her mother gripped her hands and held them tightly for a minute. "You've chosen well, Summer. Gavin . . . I like him very much. He's a good man, and you will have a happy life with him."

Summer felt the tears coming on, and she struggled to hold them back. Her face would be an absolute mess long before she got to the church, if she didn't get a grip on herself.

"Thank you, Mom, for saying that," she whispered in a scratchy voice. "I'm glad you approve of him. That means more to me than you'll ever know."

The suite door opened, interrupting her mother's reply, and Henry Stevens poked his head in. "OK. I've given you two enough time alone. It's time to go. Do you hear those bells?"

Mavis Stevens blew her nose heartily. "Come on, Summer," she said. "You've a man to marry."

TWO

Nicholas adjusted his brother's tie, then brushed a speck of imaginary lint from his superbly tailored tuxedo.

"You're ready," he said.

Gavin took a long, deep breath. "Think she'll show up?"

Nicholas chuckled. "Our Summer? Who are you kidding?"

Gavin smiled. He knew that to be true. Summer Stevens had made it abundantly clear to him, almost from the very start, that his days as a carefree bachelor were numbered. In all of his life, never had he ever met such an utterly determined woman. Stubborn, too. Just a few weeks into their association, she had told him in the most bald-faced way that she intended to have him, and that there would be nothing that he could do about it. He had been amused by her audacity at first, but very soon, he had begun to realize that she had only been truthful. There was nothing that he could do about it. And there was nothing that he wanted to do about it. She was his love, the only one for him.

Gavin brushed a tiny bead of perspiration from his upper lip. "I guess we'd better go in then."

"It'll be OK," Nicholas said. "You're going to have a great life with her. She's good for you. I mean, if we disregard the fact that she can't cook worth a damn. . . ."

Gavin's laughter exploded in the tiny antechamber, and then just as suddenly, he was serious.

"I love you, Nicky," he said. He had never actually said the words before, but they had always been there, unspoken between them.

Nicholas nodded. "I know." And the expression of deep affection that passed between the two brothers was not lost on the pastor as he poked his head into the room to declare, "It's time."

Outside the church, at almost the very moment, the antique black carriage with its high, softly padded seats came to a dainty, shuddering stop. The carriage man, positioned atop on his raised platform, muttered softly, "Whoa there, boys . . . whoa there." And the two mighty grays tossed their heads, pawed at the ground, and then stood perfectly still.

Henry Stevens was out first. In his top hat and tails, he was elegance itself. He extended a hand to his wife, and once she was firmly on the ground, he said, "Come on down, little Amber. Do you remember how you're going to hold Aunty Summer's dress?"

The child nodded. "Yeth," she lisped, "Daddy had me do it over and over."

Summer smiled behind her veil. Amber was such a sweet child, although it was common knowledge that she could be quite a handful at times. Exactly like Nicholas.

"Ready, Summer?" her father asked. Summer took a breath. This was it. It had taken four long years to convince Gavin Pagne that she was the right woman for him. In less than half an hour she would be a Champagne. *Mrs. Champagne,* to be exact. And she couldn't wait. Absolutely could not wait. Never had she ever thought it possible to be so happy. At this very moment, her dream man was standing at the altar, waiting for her. Waiting for *her. Was she ready?* She had never been more ready in her life.

She extended her hand to her father. "Let's do it, Dad."

The bells were positively shouting now. It was almost as though they were saying: "The bride is here, the bride is here, here comes the bride . . . Gavin Pagne's bride."

Summer stepped onto the ground, and waited as her mother arranged her train. Her mother said to the little girl, "OK, Amber, hold it up . . . that's right, nice and high. Careful, not too high."

The entrance to the church was lined with people, and a huge cheer went up as Summer began to walk. And from within the church, the bells ceased their shouting, and went smoothly into a rendition of the *Wedding March*. As she approached the mouth of the church, Summer's heart leapt in her chest, and then commenced an awful pounding. *He was hers. He was hers. Gavin Pagne was hers.* The words were singing in her blood, and she was almost giddy with the sensation. She carefully climbed each step, her long white train held perfectly by Amber Champagne. Both her mother and father would walk her down the aisle. It was what she had wanted: both of her parents there, one on either side. And now that she stood at the very threshold of the church, her mother pressed her hand and whispered, "Be happy, sweetheart."

Summer squeezed her mother's hand in response. She could see her bridesmaids now as they stood in neat rows, waiting for her. She felt like a princess. A queen. Surely it didn't get any better than this.

The bells faded sweetly now, and suddenly, the deep familiar chords of the organ rang out. The inner doors were thrown open, and her bridesmaids stepped to the side to let her through. In one sweep, her gaze took in the rows and rows of people, and her brain registered the fact that everyone was now standing. Her eyes raced to the altar, and she took a deep filling breath. There he was, standing before everyone, so big and tall, and beautiful. And there was Nicky. Sweet Nicky, the one responsible for all this. They couldn't see her yet, but she could see them all and she felt like laughing, crying, shouting.

But, before she could formulate another thought, the organist began to play the *Wedding March,* and as though on automatic pilot, her feet began to move and she came into view.

Gavin turned, and Summer met his eyes across the distance. There was a smile curling the corners of his lips, and her mouth reacted instantly to the sight of his wonderful face. A smile as wide as the state of Texas stretched her lips in return, and she glided up the aisle with her entourage behind her, and her parents at her side.

All the way, she kept praying that she would not suddenly awaken to discover that it had only been a dream. A beautiful, enchanted dream. But dream or not, she was almost to him now, and his hand was reaching for hers. She gave him her fingers, only now beginning to feel the trembling in her bones.

"Darling. . . ." She heard the husky rumble, meant only for her ears, and her heart soared, spreading its wings to the cosmos. She looked up at him, into his deep, dark eyes, and she loved him so much at that instant that she knew that should she die right then, she would go understanding the full meaning of her life. Tears clustered behind her eyes, and she bit her lip, holding on, holding on hard. She hardly knew it when the minister began to speak, and when her parents together answered the question "Who gives this woman?" with a resounding "We do," a long, warm salty tear traced its way down her cheek.

She repeated her vows facing Gavin, holding both of his hands as he pledged himself to her in a voice that shook. Directly behind Gavin, she could see Nicholas's smiling face, and behind Nicholas, Mik and Rob. The sweeping realization that all of these Champagnes were now hers, came over her then. And she made a silent vow that she would care for and protect them all with her life. How lucky she was, she thought blurrily. How very blessed to marry into such a family. In the deepest part of her heart, she whispered a prayer of thanks, and the words became a mental tattoo that impressed itself upon her psyche. *Thank you, God. Thank you.* She had never thought that any of this would have been possible for her. Her heart had been hard. Cold. Unbelieving. What a fool she had been. But no more. No more.

The minister was asking in his quiet reverent way, "Do you take this man . . ." And Summer was in such a daze of happy confusion that she cut him off before he could properly finish, with a "Yes" that reverberated around the entire church, and drew an answering "Amen" from the assembled guests. Her eyes were swimming again, and mercy of mercies, so were Gavin's. His answer in response to the minister's question was almost as hasty, and when he lifted her veil, she was more than ready for his kiss. Warm lips that shook just a bit descended on hers, and from a far-off distance, she heard someone sobbing. And heard the husky entreaty being whispered over and over as he feathered her lips with petal-soft kisses. "Don't cry, my love. . . . shh . . . don't cry." It was only then that she realized the sobs were coming from her.

Later, as they sat in the carriage together, Summer looked around her with shining eyes. Where was he? Where was Nicholas?

"Nicky . . ." she called, waving. "Nicky." There was a crush of people surrounding the carriage, all happily caught up in the throwing of handfuls of multicolored rice.

Gavin shaded his eyes against the sun. "There he is. Nick," he bellowed. "Come on . . . come here." He beckoned his brother toward the conveyance. "Ride with us."

Nicholas threaded his way through the crowd, completely oblivious to the fact that every female head in the vicinity had turned to observe his passage. Gavin reached out a hand to yank his brother up into the carriage, and Nicholas came aboard laughing. "Now this is what I call a wedding," he said. "There must be a thousand people here . . . easy." Then he turned to Summer with that special smile that he always reserved just for her. *"Mrs. Champagne,"* he said, "how does it feel to be an old married woman?"

Summer grinned at him. "I've never felt better." Then she turned in her seat to scan the crowd again. "I know Mom has Amber . . . but where're Mik and Rob?"

Nicholas pulled the bow tie at his neck, and leaned back in his seat. "Gone off somewhere with Harry. You know him. With this many single women about. . . ." His voice dwindled to a halt as his eyes met and held those of a petite woman standing in the middle of the church's doorway. His eyes swept over her with rapid efficiency, raking her from head to toe, with the analytical thoroughness of a scientist. He noticed the short cap of black hair, the pixieish face framed by impossibly high cheekbones, the sharp little nose and the striking hourglass figure. A thoughtful light came into bloom somewhere within the depths of his eyes. She was a tight little package to be sure, maybe a little short for his tastes, but certainly good enough for a night's enjoyment.

He turned his gaze deliberately away and forced a casual tone into his voice. "Who's that girl?" he asked.

Gavin followed his gaze, and an almost imperceptible smile curled the corners of his lips. "Amanda Drake."

Summer turned to look, too. "Amanda Drake? Do we know her?"

Gavin gave her a bland look. "She's a friend of a friend. I'll tell you more about her later."

And before more could be said on the matter, another familiar face had appeared out of the milling crowd. *Janet Carr.* She was wearing a lovely dress of soft violet, with a matching hat perched smartly atop her neatly coiffured head. She lifted a hand to wave at them.

"God Almighty," Nicholas muttered, "I hope she's not thinking of riding with us."

Gavin gave Summer a lightning glance, and observed that his wife's face had gone quite tight. "No," he said, "I'm sure she won't insist on that."

Nicholas leaned forward to tap the carriage man on the shoulder. "Well . . . just in case. Let's get going," he said. And for one quick instant, he allowed his eyes to hunt the crowd again for the petite woman he had seen at the church door. But she had been swallowed by the teeming mass of people. His searching look, however, had not been lost on his brother. Gavin raised an inquiring eyebrow at his wife, and Summer in turn mouthed a thoughtful "maybe."

Amanda Drake watched with narrowed eyes as the carriage pulled slowly away. So this was the infamous Nicholas Champagne. The ladies' man. The heart-breaker. Well, she had to admit that he was quite a looker. All six-foot-odd chocolate-brown inches of him. She could completely understand why women continually fell over themselves in their futile attempts to ensnare him. He was a supremely hand-some man, and well aware of it, too, if her reading of him had been correct. She knew his type well. Too well. He was one of that charming, debonair, totally irresponsible breed. He was probably, even now, considering a way of getting her into his bed. One-night stands were the common currency of his species. She understood that. But she hadn't jour-neyed all the way to Jamaica for just that. No, sir. It would be more, much, much more.

A flickering smile crossed her lips at the thought. Poor man. Was he in for a surprise! Little did he know that she fully intended on bedding *him* that very evening. And without question, it would be an experience he would not forget in a hurry. *Oh, the things she was going to do to him.* She could almost feel pity for the man. Almost, but not quite, for one did not pity an ornament or a nicely chiseled piece of sculpture when it fell and broke. And was she ever going to enjoy breaking his heart. All the women he had ever hurt and carelessly tossed aside would be cheering in the aisles when she crushed him beneath her heel, then kicked him to the proverbial curb. He would pay dearly for what he had done to her friend Sheila. His coldhearted callousness still made her feel slightly ill. To take away a woman's child was certainly unforgivable. But to also prevent that woman from having contact with her own flesh and blood was nothing short of sinful. Sure the Champagnes had money and power, lots of it, too, by the looks of things. But that did not matter one iota to her. She would find a way to get close to Mr. Nicholas Champagne. She owed it to Sheila, and a promise was a promise.

THREE

Pink and white roses sat on each of the round linen-covered tables, the long green stems stylishly housed within fluted vases of gray crystal. The expansive ballroom was alive with color, and laughter. And Harry Britton was the cause of it. The nicely iced, multilayered wedding cake, draped in a veil of ivory lace, stood at the center of the room, presiding over the hundreds of amused onlookers, while Harry paced before it like some ancient knight sizing up his quarry.

"I bid fifty dollars for this wonderful Jamaican wedding cake to be unveiled," he finally said, holding up a small wad of bills and shaking it above his head.

"Cheapskate," a voice from somewhere behind him said. And a swell of laughter rose in response to the comment.

It was an age-old Jamaican tradition that the wedding cake be veiled and bid upon during the reception, until the highest bidder managed to coax the mother of the bride to reveal the splendid creation just beneath the lace. But it was also expected that guests would choose to bid against the unveiling, since at the end of it all, the monies collected went to the bride. It was all in fun really, and Harry, the consummate performer, played his part like a professional.

His eyes raked the crowd, then pounced. "Nicky Champagne. . . . You're the best man. How much do you bid?"

Nicholas leaned back in his chair, and his shirt opened at the neck to reveal a column of smooth brown flesh. "You know," he said with great consideration, "I don't think I want that cake unveiled. Five hundred to keep it covered."

The crowd groaned, and seated at her table at the back of the room, Amanda Drake smiled.

"One thousand to unveil it," she said in a soft and well-modulated voice.

A hush fell over the gathering. Harry Britton shaded his eyes with a hand. "Who said that?" he asked. "Where is that wonderful woman? Come on, stand up and let the best man see you."

Amanda Drake stood and without looking at him, knew that she had Nicholas Champagne's full attention. She could feel the heated regard of his coal-black eyes as they slid over her person. She forced herself to look only at the man standing out front.

"One thousand," she said again, and the crowd cheered.

Harry beckoned her forward. "Come on up here." Then he motioned for Nicholas to join him, too. "Come on up here, best man," he said, and Nicholas uncurled himself from his chair, to pad with pantherlike grace to the middle of the room.

As he threaded his way through the maze of tables, Amanda was irritated to observe that he appeared to have an almost hypnotic effect on most of the women there, both young and old. She felt very much like screaming at them all, *"Oh, grow up, won't you."* He was just a man after all.

Nicholas came to stand beside her, and with great deliberation, she tilted her chin up to meet his gaze. It was said that the eyes were the windows to the soul, and that it was always possible to tell the real character of a man by looking deeply into them. So Amanda steeled herself for that first contact with what Sheila had described to her any number of times as the pure undiluted conceit and arrogance of Nicholas Champagne. He looked down at her from his considerable height, and her heart gave an unsteady thump as the tar-black eyes met and held hers. Then, without warning, he smiled. And the smile radiated a scorching sensuality.

Her brow wrinkled. His eyes were gentle. Kind even. Confusion swirled in her. *It couldn't be.* It had to be a trick of the light. *He was not kind. This was Nicholas Champagne. The callous philanderer she had come so far to destroy.*

"Hello," he said, and Amanda felt her mouth go dry.

Harry lifted one of her arms right then to declare to the crowd, "One thousand we are bid for the unveiling of the cake. Do I hear two?" It saved her from the embarrassing necessity of any conversation, because, for the life of her, she would have been completely incapable of it at that very instant.

Ester Champagne, seated in a place of honor at the bride's table, who had hitherto been observing the proceedings with a certain rapt attention, came slowly to her feet, much to the consternation of her nurse and the entire Champagne clan. Nicholas exchanged a hurried glance with his older brother. But Gavin motioned to him to remain where he was.

"I am the mother of the groom," Ester began quite nicely. "In fact . . . I have three handsome boys. Gavin, Nicholas, and Mik." With a murmur of encouragement from the crowd, she spread her arms and prepared to warm to her subject.

Mrs. Robbins, knowing the unpredictable proclivities of her patient, made a valiant attempt at getting her charge back into her seat before she rattled off a string of curses or some such thing. "It isn't time for the speeches yet, dear," Mrs. Robbins said softly.

But Ester would not be swayed. She gave the nurse a withering stare, and continued. "God could not have given us a more perfect day for a wedding if we had asked him to."

Again, the crowd was with her. But then, in a sudden, startling change of direction and tone, Ester leaned forward to advise the gathering at large: "I also think it my duty to inform all of the young women here today that my son, the best man, is a fornicator. So, if any of you think that he might be a good catch. . . . Think again."

The titter of surprise that followed that declaration seemed to only add fuel to the tirade that was to follow.

"And don't act as if you're any better than he is either," she said with considerable venom. "Many of you sitting out there right now are some of the biggest fornicators around." And she turned to a respectable-looking older gentleman who had the misfortune of making eye contact with her at that very moment. "You, Reverend Cole . . ." she said with a fever bright gleam in her eye, "you are the biggest fornicator of them all."

It was a full fifteen minutes before the proceedings were brought back under adequate control. It took the combined efforts of Gavin, Nicholas, and Mik to coax their mother from the room. In an adjoining enclosure, she was properly medicated and then placed on a long sofa with a sizable ice pack resting upon her forehead.

Harry Britton held court in the ballroom area, while the debacle with Ester Champagne was properly sorted out. He entertained the gathering with a seemingly unending flow of humorous anecdotes and outrageous tales. And despite her earlier resolve, Amanda Drake found herself listening to him with a degree of amusement. *He was quite a character, this Harry Britton.* It was obvious too that he and Nicholas Champagne were close friends. A thoughtful frown rippled the smooth skin of her forehead. Maybe he would help her if she approached him correctly.

As Amanda sat at her table, immersed in deep thought, Henry Stevens was mulling over a few thoughts of his own. When he had properly formulated the concerns in his mind, he leaned across to whisper in his wife's ear, "I hope to God that whatever's wrong with that woman isn't genetic."

Mavis Stevens quickly hushed her husband. "Quiet. Here comes Summer." As her daughter drew closer, Mavis said, "Summer, dear . . . is everything . . . all right now?"

Summer pulled out a chair and sat. "Gavin and Nicholas are apologizing to the reverend right now. Hopefully, we won't be asked to leave the church." She shook her head. "Can you imagine the embarrassment the poor man must've felt? Why she would've chosen him . . ." Summer took a breath, then charged on. "But she can't be blamed. She's not well."

Henry Stevens nodded. That was certainly a delicate way of putting it. As far as he was concerned, the Champagne mother was completely around the bend. "Just what is wrong with the mother anyway?" he asked.

"Now's not the time, Henry," his wife said.

"Nana's nutty," Amber explained before Summer could respond.

"See what you've done?" Mavis Stevens said to her husband. Then, to the child who was seated on her lap: "Your granny isn't nutty, Amber . . . she's just . . ." And she struggled for a way to explain it to the little girl.

"She just sees things a little differently," Summer said, jumping in. "You know . . . than most other people."

"I still think she's nutty," Amber insisted.

They were saved from further argument by the sound of a sweet, honeyed voice to the right of the table.

"Hello, Summer. I wanted to come over to let you know how much I'm enjoying the wedding."

The hairs on the back of Summer's neck rose to stiff attention, and a cold chill ran the entire length of her spine. Why couldn't Janet Carr leave well enough alone? Enjoying the wedding indeed. What a spiteful little hussy she was. Summer had been hoping against hope that she would not show up at the reception. But here she was, as large as life, and as brazen, too, by the looks of it.

Summer pasted on a smile she was light years away from feeling. "So nice of you to come. The real festivities haven't yet begun"—she paused—"but you probably already knew that."

Janet's lips curved to reveal perfect little white teeth. "Yes." And she stood there for a moment, withstanding the curious regard of both of Summer's parents. The air positively crackled with tension, and Summer ground her teeth and wondered for the millionth time why this woman would not just fade out of her life gracefully. So she had wanted to get her claws into Gavin. So she had lost him. Any intelligent woman would now accept defeat and move on. Why in the name of heaven was she still hanging around? Was she lonely? Did she need friends? Or did she now have her eye on Nicholas? Summer's brow furrowed. The other possibility didn't even bear thinking about.

Mavis Stevens, who had until now been observing the interplay between her daughter and the other woman, stepped in gracefully to say to Janet, "Would you like to sit down?"

Summer shot her mother a quick look. Couldn't she tell that this was not a woman whom she liked?

Janet accepted without further encouragement. "I'd love to. Thank you."

And before Summer knew what was happening, her nemesis had seated herself, and struck up a lively conversation with her parents. Alana Collins caught Summer's eye from across the room, and beckoned her over. Summer was glad for a reason to leave the table, and was deeply miffed that her parents did not even seem to notice that she had gone.

"Is that the girl who was after Gavin?" Alana asked as soon as Summer was seated.

"That's the hussy," Summer said.

The other bridesmaids huddled in. Racquel got directly to the heart of the matter. "What do you think she's after?"

Summer glared at the back of Janet's head. "I really, really don't know."

"Hmm . . ." Alana nodded. "Maybe Nicky."

"There's someone else in here who seems to be after him, too," Racquel agreed.

Summer gave her a quick look. "After Nicky? Who?"

"Don't look now," Racquel said, "but see that girl over there . . . the really petite one with the short hair?"

They all turned slowly in the indicated direction. Summer's brow wrinkled, and it was a second before she remembered. The girl from the church; the one Nicky had been staring at.

"All the single women in here are after Nicky, though," Summer allowed. "Even after all of the stuff we now know about his fornicating habits. . . ."

Morganna grinned. "Things that we really didn't need to know."

They all chuckled at that, and were still laughing when Harry came over to say, "What're you ladies planning? I always get nervous when I see a group of women together like this."

Alana gave him a pinch on the arm. "Shut up, Harry," she said. And in response, he leaned down to press an exuberant kiss to the side of his sister's face. There was no other woman on the face of the earth whom he loved as well as her. They were as compatible as bread and butter, as necessary to each other as water for chocolate. It had always been so, and for as long as there was breath in his body it would always be so.

"Do you see how she treats me?" he asked with a lift of a smooth black brow. "And even after all the trouble she used to get me into when we were kids."

"That's not what I heard," Summer said, laughing.

Alana nodded. "He looks pretty normal, but don't let that fool you. He's a bad one . . . this brother of mine."

Morganna leaned forward to inquire, "So, when are you going to get married, Mr. Harry Britton?"

Harry gave her a particularly mournful look. "If you were only available, Morganna O'Bannon," he sighed, "I'd marry you in a second."

They all laughed at the exorbitance of the lie. Harry Britton married. It didn't seem likely at all. Both he and Nicholas Champagne were two of a kind. Both were too good-looking and charming for their own good. And, of course, neither one was at all interested in the matrimonial state.

"We've got someone for you," Alana said, and she nodded to the table where Janet Carr was still seated. "How about her?"

Harry turned to look. "Isn't that the one . . ."

They all uttered a collective "Um-hmm."

Harry stroked the side of his chin. "Well . . . well. She is quite good-looking. I wonder why Gavin didn't choose her."

Summer gave him a playful glower. "Say that again, Harry Britton, and I'll take a shoe to you."

"That's exactly what she did to me when we first met," a deep voice behind them said.

Summer turned in her seat to proclaim, "Gavin," in a manner that seemed to suggest that it had been days since she had last seen him.

Gavin stroked a gritty finger down the side of his wife's cheek. "Did you miss me?"

And Summer went exuberantly into his arms to rain a deluge of kisses on his face. Her husband laughed in delight, wrapped both arms about her, and lowered his head to take her lips in a slow, drugging kiss.

Somewhere in the background they heard Harry sigh. "Don't they make you sick?" And they pulled themselves from each other to grin sheepishly at the gathering.

The entire room had come back to life with the appearance of the groom and, in very short order, all of the groomsmen. Harry returned to his duties as master of ceremonies, and before long, the veil on the cake was being slowly and delicately removed. Both Nicholas and Harry did the honors. With great care, they unraveled the delicate lace, layer by layer, until the beautiful ivory-white creation with its multitude of delicately whorled white roses and tiny silver balls was revealed to the room. The sudden appearance of it brought a great cheer from the watching guests. It was indeed a thing of beauty. A six-tiered sculpture of absolute perfection.

Beneath the white icing was thick dark, succulent Jamaican fruitcake. To the novice eye, it appeared to be a chocolate cake. But it wasn't. Not by any means. It was in fact a wonderful combination of soft and creamy cake, blended with a varied selection of rum-steeped tropical fruits. It was also smooth and pungent, and had the peculiar effect of going straight to the head of the eater.

Nicholas cut a tiny wedge from the side of the cake and placed the slice of dark rum-soaked dessert on a tiny ceremonial plate. Few in the room understood what he intended to do with the cake, since by custom, the bride and groom were always the ones to make the first cut. He approached his brother and new sister-in-law to the hushed quiet of the watching guests. With a tiny dessert fork, he cut the slice neatly in half. He offered one piece to Gavin, and the other to Summer. Then, with a hand resting on each head, he said in a solemn voice, "May this cake sweeten your tongues so that no angry words ever pass between you. May this cake also loosen your inhibitions so that a year from now, someone will call me Uncle."

Laughter resonated, and Amanda felt her resolve tremble a bit. Could he be this good an actor? Could he love his brother this much, and really be as cruel and despicable a person as Sheila had described? She had known many men of his type. They were invariably charming, handsome, and completely self-absorbed. They never appeared to notice the world around them. Not really. Nor did they care particularly for anyone other than themselves. Why, then, did Nicholas Champagne, a fine member of the breed she hated so well, behave in such a very contrary manner? It puzzled her. Deeply. His own mother had admitted before hundreds of guests that he was a philanderer. Fornicator, the mother had said. And Amanda had chuckled deep inside at the old-fashioned words, although her face had remained without much expression. She had thought: *Every man such as he should be so revealed. Should be so embarrassed.* Her eyes had sought his face immediately to see the effect of the damning words. But he had not appeared to feel their effect at all. If anything, he had worn a curiously blank expression. She had chalked that up to shock, though. The shock of revelation. To have his dirty laundry aired in public before a multitude of listening female ears would've unraveled some of his lascivious plans quite a bit.

So what was this intangible quality she suspected him of? That was the thing she now wrestled with. The understanding of that strange depth she had seen in him. The classification of it. She had thought she understood his kind, because he was no more than a mirror image of herself. But she sensed that he was somehow more than she was, although she pushed this awareness to the very back of her mind.

It was true that in her younger years, she had pursued men simply for the sport of it. Had bedded them for pleasure. Yes, she had broken many a heart, and had done it with a callous disregard for the carnage she left in her wake. In fact, they had called her Sunshine in art school because of this extraordinary prowess that she possessed in the bedroom. She had repented, though. She was a reformed sinner. She only used her power now for good. She only broke the hearts of men who absolutely deserved it. Men like Nicholas Champagne.

She watched him work his magic on the crowd, and suddenly everything crystallized in her mind. His game became instantly clear. He had obviously cultivated that superficial veneer of kindness, which she had noticed lurking in his eyes. There *was* no particular depth to him after all. He was simply a fisherman, perhaps a good one. And every fisherman needed his lure. His bait. So he hooked his victims with the *nice guy* routine. She could almost applaud him for it. *What a cunning disguise. What brilliance. What polish.* For a while there, he had nearly managed to catch her, too. But she was the master of this game, and this time Nicholas Champagne *had* met his match. Never had she been beaten at this. Never had she lost her heart. Never would she.

A pleased smile curled her lips. She had him figured out now. It was with delicious anticipation that she looked forward to later that evening. She would have him whimpering like a babe with just a single stroke of her peacock feather. And when she ran it with that special soft touch between his warm, trembling legs, he would see nothing but *Sunshine.*

FOUR

"May I have the pleasure?"

She looked up with questioning eyes. *Harry Britton.* How very fortunate. She had been so deep in thought that she had not noticed his approach. Had not realized either that the cake had been moved out of the way, or that everyone was now dancing.

She took his hand graciously, and said in a soft lilting voice, "Thank you. I'd love to."

He swept her into a waltz, turning her with expert hands as they moved amongst the couples on the floor. She was much shorter than he, so naturally his body blocked her view of the entire room. She was forced to look directly up at him as they moved together, and he returned her gaze with smiling eyes. He was a flirt; a handsome devil, too, by any measure, and obviously well aware of it. She never had much use for handsome men in general, but she couldn't help liking him just a bit. He seemed to be such a fun-loving sort.

"How long have you known Nicholas Champagne?" she asked now, giving him a very pretty smile. It was her policy never to beat about the bush when she was in search of information. There was little point, as far as she could see, in indulging in coy meandering niceties.

The smile spread from his eyes to his lips.

"Ah . . ." he said, and there was a trace of regret in his voice, "so it's not me that you're interested in then?"

Her black eyes danced. She had been right. She did like him. "Does that mean you won't tell me about him?"

His big shoulders rose and fell. "Nicky's always stealing my girls away from me. But what can I do?" He sighed. "Please keep in mind, though, that he is a fornicator."

Amanda laughed, and so did he. *What a charmer.* If things were different, she would have liked to be a friend of this one.

Her sleekly dressed eyebrows raised a fraction to emphasize her point. "And you're not, I suppose?"

Again the laughter spilled from his eyes. "I dabble . . . I dabble . . . but nothing too extensive."

"You lie," she said.

He turned her in a sweeping arc before saying, "You're a cynic, I think. Perfect for Nicky Champagne. He's not a cynic."

She was listening intently now. "No?" she urged.

He spun her again. "No. Nicky is. . . ." He hesitated. "Now, how would I really describe him? Nicky is a walking paradox. A simple yet complicated guy. A family man who loves his little extracurricular activities."

A hard note crept into her voice. "Don't you all?"

He left that question unanswered, and instead said, "He is capable of reform, though. Do you think you're up to the job?"

Her smile deepened. What she intended had little to do with reform.

"Should I take that smile as a yes? Or do you have more sinister plans in mind for him?"

Her heart did a triple step in her chest. What a

shrewd son of a gun he was. She thought to distract him. "So, what do you do for a living?"

He gave her a long look before saying, "I'm that breed of professional that everyone loves to hate."

She nodded. "A lawyer?"

"Um-hmm," he said. "So is Nicky."

It was beginning to make a modicum of sense now. "So, that's how you met? In college?"

"I went to school in Britain. Cambridge University. Have you heard of it?"

She hadn't, but that was neither here nor there as far as she was concerned.

Her blank look made him continue. "Anyway," he said, "Nick spent a year there after graduating from UCLA."

"You two are of the jet-setting crowd, aren't you?" she said with a wry note in her voice.

The smile was back. "I admit I was born to privilege. But Nicky definitely wasn't."

"No?"

He shook his head. "No."

The music was coming to an end, and she was almost disappointed. She hadn't gotten nearly enough information out of him.

Harry put a gentlemanly hand beneath her elbow and guided her off the floor. When she was again seated, he said, "So now that you're through pumping me . . . would you be interested in dancing with Mr. Champagne?"

She couldn't prevent a chuckle. "Is he afraid to ask me himself?"

Harry turned to look across the crowded floor. Nicholas's behavior toward the miniature Venus seated before him was puzzling to the extreme. Ordinarily he would have been all over her. It wasn't possible that he did not find her attractive either. She was a very sexy girl. A *very* sexy girl.

Harry turned back to Amanda now, his eyes glinting with mysterious lights. "I wonder," he said. Then, on an impulse of devilry, he toyed with her. "Maybe you're not his type."

She laughed, and it was a silvery, breathy sound, pleasing to the ear. "Maybe."

Harry's eyes flicked over her in a thoughtful manner. By the faint lifting of her brow, it was clear that was a possibility that had not occurred to her even once. His thoughts turned to the wager he had made earlier in the day. Could this be the girl to tame Nick Champagne? She certainly had all of the right equipment.

"Why don't we find out his feelings on the matter? Are you game? Or will you be crushed if he shows no interest in you?"

Amanda shrugged. "If he shows no interest, then there's always you."

Harry threw back his head and laughed. What temerity. Most women fell all over themselves if he paid them the scantest attention. It helped, of course, that his father was the Prime Minister of Guyana. But he had never found himself lacking in looks or charm either.

"Nick has to meet you," he said, amusement twinkling in his eyes. "You're not impressed with me at all, are you?" he asked.

Amanda gave him a very direct look. "Not much impresses me these days."

"Wait here," Harry said. And he was away from her and weaving his way across the floor of undulating bodies.

"Yo . . . Rob," he called when he was close enough. "Where's Nicky?" The teenager raised a hand and without breaking his rhythm, pointed to the French doors leading to the wraparound patio. Harry waved his thanks and kept pressing determinedly through the gyrating bodies. It took him a full two minutes to get outside, and he managed this feat by stepping on innumerable feet along the way. A few inches from the doors he was almost felled by a staggering kick to the shins. But the back end of a well-padded woman saved him.

He bent now to give the front of his leg a good rub, then straightened to cast his eyes around for his quarry. Down near one end of the patio, he spied a dark solitary figure.

"Thought you'd given up smoking, you dirty dog," he said as soon as he was close enough.

Nicholas turned, and in the half-light the red butt of his cigarette was clearly visible.

"First one in ages, bwoy," Nicholas said. He took a deep draw on the cigarette, letting the smoke curl about his lips in soft blue-gray wisps. "What happened to that girl you were dancing with?"

A smile spread across Harry's face. *So, he had been watching them.* This boded well, very well indeed. He would win that wager yet.

Harry leaned on the railing, and allowed the salty ocean breeze to hit him squarely in the face.

"That girl, unfortunately," he said, "is not interested in me. She spent the entire time talking about you."

Nicholas took another drag, his eyes squinting against the burn of the smoke. He gave Harry a sidelong look. "What'd you tell her?"

"That you're really a nice guy."

Nicholas gave a bark of laughter. "Ha. Like hell you did. You probably dragged out every single godawful thing I've ever done."

Harry grinned. "The thought did cross my mind, but I don't think it would've done me any good. It's you she's got the hots for."

"So, you're giving up without a fight? You're going to let me have her just like that?"

Harry shrugged. "I have a good day from time to time."

Nicholas straightened from leaning on the railing, and flicked the remaining ash into the night. "You have never had this good a day, Harry, my friend. You know you're a bastard through and through."

"I won't deny it," Harry agreed.

They both laughed at that, and then Nicholas inquired, "So what kind of girl is this Amanda Drake? She looked kinda repressed to me."

Harry considered that for a moment. *Repressed?* No, he wouldn't say that. He wouldn't say that at all. There was definitely something very . . . "freaky" about her, he decided. Yes, that was it exactly. He was sure of it. Amanda Drake was a full-blooded freak. All the signs were there.

"Well, let me put it like this It's not going to take dinner and a movie to get that one into the sack."

"Umm," Nicholas said, and there was a definite note of interest in his voice now. "My kind of girl." He straightened, hands in pockets. "Well," he said with a slight smile playing around the corners of his lips. "Let's go. We've left the young lady alone for far too long, I think."

Amanda watched them make their way through the crowd, and for a brief moment, her heart thrashed excitedly at her ribs. How much like sleek jungle cats they looked. Closing in for the proverbial kill. Both of them were living embodiments of masculine beauty. Her lips twitched as an errant thought struck her. Poor innocents that they were, they actually thought *she* was the prey. She was going to enjoy this immensely.

Harry came forward first, as she would've expected. "Amanda Drake," he said, "may I introduce Nicholas Champagne."

She offered her hand to shake, but the rascal bent low to kiss the back of it instead. At the feel of his lips, so warm, so firm, so infinitely sweet, a bolt of fire flashed like molten lava through her blood, and she almost pulled her hand from his grasp. Such an intense reaction she had not expected.

She forced her voice to reflect a calm she did not feel. "Nice to meet you." And she made sure that the words were said with just the right note in her voice. He smiled with his eyes first, then his lips, and a bead of perspiration ran down the center of Amanda's back. *God, he was good.*

"Thank you for coming to the wedding." He was all charm, and Amanda met his eyes directly. She took a deep filling breath. *All charm he was, and absolutely no substance.*

"My gallery received an invitation, so I decided to come."

His eyebrows flicked upward. "An artist?"

She smiled. "Yes."

Harry had melted back into the crowd, but neither one noticed.

Nicholas pulled out a chair. "May I sit?" he asked. She nodded, and he lowered his magnificent frame into the chair, and leaned forward to drape one arm lazily across the surface of the table.

"What would you say, Amanda Drake . . ." he began with a note of wicked amusement in his voice. "What would you say if I told you that you are definitely one of the sexiest women I've run into in a long time?"

A smile bloomed in her eyes despite every effort she made to control the flowering. She leaned forward, too, and whispered so that no one but he could hear her.

"I'd say . . . prove it."

He laughed, and to Amanda's astonishment, it was a completely genuine sound. *So deep. So husky. So familiar.* It was the very sound she had heard in that recurring dream of hers, the one that had plagued her for nights on end years before, and then just as suddenly disappeared into that ephemeral world where dreams go to die. It had always troubled her, too, that she could never remember the dream clearly in her waking moments. But she had known it to be a good dream. A soft dream. A dream where she was loved.

Amanda gave herself a mental shake. How fanciful she was becoming. She could only blame it on the beautiful wedding, for she had not indulged in such childish imaginings in years. Love was a lie. There was no such thing. And every rational adult who had lived for a spell knew that.

She met the dark eyes of the man across the table from her, and felt her skin warm beneath the heat of his gaze. She had to remain focused. She was here to do a job. And do that job she must.

She blinked at him for a moment. He was asking her something and she didn't know what. "I'm sorry?" she said with some amount of genuine bewilderment in her voice.

"I was asking you to dance with me."

Amanda went willingly enough into his arms, and again, as he held her, she experienced the strange familiarity again. If she didn't know better, she would surely say that they had danced this way before. The way they moved . . . so slowly, in synch, together. Not as she and Harry had done, somehow more. And his scent, his scent was the thing that bothered her the most. It made her want to rest her head upon his chest. Close her eyes. Drift away.

His hand slowly stroked the deep ridge running along the center of her back. "So, why are you so interested in me?" he asked.

And Amanda drew a trembling breath. She had to be strong. She had to be. This was her game, not his.

"I wanted to meet you." *Oh, the warmth of him, the warmth of him.* It was nothing short of exquisite. The slight hint of tobacco, mingled with something that was uniquely his very own, inflamed her senses in a way that was completely alien, completely new, and not altogether welcome.

His eyes glittered down at her in a manner that gave the impression that at that moment in time, she was the very center of his universe.

"I saw you at the church," he said, "and I wanted to meet *you.*"

Amanda experienced a slight tingling of regret. She could almost believe him. Almost. *Why was it that men were always so insincere?*

"What are you going to do with me now that you've met me?" Her game face was back. She was focused again on her goal.

He chuckled in a manner that caused the baby-fine hairs on her arms to stand at rigid attention. "Mandy . . . Mandy . . . Mandy. You are a bad child."

She looked up at him with a sweet smile. He had no idea of just how bad she was. Of just how very bad she could be. She was bad to the bone, and before the night was through, he would know it, too.

"Later," she said with soft emphasis, "I'd like to show you just how bad I can be."

His eyes took on a latent, smoldering expression. "Really? And what do you intend to do with me?"

She stroked the inner skin of his wrist with the soft pad of her thumb, and was gratified to feel his pulse accelerate in response.

"Would you have me spoil the surprise?" she asked.

Again the deep chuckle reverberated in his chest. "Will you be gentle?"

Despite herself, she laughed with him. *God, she didn't want to like him.* But he was so very, very . . . She couldn't articulate it. The right thoughts just wouldn't form in her mind.

"Have you ever run across a woman you haven't been able to charm?" she asked instead.

He grinned at her in the most infectious way. "Not yet, my dear, but I'm sure there must be at least one woman out there . . . somewhere. . . ."

The song ended, and drifted smoothly into another, but Amanda did not notice. Her entire attention was trained on her partner.

"Why are you so successful . . . with women, I mean?"

He stroked the side of her cheek with a finger. "Why?"

She nodded. "Yes . . . Why? I'm curious."

"Well," he said, and he lowered his head so that his lips were just scant inches from hers. "I like women . . . so women like me."

Amanda weighed the value of that bit of information. He was not conceited. Even though he was arguably one of the most handsome men she had yet seduced, he did not appear to have a trace of conceit in him.

"I see," she said, and stood on her tiptoes so that the soft skin of her upper lip just barely grazed the bottom of his. She took a nibble, and felt full-blooded excitement as he lowered his head just a fraction to pull the naughty bib of flesh into his mouth. A surge of white-hot electricity raced through her. And she felt the echo of an answering burn in him.

"Let's go outside," he whispered against her mouth.

FIVE

Out on the patio in a dark corner, with the wind gusting sweetly around them, Amanda gave herself up to the exhilaration of the moment. Lord, but he had a way about him. His lips were like warm tropical fruit, succulent, juicy, filling. And his tongue, his tongue, what could she say about it? What couldn't she say about it? It was rough velvet. It was indescribable silk. It was hot and soft, a curving, touching, tasting, roaming thing with a will of its own; a mind of its own. A beauteous thing made for exactly this purpose. She held him, he held her. This had never been done before. Could never happen again. This perfect mating. This absolute wonder. She was drowning, sinking, falling. *God help her, but she was just a poor mortal after all.*

"Mandy. . . ." The word was husky against her cheek.

She pulled his head back down to begin the dance again. And he cushioned her back with a hand, protecting her skin from contact with the hard wall. But the truth be known, she wouldn't have felt a dozen sharp knives digging into her flesh. She wanted more of this. Always more. She never wanted it to end. Never wanted to remember the real reason she had sought him out in the first place. *Nicky Champagne. Nicky Champagne.* The words began as a whisper in the deepest part of her mind, and ended as thick burbles of sound on her lips.

"Nicky. . . ." She could not articulate more. Her breathing was raspy. Her heartbeat thready. Almost without proper thought, her hand slid beneath his jacket to caress the sleek smoothness of his back.

She heard him speak, and the words rattled around in her mind before she actually understood them.

"We should go upstairs," he was saying.

Slowly, slowly, the fog lifted, and she could see him again. Her heart thrashed heavily at her ribs. Was she beginning to lose her touch? What was this madness? Whose game was this anyway? But his face was so sweet. His eyes so kind and clear. So he liked women. So he played around a bit. Did that make him so very bad? Why in the name of heaven had she made this promise to Sheila? Maybe the years had changed her more than she realized. Or maybe it was just the man. She didn't want to hurt him now, not the way she had intended. But she had given her word. *Her word.*

His hand was on her chin now, gently caressing and then lifting so that he could look directly into her eyes. *Oh, but he was a beauty, this man.* Smooth milk-chocolate skin, with sculpted cheekbones at just the right distance apart; a nose rising smoothly from all of this perfection, only hinting at the nobility of his ancestry. A king he would surely have been, in another time, another place.

"What's the matter? Don't you want to?" His voice, and the puzzlement there, lifted her from her reverie.

"Yes," she said, before she could rethink the decision. "I do." Then, with a smile in her eyes, and on her lips, she reassured him. "I really do."

* * *

On the way up in the huge elevator, she stood with her back pressed against the flat of his body. He had wrapped his arms about her so that he might nibble on the side of her neck from time to time. And the feel of him was pure heaven. The sensation scoured her veins and poured its residue into the thumping organ in her chest. She had never been this excited. Had never been this sorrowful, for at the end of the evening, she would leave him and the game, such as it was, would be afoot. If she knew men at all, and know them she did, she would intrigue him. He would seek her out. She would carefully entangle him in her snare. He would come to care for her, because she was very good at what she did. But then, as promised, she would walk away and never see him again.

"You're so quiet all of a sudden," he husked softly in her ear.

She stroked his arm with the flat of her palm. "I was just thinking."

He touched the lobe of her ear with his nose, and rubbed it back and forth in the most pleasing way. "About me?"

The elevator pinged, and Amanda was able to step into the corridor without answering his question. "Which way?"

He took her hand, and with a devilish smile beginning to play around his lips, he said, "Follow me."

At the door, as he fitted his key in, she asked, "Won't your brother be wondering where you are?"

Nicholas looked down at her. "On his wedding night? I don't think so."

Amanda realized that she was attempting to stall

the inevitable. But she forged ahead, pushing away the understanding of what this might mean. "I mean . . . wondering where you are . . . during the reception festivities. Won't he be disappointed that you didn't stay until everything was finished?"

"Gavin understands me," was all he said before pushing open the door and saying very nicely, "After you."

She stepped in, and remained by the door as he walked about easily, flipping on lights. Absently, Amanda noticed the palatial size of the suite. The sunken sitting room was divine with its soft white chairs and large double-doored portico overlooking the smooth midnight-blue ocean. Her eyes followed Nicholas for a bit, then drifted quite naturally to the paintings on the walls. Most of them were large foaming seascapes. Her specialty.

She went a little closer to investigate. The artist was good, very good. The play of colors and the sweeping brush strokes almost turned the canvas into a living, breathing thing. She was so engrossed by the work that she actually started at the gentle touch on her arm.

"Have you forgotten about me?" came the playful jest.

Amanda turned to face him. There was no doubt about it, she was getting soft. But why did he have to look at her in that particular way? With those eyes, those darkly sinful eyes.

"The suite is wonderful," she said. "And I really love the paintings."

Nicholas smiled. "I'll show you around, if you like?" He had shrugged out of his jacket and draped it carelessly across a chair. His shirt was now unbuttoned to mid-chest to reveal a gorgeous glimpse of chest. Amanda bent forward to press a kiss to the very center of his breastbone. She didn't want a tour. She didn't want to see how the other half lived. She didn't want to hanker for a softer, easier life than the one she'd had so far. No, she didn't want a tour.

"Where's the bedroom?" she asked between a peppering of soft kisses to the broad expanse of his chest. He scooped her up with little effort and carried her across the floor. The bedchamber was off the sitting room, and was decorated in swirling colors of blue and white, with thick ivory-colored carpeting running from wall to wall. Nestled in a cozy alcove was a large antique whitewashed bed. And her heart gave an unsteady thump as she felt her back touch the soft chenille spread.

His fingers did not fumble even for a second as he began to undo the tiny buttons holding the front of her bodice together. Amanda stilled his hands with hers.

"Let me," she said softly, and pushed at him so that he was now lying on his back. Her hands were deft and sure as she peeled his shirt away. The flats of both thumbs went to caress the sleek hairs in his armpits, and then she bent to gently bite the skin of his neck. Her tongue, like an industrious worker bee, darted deep into the heart of one ear, and at the gentle tremor that rippled across his skin, she whispered, "Do you like that?"

"Umm," was the heated reply.

He lifted onto his elbows and allowed her to tear his shirt away. And she did this with grand finesse, tossing it into a corner of the room. In the half-light, her eyes glowed like those of a lioness, and Nicholas muttered, "You are an amazing woman, Amanda Drake."

She was sitting astride him now, with her legs

curled on either side. And in her hand she held
what appeared to be a long feather. Nicholas's eyes
narrowed to watchful black slits. *Now where had she
gotten that?* He sank back against the pillows. Harry
had never been more right. This girl was a bedroom
general. An artisan. That she was completely unin-
hibited was clear. This was a fine way indeed to
break his self-imposed fast. It had been more than
six months since he had been with a woman. He
had received many tempting offers, it was true. But
none had stirred him like this. He had long imagined his heart to be a dead thing. Numbed, no
doubt, by his endless pursuit of meaningless pleasure. He now needed something more substantial.
This was not the girl to plan such a life with, but
God knows she would be well worth the tumble. A
fitting tribute to the riotous life he was now determined to leave behind.

Nicholas closed his eyes. *Lord, what was she doing
with that feather?* Had he ever experienced such
heights of sensation? The way she moved over his
skin, touching, tasting, stroking. Her hands were at
his belt now, sliding the leather out of its buckle.
In all of his many years of hearty carousing, never
had he met one such as her. She would be wild and
insatiable, he knew. Exactly what he needed in order
to bid a fond farewell to the past. It would be one
last hurrah of the absolutely freaky kind. He would
have to remember to thank Harry later.

Amanda hauled his nicely creased pants from him
and tossed them to lie in the corner with his shirt.
She looked down at him with bemused eyes. *What
perfection.* A supremely formed six-pack framed by
smooth, rippling abdominals. And not an ounce of
fat or flab on him anywhere. She bent to nip the

skin just above his briefs, and she felt his fingers wrap around her arms.

"Are you trying to drive me crazy, woman?"

Amanda smiled at that, and there was a trace of regret in her eyes. *Not yet, my sweet. Not yet.*

She hovered over him for a moment, then bent to steal a kiss. Her lips clung to his, and she allowed herself to linger warmly over this final indulgence. His arms wrapped around her, and she knew the exact moment when he began to shift his weight. She closed her eyes, steeled herself, and then spoke. "Nick . . . would you like to try something a little different?"

She had his attention with that. He paused in his roll and said, "Different?"

"Umm," she agreed. "I have something in my bag. . . ."

His eyes were wickedly amused. "Another feather?"

She stroked the curve of his jaw with a finger that trembled just a bit. "No, better than a feather."

He smiled. "Well, go get it, darling . . . go get it."

She was away and back in scant seconds. And Nicholas watched her with hooded eyes. *What a woman. What a woman.* There was absolutely no preamble in her. She just got right down to the heart of the matter. Now why couldn't all women be exactly the same? Life would be so much easier if there were no more coy pretenses. No more games.

In the darkening room, it was hard to see exactly what she held in her hand. It looked vaguely like . . .

"Handcuffs?"

"Handcuffs," she said with a perky smile. "Now come on . . . don't be a prude."

Nicholas laughed. *A prude?* Now that was something he had never been called.

"Give me your wrist," Amanda coaxed softly. "It's going to be supremely delicious this way."

Nicholas proffered his wrist. "I like delicious."

Amanda knelt above him, allowing the tops of her bosom to spill softly from her bodice. She fastened one wrist to the rails of the bed, and then asked for the other wrist. He gave it without hesitation. The deed was done in only moments, and then she sat back on her heels.

"Now what?" he said with great curiosity.

Amanda crawled to the end of the bed. "Now I undress."

Nicholas flexed his arms in the restraints. "Ah . . . I see. A striptease."

She nodded. "But first let me hang up your clothes. I hate to see a messy room. I'm really not at my best if there's any clutter around."

Nicholas watched as she darted about the room, picking up the discarded articles of clothing. He shook his head in the darkness, and muttered to himself, "What a weird, freaky chick." He heard her mumble something about dry cleaning, and the first niggle of worry penetrated the sensual haze that he had been in. *What in the name of heaven was she up to?*

"Amanda?" he called.

He heard the sound of running water coming from the bathroom. What was she doing? *Washing his clothes in the bathtub?* Had he picked up some sort of mental patient?

"Amanda?" His voice was more urgent now, and he rattled at his bonds.

Her head suddenly appeared around the bathroom door. "Yes?" she said sweetly.

Nicholas took a breath. She was fully dressed, in heels and all.

God almighty, he had picked up a psycho. It was his fault, of course. Entirely his fault. Had he not promised himself earlier in the year that he would never do this sort of thing again? She probably had a big butcher's knife in her purse, too. She certainly seemed to have everything else in there. Maybe she was planning to cut off one of his ears, or to carve his privates up into little tiny pieces.

The thought of that possibility galvanized him into speech. He had to reason with her. The insane were a delicate bunch, but they could be reasoned with on occasion.

"You hate men, don't you," he said softly.

Amanda blinked at him. What was he on about? Hate men? She didn't hate men at all.

"Why would you think that?" she asked. Then the understanding hit her. He thought she was a maniac of some sort. A chuckle brewed somewhere deep in her chest. Maybe she should prance about the room with her feather. Do some cartwheels and back flips.

He was speaking to her again in that same tolerant, gentle way. "Why don't you come over here and free me, sweetheart? We can forget that this thing ever happened. You really don't want to do anything you're going to regret later."

Amanda walked slowly to the side of the bed, and stood looking down at him. She was sorry to have done it now. But at the time she had conceived the idea, it had seemed like the perfect way in which to embarrass him, to shake his confidence and conceit. But after meeting the man in person, she had to admit that he did not seem to be at all like the creature Sheila had described. If she remained there any longer, she would forget all about the promises she had made, and release him.

She met his tar-black eyes, and was surprised to observe that there was not a trace of anger there. He seemed, if anything, vaguely puzzled. She couldn't stand any more of it.

"I'm going to leave the key on this table," she said, holding up the metal so that he could see exactly what she was leaving.

"You're just going to leave me here . . . like this?"

She turned on her heel and made a beeline for the bedroom door. Over her shoulder, she said, "Someone will find you soon enough."

Nicholas heard the outer door to the suite close, and he rattled at his bonds again. What in the name of heaven had possessed him to allow her to handcuff him to the rails of the bed? He should have seen it coming, though. It just wasn't normal for a woman to be that instantly passionate. She had responded to him like a house on fire from the first second their lips had touched. He should have been suspicious at that, but she had blinded him with her passion. Numbed his hunter's instinct. He could count himself lucky she had not turned violent. What an absolutely crazy witch. Why had she done this to him? Did she make the rounds of weddings and other social events, looking for men to tie up? Was that how she had her fun?

He turned his head to look at where the tiny key lay glistening on the surface of the bedside table. He leaned across as far as he could go, reaching, straining against the restraints, until he was forced to flop on his back again, frustrated. God Almighty, once he was out of his bonds he would search for that woman and get an answer out of her. If it turned out that she was crazy, then he would understand and let it go. But should she have one glimmer of sanity left, just one single shred of lucidity, he would. . . . Well, he didn't know just yet what he would do. But rest assured, it would be something fitting.

He struggled up again, and this time made a lunge for the key with his feet. His right leg careened into the large ceramic lamp standing on the table, and it teetered for a moment, as though undecided, then crashed with abandon to the floor. Nicholas swore heatedly beneath his breath.

A laughing voice from somewhere in the vicinity of the bedroom doorway distracted him from the problem at hand.

"Nick Champagne . . . what are you doing to the hotel's property? Do you know how much that lamp probably cost?" Then the shadow in the doorway collapsed into gales of laughter.

Nicholas squinted at the door. *Harry*. He should have known he was behind this.

"Harry," he grated. "You are one son of a . . ."

Harry came fully into the room. "Don't say it," he said, still grinning. "I had nothing to do with this. Your little girlfriend told me that you might need a bit of help up here. So"—and he came to sit on the bed—"here I am."

Nicholas pulled himself onto his elbows. "You put that crazy psycho woman from hell up to this, didn't you?"

Harry was all innocence. "Me? C'mon. I know I'm good. But . . . not this good."

Nicholas shoved him with a leg. "A likely story. Get me out of these things." He jangled the cuffs against the metal of the bed. "The key's somewhere over there. It may have fallen on the floor."

Harry got off the bed and took a look around. "Over here where?" he asked after a moment of looking.

"On the table . . . or the floor, Harry. It's there. I was trying to get at it just minutes ago."

The sound of the suite door opening and closing brought both of their heads up. "Jesus Christ," Nicholas said, "is the entire reception on its way up here now? Was that part of the plan, too?"

A shape loomed in the doorway, and Nicholas recognized his older brother before he had the time to even say a word. God, this was all he needed. Gavin here, too. Nicholas knew what his brother would have to say about the pickle he was in. He knew it as surely as he knew his own name. Gavin had spent his entire life getting him out of one scrape or another. And it had finally been mutually acknowledged between them that there would be no need for such rescues henceforth. Now this.

Gavin flicked the light switch, and grated in a voice that was filled with amusement, "So, this is where you are."

"Please tell me that Summer isn't directly behind you," Nicholas groaned. That would be the crowning glory of the entire evening, if his sister-in-law were to show up, too. Gavin came over to the bed, and stood with both hands in his pockets. And for what seemed an interminable stretch, he said nothing at all. Nicholas waited for the words that were certain to be forthcoming.

"Isn't this a sorry sight," Gavin finally said. "Need I ask how you got yourself into this one?"

Harry, who was still down on his hands and knees, scrabbling around for the key, looked up with humor dancing in his eyes. "His future wife's idea of romance."

Gavin threw back his head and guffawed. "Little Amanda Drake did this?"

Nicholas was not amused. "Future wife? That psycho? Not in a million years, I promise you. I'm certain she had one of those big knives in her bag. You both could've come up here and found me cut to pieces."

Gavin broke down again. "Amanda Drake?" he said again in a disbelieving manner. "What happened? Did she wrestle you to the bed?" Harry slapped his knee and cackled. "Maybe she's a Navy SEAL or something."

Nicholas gave them both a dark look. "I'm glad I'm providing you with the evening's entertainment."

Gavin wiped the corner of an eye. "OK . . . OK. Let's get you out of these things."

Harry uncurled himself from his crouched position. "We're gonna have to get a blowtorch and cut him out of them. 'Cause that key is not down here. Sure she left it?"

Gavin forestalled Nicholas's response. "We won't need the key. I think I still remember how to pick a lock."

He removed a key chain from a pocket, had a look at his selection of keys and paper clips, then sat on the edge of the bed and went to work on the lock. Within very short order, Nicholas was removing his left wrist from the cuff, and waiting as his brother worked on the right.

By the time Gavin had sprung the lock on the other cuff, Nicholas was well on the way to regaining his usual good humor.

"I may not have any clothes to wear," he said ruefully. "I think the nut job wet them all before leaving."

The lock on the second cuff sprang back as Gavin said, satisfied, "OK. That should do it."

"Thanks," Nicholas said, and he pulled his wrist out to vigorously massage the circulation back into his arms.

"I'm going to get on back down to my beautiful wife," Gavin said, standing. "She's probably wondering where I am as we speak. And don't worry," he continued before Nicholas could say a word, "I won't say anything about all this. Though you've got to admit, it is kinda funny."

A reluctant smile twisted the corners of Nicholas's mouth. "How do you happen to know this Amanda Drake woman?"

Gavin gave his brother a hooded look. "I'm a fan of her work."

"She's an artist or something, isn't she?" Harry asked.

Gavin nodded. "A good one, too. I think she and Summer would get along. Creative types, you know? Maybe we should—"

Nicholas interrupted him. "Did she tell you what she had done to me up here? Is that why you came up?"

Gavin shrugged. "I put two and two together. I saw you leave with her. I saw her return without you . . . and then Harry left. I figured I'd better check things out."

"Well," Nicholas said, "this is definitely a wedding you won't forget. What with impromptu speeches about fornication, and then . . . this thing."

Gavin chuckled. "Get some clothes on and come back down. We're going to cut the cake in a bit, and I know you don't want to miss that."

Harry emerged from the bathroom just then, holding apparel that had been neatly folded on padded hangers. "Your clothes, I think," he said. "Bone-dry, too."

"God save me from the lunatics of this world," Nicholas said with a shake of his head. Gavin smiled. God would save his little brother, with a bit of help from Amanda Drake, of course.

SIX

Nicholas stood on the wraparound veranda of the newly built Champagne Manor house. It was a breezy Saturday, and a month since his brother's wedding. A month since he had been handcuffed to the bed by the nut job Amanda Drake. In the early days following the wedding, he had considered looking for her. There had been burning questions in his mind. He had rethought the events leading up to their meeting, and he still could not make heads or tails of why she had behaved in such a curious manner. Women far and wide adored him, after all. So, why a woman he did not know, had not even seen before that infamous day, would do such a thing was completely beyond him. He had gone to the local artists' gallery, looking for her, but had been told that she was off on assignment and that no one knew where she was exactly. A likely story, it had seemed to him. He had even checked with them once a week to see if she had returned from her mysterious seclusion, but each week, the answer had been the same. Assignment. She was still on assignment.

He took a healthy swig of his Red Stripe beer, and glared at the glittering blue ocean. The problem with the world, as far as he was concerned, was that there were far too many crazies walking around on the streets. His mother, for example, was completely out of her noodle. Gavin had finally brought her down from the States, and installed her in the fully renovated beach cottage that Summer had painstakingly decorated. But was she appreciative? *No.* Every day she found something new to complain about. The colors on the walls made her dizzy. She heard strange sounds coming from the catacombs running beneath the house. The pots weren't the right color. Even the ocean didn't please her. It was too loud. Gavin was patient with her, and Summer bent over backward to accommodate her many demands. He, however, stayed far away from the entire confusion. He still wasn't completely sure how he felt about his mother. He understood that she was not well, and that it wasn't her fault. But she didn't really feel like his parent at all. She was just this stranger who was somehow related to him. She made him nervous, too, the way she would stare at him for minutes on end. He couldn't be at all certain that she wasn't hatching some devious plan to do him injury. He took another swallow of the bitter, and nodded at no one in particular. Yes, there were far too many crazies around.

The slam of a car door, and the crunch of feet on the gravel walkway leading up to the house, caused him to straighten up. He followed the curve of the veranda all the way around to where the pathway kissed the wooden stairs. He heard the voices before he actually saw them.

"Come on, Amber," Summer was saying, "let's go find Daddy, and show him all the great stuff we got for you."

"I got somethin' for Dada, too. A swerpise," the little girl agreed.

"Surprise," Summer corrected.

Nicholas smiled as he rounded the corner. He held out his arms. "My two favorite girls."

Amber bounced up the stairs ahead of her aunt. "Dada . . . we got you a swerp . . . surpise?" She looked back at Summer for confirmation that she had finally gotten it right.

Summer grinned, and gave her a playful smack on the rump. "OK, I know you can't wait. Show Daddy what you got for him."

"Give me a hug first," Nicholas said, bending. And the little girl gave him an exuberant squeeze. "And a kiss."

Amber planted a large wet one on her father's cheek, and Nicholas smiled. "OK, now you can show me."

Summer put down her shopping bag, while Amber hopped from one foot to the other, caught up in a frenzy of excitement. She removed two sizable brown paper bags.

"It's curry stoat," Amber supplied helpfully, unable to wait for the unveiling of her gift any longer.

"Curry goat," Summer said. She unfurled the bag, and peered into its aromatic depths. "With peas and rice. And coconut biscuits for dessert."

"Yummy," Nicholas said, rubbing his stomach. "Thank you so much, sweetheart," he said. "Give Dada another kiss."

And his daughter lathered his face with kisses.

"Can you take these two little bags in to Mrs. Carydice?" Summer asked.

Amber nodded immediately. "Yeth," she said, and before another word could be said, she was off and running for the front door at top speed.

"Careful," Nicholas bellowed after her, "don't fall."

Summer flopped onto the top stair, and fanned

herself vigorously with a hand. "It's really hot today, isn't it?"

Nicholas sprawled beside her, his long legs draped easily over the wooden runners. "It's going to get a lot hotter before it cools down. The weather report said it might top a hundred tomorrow."

"Jeesh," Summer said, "I never thought it could get this hot so close to the ocean." Then, in a sudden tangential change, she asked, "Where's Gavin?"

"Out with Harry. I have a feeling those two are planning something."

Summer reached across to give him a consoling pat on the back. "What could they be planning, Nicky, my love? They're probably just looking for more furniture for the house. We still have a lot of work left to do. The rooms upstairs aren't properly furnished yet."

"Hmm," Nicholas grunted, and raised the narrow brown bottle to drain the remaining swallows of beer. He lay back on the stairs, with his head pillowed on his arms; his eyes squinted against the bright sunlight.

Summer looked down at him. "Tell me, Nicky," she said with a brisk note in her voice. "You've been moping about like this ever since Gavin and I got married. What's the deal? Are you feeling lonesome up there at the main house? With Mik and Rob off at college, and Gavin down here with me?"

Nicholas gave her a sidelong glance. "Moping about? Me? I never mope, my girl. Never. You should know that."

"Well," Summer said, tickling him about the rib cage, "you're not your usual happy self. And you haven't been going out at night with Harry either." She pulled back one of his eyelids to peer at his very healthy-looking eyeball. "You're not coming down with the croup or something, are you?"

Nicholas chuckled, and batted her hand away. "Do you even know what the croup is?"

Summer grinned. "It sounds like something perfectly terrible, whatever it is. And it would have to be something pretty serious to make you swear off your most favorite activity."

Dark eyes swung in her direction again. "My most favorite activity?"

"Girls."

He turned away. "Girls are highly overrated. Crazy, too. There're a lot of crazy women around."

Summer released a silent sigh. So that was it. His mother. It was true that taking care of her was no easy task. She was belligerent, cantankerous, and downright ornery most of the time. But once she got used to company, she wasn't nearly as bad. Nicholas, though, made no effort at all to spend any time with her. He appeared agitated and ill at ease whenever she was around.

"Maybe if you spent more time with her, Nicky," Summer suggested.

Nicholas came out of his sprawl like the recoil of a spring. "More time with her? Not on God's green earth would I ever again. She's got a few screws loose . . . more than a few if you ask me."

"Well," Summer continued with great patience, "we always knew that. But you shouldn't blame her for it. She's sick."

Nicholas nodded in agreement. "You can say that again." He groped around in his jeans pocket for a moment, and then removed a crushed pack of cigarettes. He pulled one from the box, tapped it on the stairs, cupped his hands to light it, then dragged harshly on the glowing tobacco.

Summer wrinkled her nose. "I thought you had given that up."

Nicholas dragged again. "A man has to have his vices. If I've given up on girls, then I've got to have something else."

Summer ruffled a fond hand through his thick black curls. This thing with his mother was driving him crazy.

"You know," she said after a moment of thought, "you need a haircut. Look at this." And she unraveled a long black curl. "Must be four inches at least."

He leaned forward to grind the cigarette head into the gravel. "Feel like giving me a trim?"

Summer gave a prolonged "Hmm," as though the request was something that required deep consideration. Then, with a sparkle in her eyes, she said, "OK. But on one condition."

Nicholas smiled. "No free lunches, huh?"

"Free? Does anyone get anything for free these days?" And humor danced in her brown-gold eyes.

"OK," Nicholas agreed, "tell me."

"No, no, my sweet. You're going to promise to tell *me* exactly what's on your mind. . . ."

Nicholas began to speak, but Summer quieted him with an "Ah, ah, ah . . . yes, you will tell me exactly what's been bothering you these many weeks. I'm tired of guessing." She held up an imperial hand. "And if it's your mom, as I suspect . . . then we'll think of a way to work this thing out."

She stood with a flourish, grabbing the bags that were sitting on the top stair. "I'll be back in a minute with my trim kit."

Nicholas watched her go with a wrinkled brow. Was his mother the person she had been telling him to visit just minutes ago? God, he was really hung

up on this Amanda Drake chick. Of course Darling
Summer knew nothing about the incident in the
hotel suite. Gavin had promised not to say a word
about it. Not even to Summer. Especially not to
Summer. There was an unspoken code between
men, between brothers, that things like this not be
bandied about. Not that he thought for even one
second that Summer would spread the story around.
But it would be a trifle embarrassing if she knew.
Her opinion of him was important. It wasn't a thing
to be sullied with trivialities and tales of psychotic
women. He just had to get the Drake woman out
of his mind, that was all.

The screen door swung open, and Summer re-
emerged carrying a large pitcher of lemonade. The
housekeeper, Mrs. Carydice, followed directly behind with a trolley of steaming dishes.

Summer beamed. "A little snack." She was all efficiency now. "Come on up, Nicky. We'll eat first;
then you get your trim." She moved a deck chair
to make room for the trolley. "You can leave it right
here, Mrs. Carydice, we'll be fine. And Amber can
have some coconut biscuits when she's finished eating."

Mrs. Carydice pushed the trolley into the spot between the loungers. "Sure you nah want me fe'
dish?" she asked.

"No, that's all right," Summer said with a smile.
"We'll help ourselves."

The housekeeper returned her smile, nodded,
and disappeared indoors again. Nicholas came to
sit before the spread. He reached across and began
taking the lids off things.

"You didn't cook any of this, did you?" he asked
with a trace of humor in his eyes.

"No," Summer said with mock ire in her voice,

"I didn't *cook* any of it. I really don't understand why no one in this family likes my cooking."

Nicholas laughed. "Because you stink, darling."

She gave a reluctant chuckle. "Now that's more like the Nicky I know. So, what do you want? We have some of Amber's curry goat here. . . ." She unveiled dishes one after another. "And here's the peas and rice. Some ordinary white rice. Boiled green bananas with mackerel. . . ."

"All this for me?"

Summer leaned across to kiss him on the cheek. "Comfort food," she said. "Now, what do you want?"

Nicholas handed her a plate. "Fill me up with a little of everything."

Summer went around the dishes, giving him a healthy sampling of all of the fragrant niceties. "There," she finally said when his plate was full to overflowing. "That should hold you over for a while."

After they were both digging into the plates before them, Summer looked up to remark, "You know, Nicky, you should really find a nice steady girl." She took a bite of a savory chunk of curry goat, chewed with obvious enjoyment, and then went on. "Do you remember that girl at the wedding? Amanda . . ."

But she was prevented from saying anything more by the violent fit of coughing that seized Nicholas at that very moment. She quickly poured a glass of lemonade. "Drink," she said.

She watched him as he gulped down the entire glass in just a few swallows. A suspicion was slowly beginning to form in her mind. Could it be that Nicholas was interested in this Amanda girl? He had been totally unlike his normal self since the wedding, and now that she thought more carefully about it, she had not seen him this upset before.

"More?" she asked, and reached forward to pour him another glass. Her smooth brow furrowed a bit in thought. It couldn't possibly be his mother that he was this bothered about. She had been with them several months before the nuptials, and although it was clear that Nicholas still harbored some kind of resentment toward her, he had not seemed this upset about things.

"Thanks," Nicholas grated after he had swallowed the second glass. "Food went down the wrong way."

"Um-hmm," Summer said in a noncommittal way. "Anyway . . . I was saying, that nice-looking girl—Amanda something was her name. Remember her?"

Nicholas packed way too much food into his mouth, and chewed for a good long while without answering. A smile bloomed in Summer's eyes. *It was the girl.* Well, heaven be praised, this was a good sign indeed; and she hadn't an inkling of it before now. He had been so secretive. Well, she would talk to Gavin about inviting the girl around for dinner or some such thing. Sweet, darling Nicky; why hadn't he told her? Didn't he know that she could help?

Nicholas wiped his mouth on one of the paper napkins. "I seem to remember an Amanda . . . but there were so many women at the reception, I could be thinking of someone else entirely."

Summer put a flavorful forkful of peas and rice into her mouth. "Well, anyway," she said mildly, "you should find some nice girl to hang around with. Someone who can cook," she added, "not anyone like me."

They exchanged a fond glance. "Oh, you're not

so bad," Nicholas allowed. "It's just this cooking thing that we have to work on."

"Don't change the subject," Summer interrupted. "So, what do you say? Will you look for someone? You couldn't have gone off girls so completely. You like them altogether too much."

Nicholas partook of several mouthfuls of food before lifting gleaming black eyes. "What about Janet?"

Summer paused in her eating. "By Janet, you mean Janet Carr?"

"Janet Carr. Yeah. Why not? She's available, isn't she?"

"Available, and devious," Summer said, spearing the remaining chunk of meat on her plate with a mighty jab of her fork.

"You shouldn't be so worried about her anymore. You won," Nicholas said with a little smile beginning to curl the corners of his lips. "Besides, Gavin was never interested in her . . . and your parents seemed to like her plenty."

"My parents like everyone. Are you finished?" And she stood to remove the trolley from between them.

Nicholas leaned back on the lounger as she busied herself with stacking the plates in orderly piles. Her frenetic activity amused him. It was clear that Janet Carr was still a major thorn in her side. He had only offered the suggestion to get her off the very determined track she'd been on. He didn't want to go out with anyone at all at the moment.

"I thought you didn't even like her." Summer turned back to him now.

Nicholas shrugged. "She's OK. I wouldn't ever want to marry her, though, if that's what's worrying you."

"Well, thank God for that." She seated herself in a straight-backed chair, and said in a very brisk manner, "OK. Let's see what we can do about all this hair."

Nicholas came to sit before her. "Don't cut bald patches into my hair now because you're mad at me."

Summer picked up the scissors and glowered at his curly black top. "I'm not mad at you. You're free to go out with whomever you like." She picked up a curl and snipped off the end of it. "Even if the person you choose is the worst ah . . . ah . . ."

"Yes?" His eyes twinkled merrily at her.

"Oh . . . you're teasing me." And she rewarded him for the bit of fun at her expense by giving his earlobe a sharp pinch.

"Ach . . . you vicious little wench." He turned, wrestled her to the flat of the lounger, and then proceeded to tickle her into a shrieking tangle of limbs.

It was this scene that greeted Gavin and Harry as they pulled up to the side of the veranda in a flatbed truck loaded with furniture, lamps, and other knickknacks. Both men emerged from the truck to Summer's pleas of, "No more . . . please, no more."

Gavin shook his head and said to Harry, "Can't leave those two alone for a minute. Nicholas?" he yelled. "We need some help down here."

Nicholas paused in his very thorough tickling of her sides. "Saved by your husband," he said. He pulled his sister-in-law to her feet, and Summer ran a hand across her eyes to wipe away the tears of laughter. Now this was the Nicky she knew. He was always such a carefree kind of guy, and she didn't like to see him unhappy at all. She would definitely talk to Gavin about having Amanda-Whatever-her-name-was around for a meal.

She went to lean on the veranda railing as the items she had bought just days before in Kingston were unloaded. She had forgotten that Gavin was picking them up today.

"Careful with that one, honey," she said to her husband as he lifted a fine hand-carved Jamaican lamp from the back of the truck. Gavin looked up at her and smiled. She looked so beautiful, standing there with her glorious raven hair blowing about her head like a dark cloud of silk.

"I've got something for you," he said, patting his pocket.

"Really?" Summer beamed. "I'll come down."

She clattered down the stairs in her sandals, gave Harry a "Hi, handsome," then wrapped her arms about her husband. "So, what'd you get for me?" she asked perkily.

Gavin gave her a kiss on the tip of her nose before removing a thick envelope from his pocket. "From your parents."

She accepted the letter with a happy note in her voice. "They promised to write as soon as they got back to the States."

She wandered across to the stairs, and sat. It was a rather bulky package. She tore the seal with eager fingers. She had been onto her parents now for months, begging and pleading with them to sell their house in Mammoth Lakes and move to Jamaica. But they had been adamant that they were comfortable exactly where they now were. Too many memories wrapped up in the old house, they had said. She had a feeling, though, that there was more to it than that. Maybe they thought they would be

in the way. That maybe she didn't need them anymore now that she was married.

Summer peered into the envelope. There were
two smaller envelopes inside. She pulled them both
out with great curiosity. One was addressed to her,
and the other . . . She stared at the other in
stunned disbelief. *Janet Carr?* A letter addressed to
Janet Carr? What could her parents be thinking of,
writing a letter to that woman? Of all people, why
her?

She scooted to the side of the stairs as the men
approached with a long white leather settee.

"You're going to have to get up, darling," Gavin
said when they were almost upon her.

Summer shoved both envelopes back into the bigger one, and said, "That goes in the breakfast
nook."

She followed them up the stairs and into the massive entry foyer that was still almost completely without furnishing. Her mind was still reeling. Her
parents were always such good judges of character.
Couldn't they see that Janet Carr was nothing more
than a demon clothed in flesh? A man-hungry
harpy? How could she have done such a very thorough job of pulling the wool over their eyes at the
wedding? Admittedly, if pressed, the woman could
be charming. But the charm was nothing more than
so much superficial fluff.

"Where do you want this?" Nicholas grunted.
"I'm about to get a hernia."

"I'm already on my second one," Harry agreed.

Summer chuckled despite her current upset over
the letter. "Come on. It's not that heavy, is it? OK . . .
OK," she said at the looks on their faces. "Underneath that bay window should do . . . for now."

The settee hit the designated spot with a thump,

and Nicholas straightened to massage the middle of his back.

"Lord, what did they make that thing out of," he asked, "lead?"

Harry grinned. "I'm going to need another vacation to recover from this one."

Gavin slapped them both on the back, and said cheerily, "Come, men, there's more in the truck."

Summer stood looking around the roomy alcove after they had gone. It would be beautiful after she was through with it. The professional designer in her could see the wonderful possibilities of the space. It was the perfect room in which to have sleepy Sunday morning brunches, or to entertain an intimate group of friends. With the salty ocean air pouring through the large bank of windows, and the furnishings positioned just so to properly reflect the light, it would be marvelous. Her brow furrowed as she looked at the walls. They were very bare. No character in them yet. She wanted to choose paintings that matched the light and airy feel of the house, but had not yet found any that pleased her.

The men were back with a collection of very tall stone washed lamps before she could set her mind to worrying over the Janet Carr letter once more.

"Just put them all over there in that corner. I'll move them around later."

"You're not moving these around on your own," Gavin said. "They're way too heavy for you to lift."

Summer made a clucking noise with her tongue. "Do you think I've no strength in these arms of mine?"

"Promise me, darling," he insisted. "They're really heavy."

She smiled in response to his gentle coaxing. "Anything for you."

Nicholas left them together. It warmed his heart to see his older brother so very happy. It was almost enough to fill the gaping hole that had been eating at him for so many months now. Almost enough.

He walked toward the back of the house in search of little Amber. The housekeeper was keeping her well entertained, he knew, but he needed to see her cherubic face. He poked his head into the country-style kitchen, and said the name uppermost in his mind.

"Amanda?"

SEVEN

The woman whose name had come so unbidden to the lips of Nicholas Champagne sat more than fifty miles away, in a fragrant spot beneath the sprawling branches of a giant gennip tree. Before her, some distance away, was the stark white face of Rose Hall Great House, one of the primary tourist attractions in Montego Bay.

Amanda sat now before her canvas with splashes of paint on her clothing, a slight frown rippling the smooth skin between her brows. There was a monstrous serenity to the house that she wanted to capture. She had done some research on the place, and had been horrified to discover that in centuries past, Rose Hall had been the centerpiece of a thriving sugar plantation; a place where African bondsmen had been slaughtered by the hundreds, and in so many different ways. She had been told tales that still haunted her dreams at night. Tales of beheadings, of male slaves being candied in giant vats of boiling molasses, of women and children being buried up to their eyeballs in the nests of flesh-devouring ants. It seemed curious that a place where such evil had existed should be so very quiet now. So very still.

She wiped the corner of an eye with the cotton edge of her sleeve. In this great silence, she could

see things so very clearly. She could see how these
Africans, chained to the land as they had been, must
have suffered. This ground that she sat on now with
such calm, with such ease, would have been ground
where great souls with backs split open fell; with
bloodied backs, torn raw by the lash of the over-
seer's whip, they would have clawed at this ground.
Prayed on this ground. Died on this ground.

Amanda muffled a sniffle, and bent again to her
paints. Yes, this was hallowed ground, and she had
to capture the spirit of the people who had been
there before. It was important. More than that, it
was essential.

So intent was she on her purpose that it was several minutes before she realized that she was being
observed. It began with a prickling sensation on the
back of her neck that spread slowly to the flesh of
her scalp, and then on into full-blown awareness.
She turned slowly, expecting to see one of the children she had spoken to earlier in the day, but instead, not fifty paces away, half concealed by the
reedy stalks of sugarcane that grew so prolifically
around the property, was the very distinctive black
head of a Spanish bull. She recognized it as such
because it appeared so similar in description to the
many photographs she had seen of the bovine
breeders that had been brought to the island in the
nineteenth century. It was a massive creature, with
thick, yellowed horns; red, spiteful eyes; and foam
dripping from the environs of one nostril.

From where she sat, Amanda could smell the
foul odor that emanated, and instinct born of self-
preservation told her to run. To forget about her
expensive paints, and gloriously half-finished canvas, and run as fast as she could for the house
ahead, before the vicious beast was upon her. But as

she slowly uncurled from her seat to do exactly that, the animal pawed at the ground with its right hoof, lowered its head, and prepared itself to charge.

With her heart thundering in her chest, Amanda cast a quick eye around. There was no one to help her. No groundskeeper, no tourists, no one at all. She was pretty certain that she would be unable to outrun an enraged bull in full charge. She might make it halfway to the Rose Hall Great House, but the beast would catch her for sure before she managed to make it all the way. She knew she had only seconds to decide, and she looked down at her skirts, and made the only choice she felt she could. She would have to climb the gennip tree minus her skirt. There was no time for false modesty now. It was simply this. Climb the tree in her underwear, or be gored and trampled to death by a mad bull. She chose the tree.

She ripped her skirt from her body, and made a pell-mell dash for the tree. Behind her, she was certain she could hear the thundering hooves of the animal. She had never climbed a tree in all her life, so she tackled the scaly trunk in a wild and ungainly manner. Her nails clawed at the tree, and she hauled herself upward in a panicked desperation she had never before experienced. Halfway to a sturdy overhanging branch, she felt her underwear tangle on the scaly bark. By now, any regard previously given to modesty was completely gone, so she wasn't at all perturbed by the ripping sound the silk made as the bark tore the fabric from her. She clambered on, with steadfast determination, scratching and clawing her way into the densely leafed tree. By the time she had made it to the branch, she was completely out of breath, and the roar of the blood in her veins was only outdone by the cacophony of her breath as it rushed back and forth through her tortured lungs.

After she had worked up enough courage, she peered down through the leaves. *Where was it?* Where was the horrible creature? Below, a gusty wind had swept up her skirt, taking it along on a soaring rollicking ride into the still-water pond to the right of the house. And her underwear, or what remained of it, hung like a tattered flag, suspended from the bark, halfway up the trunk of the massive tree.

She closed her eyes, opened them again. No bull. She gave the area a wide sweep, while somehow managing to continue clinging to the branch. How could it have disappeared just like that? Maybe it was hiding, she thought irrationally. Waiting for her to come back down. She drew a deep, shuddering breath. Well, she wouldn't come back down, that was all there was to it. Eventually someone was bound to come along. She was perfectly willing to wait until then.

She had just settled in for a good long wait when out of the corner of her eye, she observed a brunette emerge from the thicket of cane. The woman, strangely, was dressed in a long flowing ankle-length white dress and a large-brimmed white hat.

Amanda hissed at her from her perch in the tree. But the woman appeared not to hear her, and she walked with the kind of unconcern that told Amanda that she had no clue that there was a mad bull about.

"Miss," Amanda tried again. "Miss." But the woman only parted the reedy stalks, and as suddenly as she had appeared, vanished again into the field of cane. Amanda stared. What a strange woman. Perhaps she was deaf, Amanda decided.

"Lawd Jesus, have mercy. Is wan half naked woman dat inna de tree?"

The sudden exclamation so startled Amanda that she almost lost her grip on the branch to which she had been clinging.

"Madam," the woman beneath was saying with some degree of patience, "we do not allow dis kind of vulgarity on our property. If you want to climb de trees, den please do it fully clothed."

Amanda was so relieved to see the stout woman just beneath that articulate speech for a brief moment failed her. "Bull . . ." she stammered. "The bull . . ."

The woman beneath was not impressed. "Is what she saying?" she muttered to herself in an irritated manner. Then more loudly, so that Amanda could hear her: "If you don't come down outta de tree right now, me will have fe go get de constable."

"There's a bull hiding in the cane," Amanda said very clearly now.

The woman rested her arms on her ample hips. "Bull? What kinda bull?" Then she started muttering to herself again. "Lawd save me from all dese tourist dem, you see. Dem come up in 'ere and smoke all dis ganja weed, and den go crazy."

"I haven't been smoking anything," Amanda said very distinctly. "I'm up here because there's a wild bull down there, and if you're not careful. . . ."

But the woman cut her off with a laugh. "Oh," she said, as though what Amanda had been saying all along had only just made sense to her. "Is rolling calf you a talk 'bout?"

The patois was thick, and Amanda had no idea what the woman was talking about. "Rolling what?" she asked.

The woman seemed much kinder now. "Come down outta de tree, dear," she said. "Come down."

Amanda gave the ground a very dubious look. She wasn't at all certain that she wanted to leave the confines of her safe perch. Her ascent into the tree had been nothing short of miraculous, and she was sure that she would be unable to manage it again at short notice.

"It's all right, dear," the woman encouraged again. "See here"—and she swept her arms in an expansive gesture—"no bull. Dere's no bull. Come down, and me will explain."

A short while later, Amanda was clothed in a borrowed pair of baggy jeans, and nicely settled in the caretaker's little cottage. Over a pitcher of pink fruit punch, with her canvas and paints neatly positioned beside her, Amanda leaned across to accept a slab of guava jelly from her host.

"No . . . no, you eat it jus' so," the woman said when Amanda attempted to spread the chunk of guava on a grainy cracker.

"Without the cracker, you mean?" Amanda asked.

"Yes, yes, without de cracker." And she picked up a slab and sank her teeth into the confection to demonstrate her point.

Amanda followed suit in very short order, and chewed the guava jelly, which had a surprisingly sweet, yet tangy taste to it. "It's good," she admitted after a bit. "It's kind of sweet and sour at the same time."

Her host poured a substantial glass of punch, set it before Amanda, and said, "My name is Winifred, by the way."

Amanda smiled ruefully. "I'm Amanda Drake . . . and I don't usually climb trees at all."

Winifred laughed. "Girl," she said, "you not de first one to talk 'bout Rolling Calf 'pon dis ya property."

Amanda bit into a crunchy cracker. "What do you mean when you say Rolling Calf?"

Winifred leaned in. "You heard all de stories dem about The White Witch of Rose Hall?"

"Well, I know Rose Hall used to be a sugar plantation, and that a lot of slaves were killed here. But I hadn't heard of a witch. . . ." Amanda began.

But Winifred, enthused by the telling of the story to someone who had never heard it before, charged on. "In anotha' time, you see . . . Annie Palmer was de owner of Rose Hall. And she was wan wicked, wicked woman."

Amanda lowered her voice in keeping with the spirit of things. "Was she the one who was responsible for all of the killings?"

Winifred slapped her leg. "All dat and more. Listen me. She was well practiced in de arts, you know?"

Amanda didn't know, so she remained quiet and just let the story happen.

"You know . . . de black arts. Voodoo, obeah, and all dem t'ings. But"—and Winifred held up a finger in an authoritative manner—"but de black arts can be used fe good or fe evil. And dere was not a drop of good inna dat woman."

Amanda took a sip of punch. She still didn't see the connection between Annie Palmer and the bull she had seen earlier. But she was more than willing to let the story unravel. Winifred paused for effect, as any good spinner of yarns would.

"Annie had three husbands. And all of dem died

under mysterious circumstances. One of dem fell down de stairs in de great hall . . . broke his neck clean off. You can still find his blood up dere on the walls."

Amanda shivered. "You mean . . .there are still bloodstains on the walls . . . right now?"

Winifred nodded. "Dis ya part is not legend. Annie Palmer was a bad woman . . . a witch . . . and she killed a lot of the slaves and ate dere hearts . . . fe get more power, more strength. And people say whenever she was planning some evil, she would put on a long white dress—"

Amanda stopped her. "And a white hat?"

"Oh, dis part of de story you know?" Winifred smiled.

"I saw a woman earlier . . . in a white hat and dress. When I was in the tree," Amanda said.

Winifred gave a mournful shake of her head. "Dat not a good sign. Not a good sign at all. If it was just de Rolling Calf you did see . . . But dis mean bad things. . . ."

"Bad things?" Amanda asked. It was beginning to dawn on her that the whole routine with the bull and the woman walking in the cane field must be part of the sideshow that was put on for the tourists visiting Rose Hall. But since she wasn't a tourist as such, they could at least have warned her of it. How they must have laughed at her as she climbed that tree.

"I can't say what will happen," Winifred was saying, "but nothing good can come of it."

Amanda hid a smile. "So, whatever happened to this Annie Palmer witch?"

"Well, " Winifred said, "she died by de hand of one of her slave lovers. He squeezed de life right out of her. And people say dat she still wanders de property today dressed all in white."

"With her pet bull?" Amanda chuckled.

Winifred gave her a solemn look. "Rolling Calf is nothin' fe laugh 'bout."

"Sorry," Amanda said, and she managed to school her features appropriately before asking, "So is Rolling Calf a pet name people around here give to the bull?"

"No," Winifred said, shaking her head. "Me can't say how de name Rolling Calf come about. But you can see Rolling Calf anywhere. It's not just here at Rose Hall. It mean evil . . . evil's coming."

Amanda sucked in a breath. Well, maybe she did deserve to be followed around the countryside by a slobbering red-eyed bull. She was still deeply remorseful over what she had done to Nicholas Champagne. The very day following the wedding, she'd made herself sit down and compose a long and wordy letter to Sheila. In it she'd thanked her for what she described as their long and unbreakable friendship. Expressed yet again how much she appreciated the fact that Sheila had gotten her out of more than a few unpleasant scrapes while they roomed together in college. Amanda had also added that she would be eternally grateful to her *best friend*, and hoped that her decision would not affect their friendship in any way. But, she went on to stress, what Sheila had asked of her now was entirely too much, and she could no longer take part in any scheme that involved causing Nicholas Champagne further distress.

After she had sealed the letter and sent it on its way, she had puzzled for several minutes over her reversal in attitude. It was true she had attended the wedding with absolutely no kindly intentions toward

Nick Champagne. But after meeting the man, after being held by him, a tidal wave of doubt had washed away any harsh feelings she had hitherto possessed. So he was a ladies' man. But a more charming rascal she had yet to come across. The plain and unvarnished truth of it was that she liked him. That being the only satisfactory answer she could resurrect to explain away her feelings, she had packed up her many bags and run, all the way to the other end of the island.

She'd thought to immerse herself in her work, to numb her mind to the smell and taste of him. But try as she might, thoughts of him would intrude, and on occasion at the most inopportune times. She had already decided, of course, that she would never see him again. He did things to her equilibrium that she neither liked nor understood. Besides, what would she say to him if she did see him again? How could she possibly explain away her actions? He already thought her to be a raving lunatic.

No, for once in her life, she was going to do the right thing. The noble thing. If Sheila intended torturing Nicholas Champagne further, she would just have to do it herself.

"Thank you so much for the snack . . . the story . . . and everything," Amanda said now, standing. She'd had quite enough of this Rolling Calf and Annie Palmer business. She had an art show to prepare for, and a painting to finish. So it was high time that she got on with it.

EIGHT

Nicholas pulled up to the tiny frame house in a cloud of dirt and pebbles. He hopped down from the Land Rover, walked briskly to the door, and rang the bell. In just seconds it was being pulled back to reveal a smiling Janet Carr.

"Well, well, well . . . if it isn't Nicholas Champagne." She stepped back, and motioned him in with a chirpy "Come in . . . come in. It's not often I get a visit from one of the handsome Champagne men."

Nicholas wiped his feet on the coconut-hair rug, and stepped into the brightly decorated living room.

"Nice place you have here," he said.

She shrugged. "It's home. For now."

Once he was nicely settled in a comfy bucket-shaped sofa, Nicholas leaned forward to remark, "You've been keeping to yourself these days."

Janet came to sit beside him, and with unconscious coquetry, she hitched one smooth bronze leg over the other. Her obsidian eyes flashed at him.

"I got the distinct impression the last time I paid a visit to the estate that I was definitely not welcome."

"Now, where would you have gotten an idea like that?" he teased.

"Your new sister-in-law for one. What's her name again?"

Nicholas chuckled. "You know what her name is. I can't figure out why you two don't get along."

Janet gave him a dour look. "You know the answer to that as well as I do."

Nicholas leaned back in his chair. He was well aware that he was treading in dangerous territory. Janet had never truly accepted Gavin's non-interest as final. But there was no point, as far as he could see, in her hanging on to the fantasy any longer.

"Well, maybe," he said after a deliberate pause. "But that's all over with now. And it was always all over with . . . as you know."

Janet's eyes were dark and turbid now. "He might have changed his mind. If she hadn't shown up. He might have."

Nicholas felt a surge of pity for her. He didn't have the heart to tell her in so many words that Gavin would never have changed his mind about her. Maybe she did have genuine feelings for his brother after all. For the most part, Nicholas had always figured that her interest lay more in getting her hands on the vast Champagne holdings than in anything else. But maybe he had been wrong about that. Maybe they all had been.

"Gavin is married now, sweetheart," he said gently, "and whatever might have been is over. You know how seriously he takes any commitment he makes. There is no chance"—and he repeated his words so that she would not miss his meaning—"no chance at all that he's going to go back on the promises he made to Summer. Do you understand?"

Janet turned away to stare at a photograph on a facing wall. "I hate her," she said thickly. "I hate her like I've never hated anyone before in my entire life. And I don't care if you know it. I don't care if you tell her of it too. I know how close you both are," she finished with a nasty tone in her voice.

Nicholas fished around in his pocket for the letter. It was the only reason he had come, and now he wanted to deliver it and remove himself from the present situation as quickly as possible. He sensed that Janet was in the process of working herself into a volcanic rage, and he didn't want to be around when the lava began to flow.

"I've got something for you," he said.

"For me?" Her voice lightened, and Nicholas knew without asking what she was thinking, and he pitied her for it.

"A letter," he said as gently as he could. "From Summer's . . . the Stevenses." He had been about to say *Summer's parents,* but had changed his words swiftly, thinking it a much wiser thing not to mention Summer's name again.

A genuine smile sparkled in Janet's eyes for an instant. "Oh, that nice couple I spoke to at . . . How sweet of them to remember me at all." She accepted the envelope, then said, "I can't understand how they could have raised such a . . . a . . ."

Nicholas's brow flicked upward. Where had he heard this before? Both women were so similar in their expressions of dislike for each other it was uncanny.

". . . a . . . conniving . . ."

"You know," Nicholas interrupted, "you two are very similar. Have you noticed that?"

Janet's eyes spat daggers at him. "Us two? Us two? Meaning that she-devil your brother went and married?"

Nicholas stood, hands in pockets. This was getting to be entirely too much for him. Janet hated Summer. Summer hated her right back. If left alone in a room together, the two women would rip each other to shreds, he was convinced of it.

"Well," he said after a moment's pause, "you take care of yourself and . . ." The words he had been about to say halted in his throat as his eyes fastened on the chain that hung from about her neck.

"Where'd you get that?" The question was rapped out with the velocity of a gunshot.

Janet's long fingers clutched at the oval-shaped pendant at her neck. "What? My necklace?"

Nicholas nodded. He had thought this woman to be many things over the years, but a thief was not one of them. Unless he missed his guess, though, Janet Carr was now in possession of his sister-in-law's favorite pendant, something she was hardly ever without.

"What does it matter to you where I got it?" Janet fingered the oval again in a caressing sort of way. "It's very old, and I've always had it."

"Mind if I take a look?"

She lifted her short length of hair to fiddle with the clasp. "It's just a keepsake really. My aunt used to have it locked away in a little jewelry box. She gave it to me just before she died."

"Here," she said once she'd gotten it free. "It's not worth anything." And she plunked the pendant into his palm.

Nicholas spent a moment looking at the ornate metalwork on the front, and then turned it over to examine the back. It was similar, very similar, but definitely not the same one Summer owned. "What was your aunt's name?"

A furrow wrinkled Janet's brow. "Sandra Carr . . . why the sudden interest in my poor dead aunt?"

"Ah," Nicholas said, "that explains the initials on the back then."

He returned the pendant to her, and Janet fastened the chain about her neck again. "You know," she said after spending a moment over the clasp, "you're getting stranger and stranger each day, Nick Champagne. It must be all the womanizing . . . it's finally beginning to affect your brain."

"And what would you know of all that?" Nicholas said, grinning.

"I think every woman in Ocho Rios has heard of . . . all that. You're a legend," Janet said with a matter-of-fact look.

"Come, come . . . a legend? I'm not as bad as all that. Surely?"

"Everyone knows you're the Champagne wild child, Nick . . . the thorn in your older brother's side."

Nicholas reached across to pinch the tip of her nose. "A man of my years can hardly be called a wild child," he said.

She gave a reluctant chuckle. "Well, that sounded a bit better than saying 'wild man.' "

"You know," Nicholas said, and there was a thoughtful gleam in his eyes now, "I think you set your sights on the wrong Champagne man."

"Well, well . . . what is this? A proposition?" she bantered with him.

"Nothing nearly so vulgar, darling," Nicholas said, playing along with her sudden change in mood. "But I might have something to offer. What do you think?"

Janet exploded into laughter. "You! I would never be able to take you seriously."

Nicholas gave her a winning smile. *Now who had*

*said that he couldn't charm every woman? The nut job
Amanda Drake, wasn't it?*

Janet went to him, and his arms wrapped about
her in a brotherly manner. She rested her head on
his chest, and he tightened his grip as he felt her
shoulders begin to shake. For long minutes he just
held her, rocking them both gently from side to
side. Finally her dry sobs ceased, and she looked up
at him with tear-reddened eyes.

"Do you know why I wanted Gavin so much?"

Nicholas wiped a runaway tear from the corner
of an eye. "Tell me," he said softly.

"Well, it wasn't so much that he was good-looking.
It was a bit of that, of course. But it was more because he . . . he . . . had you all."

"Me, Mik, and Rob?" Nicholas asked, not seeing
her point at all.

Janet sniffled a bit before continuing. "Well, all
of you together were a family, you see. A nice warm
family. Something that I've never had . . . always
wanted, but never had."

"Oh," Nicholas said, and proceeded to hug her
again. "But what about your aunt? Didn't you have
lots of cousins and uncles . . . and your parents . . ." he said suddenly, realizing that he had
never bothered to ask her about them before.
"What happened to them?"

He felt her shoulders lift in a shrug. "They died,
I guess."

Nicholas tilted her chin up. "You guess? You
mean you don't know for sure?"

Janet pulled away from him. "I could never get
my aunt to talk about it. All she would ever say was
that they didn't want me and that I would be better
off if I just forgot about them altogether."

"Uhm-hmm," Nicholas said, and he was thoughtful again. "Tell you what," he said with a coaxing note in his voice. "Why don't you come out with Harry and me tomorrow night?"

Her eyebrows lifted. "Harry Britton? Is he still here?"

"He's spending a few months with us . . . before returning home to Guyana." Nicholas smiled. "Do I detect a note of interest there?"

Janet gave him a watery smile in return. "And what will *Summer* have to say about all this?"

Nicholas wrapped an arm about her. "Don't you worry about that. Just leave everything to me. OK?" And he placed a very chaste kiss high on her cheek, but his mind was already far away. There were so many things to do. Plans to make. He was suddenly happy again. Happy and hopeful.

NINE

Amber bounced on the large bed in the middle of the room while Nicholas lathered his face over the bathroom sink.

"Dada?"

Nicholas stuck his head out. "Yes, sweetheart?"

"What're you doing?"

"Shaving."

"Why?"

Nicholas smiled. "Because I have to."

His daughter was going through the *why* phase. She wanted to know the reason for everything. And sometimes, he just didn't have the right answers for her.

"Will I have to when I'm old?"

Nicholas patted some more foam unto his face. "No . . . well, not your face anyway."

"Why?" The bouncing continued unbroken.

"Because girls don't have to."

"Only boys?"

He chuckled. "Yes. Only boys."

"Why, Dada? Why only boys?"

Nicholas picked up the razor and scraped away a smooth line of foam. "Because that's the way God made things."

The bouncing stopped suddenly, and her tiny face appeared around the lip of the bathroom door.

"But Dada . . . I want to shave too. Please?"

Nicholas gave one of her chubby cheeks a squeeze. "OK. You can shave just this once. Promise?"

She nodded. "Pwomise."

He lifted her to sit before him on the lip of the sink, squeezed a large portion of foam into one hand.

"OK," he said, "tilt your face a little."

He patted on a large Santa Claus-looking beard while she watched him with intent black eyes that so resembled his own it was scary.

"Dada," she said when he was almost through. "Can I come with you tonight?"

Nicholas gave the beard a final pat. "No, darling. Tonight's for grown-ups only."

"When I'm a grown-up . . . then can I come?"

He nodded in a very solemn manner. "When you're a grown-up."

"Will I be a grown-up tomorrow?"

Nicholas laughed. "No, not tomorrow. It'll be many years before you're a grown-up."

The little face looked disturbed by the suggestion. "How long is a year?"

Nicholas removed the blade from one of his razors and handed the shaver to her. "A year is . . . well, it's a long time for a little girl." He gave her a hug. "When you're a grown-up, you'll want to live somewhere else, you know. Don't you want to stay with your poor lonely Dada?"

Amber gave her father an outraged look. "But I'll always stay with you, Dada. Forever and ever."

Nicholas kissed the round of her forehead, and for a minute tears pricked the backs of his eyes. How he loved this little person. Everything about her amazed him. It was still incredible to him that he was responsible for this little life being here. It was a completely mind-boggling accomplishment.

He held her hand and showed her how to scrape the foam from her face.

"Dada?"

"Yes, sweetheart?"

"Will I stay with Aunty Sumsum and Uncle Gavin tonight?"

"Um-hmm . . . you love your Uncle Gavin, don't you?"

"Yes." She nodded. "But he has a big voice . . . and he doesn't let me play with the fish."

Nicholas stroked the final bit of foam from his chin. "The fish?"

"In the big 'quayrum."

"Aquarium," he corrected. He lifted her down from the sink. "You can't play with the fish. They'll die if you do."

She thought on this for a second. "Uncle Harry sez he'll get me a kitty," she said with a hopeful note in her voice.

Nicholas looked down at her, and was tempted to laugh again. She was such a crafty little schemer. Harry had probably promised her no such thing. This was just her way of asking for a pet.

"Are you sure Uncle Harry said that?"

She nodded vigorously. "Well, he was going to . . . but . . ."

"Go and sit on the bed while I finish dressing," Nicholas said. "And if you're a good girl tonight and don't give Aunty Summer any trouble, I'll get you a kitty tomorrow."

He was rewarded with a squeal of delight. "When tomorrow? Soon as I wake up?"

"Only if you're good. Now . . ." And he pointed

at the bed. She went silently, although she skipped quite a few times before she got there.

Nicholas splashed a handful of water onto his jaw, patted his face dry, then went to his closet. He was deep within its confines when a voice said right beside him:

"Dada . . . can I choose?"

Nicholas turned. "Didn't I just tell you to sit on the bed?"

She pouted. "But Dada, I can help. I know 'xactly what you should wear."

He sighed. The child was relentless, and quite stubborn too.

"What do you think I should wear then?" he asked.

She yanked at the tail of a silky blue shirt. "This one," she said.

Nicholas lifted the shirt from its hanger. It was one of the more stylishly cut shirts he owned.

"And what pants?"

She scurried into the very back of the closet. "The one with the tiny legs."

He followed her. "One of the black ones, you mean?"

"This one," she said triumphantly.

"Hmm," Nicholas said. It wasn't a bad choice. Maybe the child would be artistic when she grew up. She certainly appeared to have an eye for color.

He held up both pants and shirt and said to her, "Are you sure this looks OK?"

She propped her little hand beneath her chin and studied him for a minute in a very adult fashion. "Yeth," she finally said. "You look pretty."

He smiled. "And what about my shoes?"

She giggled. "Red?"

He chased her out of the closet. "You know I don't own any red shoes, little girl."

"Can I get red shoes?" she asked with a beaming smile.

"Well, which do you prefer . . . red shoes, or a kitty?"

"I want both, Dada."

Nicholas slid into the shirt and began to button the front of it. "Well, you can't have both."

"Can I ask Aunty Sumsum to buy me the shoes . . . if you buy me the kitty?"

"No. And you're in danger of not getting that kitty."

She was silent for a full minute, and Nicholas experienced a twinge of misgiving. He didn't like being hard on her, but if he didn't look out, she would have him wrapped neatly about her little finger.

"Come here and let me comb your hair," he said when he was into his shirt and pants. She bounded over to give him the most cherubic of smiles.

"Stand still now." And Nicholas swept the corkscrew black curls together with a hand, and secured her hair in a haphazard knot atop her head. He had not yet mastered the fine technique of combing and braiding, and didn't think he ever would either. His fingers were of the wrong length for such intricate work, and he also didn't have the patience for it.

"There," he said. "You look OK."

The knot had begun to sag on one side of her head, giving her a rather lopsided appearance.

"I don't like my hair like this, Dada," she said after a moment spent looking in the mirror.

Nicholas ran a hand across his forehead. Lord, she was turning into a very vain miss. "How do you want it then?"

She sat again on the bed, and handed him the comb. "In two pigtails," she said.

He undid the knot and placed her before him. He took a filling breath, and then made a jagged part down what appeared to be the middle of her head. He secured one bunch of curls with a hand, pulling the hair at right angles to her head. He figured if he pulled hard enough, it would stay.

"Keep still, Amber," he said after several unsuccessful attempts at getting the hair to cooperate. "Why do you keep moving your head around?"

Beads of perspiration broke out on his forehead after several minutes of this activity, and he muttered beneath his breath from time to time about having "a good mind to shave her completely bald."

A knock at the door interrupted his struggle. "Harry?" he said.

And the man himself poked a head around the door. "No," Harry said before Nicholas could say a word. "I don't know a thing about hair."

"Just hold this part while I get a ribbon around the other," Nicholas said, then to his daughter who was squirming on the bed: "Amber, sit still I tell you."

Harry came forward with a look of great trepidation on his face.

"OK," Nicholas said, "hold this part." And he released a bunch of unruly curls into Harry's hand. "Just keep it all together while I get the ribbon around. Jesus, God what is with this hair?"

Amber gave her father a very stern four-year-old stare. "Don't swear, Dada, it's not nice."

"I'm sorry, honey, but your hair . . . your hair has a mind of its own."

"Look," Harry said after it became apparent that they were making no progress at all. "How about if

I hold both bunches of hair . . . and you wrap the ribbon around each one?"

Nicholas wiped a goodly portion of sweat from his brow. "OK . . . I'm willing to try anything at this point. Amber, darling, I'm begging you, please sit still."

"I'm hot, Dada."

"I know you're hot. I'm hot. Uncle Harry's hot, too."

"Right," Harry said, "I've got both parts. Now wrap the ribbon as fast as you can, knot it and then I'll let go. Got it?"

"Don't move your hand," Nicholas said.

"I'm not moving my hand. You focus on doing your part."

Nicholas wound the ribbon quickly around the swatch of hair and put an industrial-sized knot in the delicate satin. "OK. Move your hand."

Harry took his hand away, and the curls puffed over the ribbon, but stayed in one place.

Nicholas smiled. "Perfect. It worked."

"Do the same thing with the other one," Harry said.

"Don't rush me. Don't rush me. This thing requires a lot of skill. Amber, do not under any circumstances touch that ribbon."

"But Dada . . ."

"Did you hear what I said?"

There was a flurry of activity over the second bunch of hair; then Nicholas gave a very satisfied "There."

Amber bounced. "Dada . . . can I look? Can I look now?"

Harry shook his head. "You think I'm kidding when I say I'm never getting married? I don't have the nerves for this sort of thing."

Nicholas wiped his forehead on a rag, flung the cloth into the sink from where he stood halfway across the room. "You'll probably be married before me. . . . OK, Amber. Go have a look."

The little girl slid down from the bed and clattered in her sandals to the mirror in the bathroom.

"Well, what do you think?" Nicholas asked when there was no immediate response.

She came slowly out of the bathroom with a very woebegone look on her face. "Dada . . . I look like a cow," she said.

Harry turned away to hide a chuckle. Nicholas got down on a knee. "What do you mean . . . a cow?"

"Well," she said in a very solemn voice, "I've got two horns."

Nicholas walked across to the phone, and dialed. When Summer answered, he uttered one solitary word: "Help."

The exhibition was going very well. More than half of the paintings had been snapped up within the first half hour, and people were now milling happily, sipping on long glasses of chilled wine.

"Amanda? Amanda dear. Would you come over here for a minute?" Mr. Browning, the owner of the gallery, was a short bespectacled man with a rather round stomach and merry little eyes. He beckoned her over now with a satisfied note in his voice.

"This is the artist," he said, and he nudged Amanda forward with a fatherly hand. "Mr. . . . Potter here is from Coral Cliff Hotel, and he's most interested in your painting of Rose Hall Great House."

Amanda came forward with a smile. "Hello, Mr.

Potter," she said. "Yes, this one is a favorite of mine. Would you believe that as I was painting it, I actually thought that I saw a Rolling—" The words she had been about to say froze into splinters of ice, and wedged in her throat. *Good God Almighty, what was he doing here?*

Mr. Potter smiled benevolently at her. "A rolling? I'm afraid you'll have to explain that one, Miss Drake. It's too hard for me to keep up with all of the slang these days. . . ."

And his voice faded away to become a faint buzzing in Amanda's ear. At that very moment, she was as far away from him in thought as one could possibly get, her eyes glued to the beautiful Adonis as he strolled casually into the showroom with a tall woman on his arm. Amanda's eyes flickered over him, and the breath in her lungs became hot and short. He was unbelievably elegant in a navy-blue top and pair of cream-colored slacks. Oh, but he was magnificent, standing head, and in some cases shoulders, too, above most of the men in the room.

"Miss Drake?" A sharp voice calling to her from a distance brought her slowly out of her stupor. "Miss Drake, are you unwell?" It was Mr. Potter, and he appeared greatly concerned by her sudden catatonia.

Amanda mustered a smile and a very reassuring: "Oh, I'm fine, Mr. Potter. Really. There's no need to get anyone."

"Maybe you should sit down for a minute?"

Amanda took a filling breath. She didn't need to sit down; maybe she needed to stand on her head so that some of the blood that had drained away could make a rapid return, but she most definitely did not need to sit down.

She smiled at the little man and reassured him again. "I'm fine. Now what painting were you interested in? The seascape, wasn't it?"

TEN

"This place is packed, Nick," Harry said with some amount of disgust in his voice. "Why in the name of heaven did you want to drive all the way to Montego Bay just to see some local artist? Aren't there plenty enough to go around in Ocho Rios?"

Janet linked arms with both Harry and Nicholas. "Oh, come on, Harry. This'll be fun. It was my idea really. Not Nick's."

"You heard that, Britton," Nicholas said with a tinge of humor in his voice. "It wasn't my idea. So quit giving me a hard time."

Harry sighed. "What is so special about these paintings anyway?"

Janet pulled them both along. "I saw the ad in the Ochi newspaper. Apparently, the artist has developed an interesting new style of painting. She uses dots and dashes instead of smooth strokes."

"Dots and dashes? Isn't that what Monet did?"

And, before long, they were knee-deep in a discussion that rambled from Monet to Picasso and Van Gogh.

The sight of a passing waiter with his empty tray held high made Janet say, "Nick, darling, can you get us something to drink?"

"Do you see that?" Nicholas joked. "She chooses me for all of the grunt work."

"Well," Harry said, and he blew on his nails, only to dust them against his shirt, "it's only natural. I am better-looking."

They all laughed at that, and Nicholas said with a shrug, "I don't have a response for that. I guess I'd better go get the drinks." And he headed off, weaving his way across the very crowded room.

Halfway to the bar on the other end, an older woman with beautifully styled silver-gray hair stopped him to remark, "Darling . . . now you're the most beautiful piece of art I've seen here all night." And she slipped a card into the front of his shirt, patted Nicholas on the rump, and whispered a very suggestive "Call me."

Nicholas grinned at her, and kept moving. If she had been maybe twenty or thirty years younger, he might have given her a tumble, but his tastes did not yet run to the seduction of sexagenarians.

"Excuse me," he said as he attempted to maneuver around yet another cluster of gabbing women. The cluster turned as one, and Nicholas smiled. *Young women.* The kind he had an especial fondness for.

"Hello, ladies," he said in a rasping tone.

The boldest of the group looked him over with glittering eyes. "Hello yourself," she said, and ran her tongue around the edge of her wineglass.

A predatory gleam burst into fiery life in the depths of his eyes. *Now here was his kind of woman.* He gave her a very deliberate head-to-toe perusal, pausing on the gentle swell of bosom, and then moving slowly back to settle on her eyes. Maybe he had been wrong to swear off women of late. He had almost forgotten the thrilling rush of adrenaline that always surged through him when he was on the scent of the chase.

"Like what you see?" the girl asked, and the others in the group giggled at her audacity.

"Sweetheart," he said, "you look good enough to eat."

The girl sipped from her glass, and purred a throaty "Well, I hope you're hungry then."

Amanda, who had been watching his progress from across the room, pulled back behind the large whitewashed column that ran from floor to ceiling, and ran a palm across her forehead to smooth away the drops of perspiration that glistened there. Thank the Lord he didn't appear to realize who the artist was. Or maybe, he had blocked the entire incident at the wedding so completely out of his mind that he had forgotten her name. Maybe he had even forgotten her face. She rested her head against the flat of the column and closed her eyes for a second. It was really silly hiding in this manner. She had never felt the need to hide from any man before in her entire life. If he were anyone else, she would have been able to handle the situation nicely. Why was it that she couldn't now look him in the eye and brazen the thing through? So what if she had chained him to a bed and then abandoned him? Maybe such things happened to him every week. It wouldn't surprise her at all if that were really true either. By the looks of things, he was constantly besieged by women, young and old alike, who were more than willing to indulge his every whim.

"Amanda, dear . . . Amanda!"

She opened her eyes and cringed inside. Mr. Browning again. Why did he continually holler her name in that manner? This was not an auction at a meat market, for heaven's sake. It was supposed to be a classy art event.

"Amanda!"

She gritted her teeth. "Coming." She emerged from behind the column and collided solidly with a completely immovable wall of steel. She knew instinctively, before she even raised her eyes to his, to whom the steel belonged, and her heart charged into a frenetic pounding in her chest. *Oh, God, how had he come upon her so very suddenly?* He had been across the room just a minute before, talking to an entire pack of slobbering women. *Maybe he wouldn't remember her. Maybe he wouldn't remember what she had done.*

She raised her eyes slowly to meet the coal-black depths of his. Her throat clenched in a twisting awkward movement. *He remembered.*

He spoke first. "So . . . it's little Amanda Drake. The performance artist." Amanda sucked in a little breath. She didn't blame him for being upset. It was good that this had happened now. She had been dreading running into him again for weeks. Now it was over, and she didn't need to worry about it any longer.

She forced a certain boldness into her voice that she didn't really feel. "Nick Champagne." Her voice was breathy, soft.

"You remember me then?"

Her throat contracted in an involuntary swallow. "Of course I remember you," she croaked.

He stroked the side of his chin. "Yes . . . the last time I saw you I was sort of handcuffed to the frame of a rather large bed, wasn't I? So . . . how have things been progressing in that regard?"

Amanda blinked owlishly at him. "What do you mean . . . in that regard?"

His eyes were as silky as black satin. "I'm concerned for your well-being is all. Have you been taking your medication?" He gave the ceiling a quick glance. "I wouldn't like to suddenly discover you swinging from the rafters in here with a feather stuck between your teeth."

Amanda sniffed crossly. "I am not on any medication as you very well—"

But he interrupted her. "Now that's something I really think you need to reconsider. I'm a firm believer in the virtues of modern medicine, you know, so if you need the help, then for God's sake get it."

Amanda drew herself up. "You're an extremely rude man," she said, and because she could think of nothing else to say that was suitably cutting, she turned abruptly on her heel and left him. *Medication indeed.* He was the one who needed medication, not her. Philanderer that he was. Frolicking all over the place with every living female who still had a pulse beating somewhere in her. Fathering children here, there, and everywhere. He was the one in need of medication, possibly a good dose of shock therapy, too.

"Amanda!" came the bellow from somewhere near the door to the establishment.

"Coming, Mr. Browning. I'm coming."

Nicholas walked back with three fluted glasses of white wine. *Good, he had gotten that off his chest.* Now he would forget her. He would forget her so completely that the next time someone said, "Amanda," his natural response would be: "Amanda who?"

"What are you looking so very stern about?" Janet asked as soon as he was close enough.

Harry's eyes followed Amanda as she barreled a

path through the crowd. "Ah . . . now I understand," he said with a grin. "No handcuffs this time?"

Nicholas gave him a dark look, and drank deeply from his glass of wine.

Janet's eyes flashed between them both. "What do you mean handcuffs?"

Harry chuckled. "Oh, it's an old joke. Nick tells it best."

Janet looked at Nicholas, who was glowering into his glass of wine. "So tell it, Nicky. Sounds like a good one."

Nicholas swallowed the rest of the chilled wine, wiped his mouth with a linen napkin, and rasped in a voice that did not encourage further discussion: "I think I've seen enough. Let's get outta here."

ELEVEN

The month of July rolled in, in a sweet blue haze. It was hot, but not swelteringly so, and the trees all around the sprawling Champagne estate were bursting with ripe wonderful fruit. There were luscious red-gold mangoes, plump gennips, oranges, lemons, and an assortment of other fruit swaying from the branches. The trees labored through their multiple pregnancies without complaint, hissing and singing beautifully as the brisk ocean breeze raced through their leaves, casting off the occasional fruit and sending it rolling to some warm and forgotten spot.

School was out, and hordes of children ran happily along the sandy beaches with multicolored kites trailing drunkenly behind them, their laughing voices flavoring the wind with the very essence of summer. The scent of happiness was in every breath of air. It was a time for cricket, for barbecuing huge slabs of beef, for being swept up by the simple glories of living.

Nicholas stood over a large smoky grill in the expansive backyard behind his brother's house. Behind him, Amber splashed around in the smoothly designed black-bottomed pool, shrieking every so often, "Look, Aunty Sumsum . . . look at me." Summer was stretched out on a deck chair, her long limbs glinting like burnished gold in the soft sunlight. With a pair of very chic-looking sunglasses perched on her nose, she looked not unlike a movie star relaxing in some secluded spot in the south of France. She raised her hand now to further shield her eyes from the sun.

"Careful, Amber, love," she said, "so you don't slip and fall."

Nicholas turned from the grill to say, "Amber, stop that running."

The little girl, whose aquatic ability was quite phenomenal, took a flying leap into the pool to land in the water with a giant splash. Gavin emerged from the patio door with a cell phone tucked beneath his chin.

"Amber," he bellowed. "Stop that right now."

The little head bobbed up from beneath the silky surface of water. "But Uncle Gavin . . ." she began.

Gavin ended the call and walked to the water's edge. "Would you like a spanking?"

Satin eyes locked with his, and the child shook her head in mute acquiescence.

"OK then," Gavin said. "I don't want to see any more of this running and jumping into the pool. Do you understand? If you fall and hit your head on the concrete, we'll have to rush you to the hospital."

"OK, Uncle," she said in a meek voice that didn't fool him for a second. She was becoming terribly spoiled, he knew, being the only child around so many adults. It was true that he doted on her as much as anyone else. It was very hard not to. She was a completely delightful child who also happened to possess a particularly precocious tongue.

Summer uncurled herself from the lounger. In a soft undertone she asked her husband, "Is everything arranged now?"

Gavin slid the phone into the back pocket of his cotton shorts. "First thing next week," he said. "How's that?" And his brows flicked upwards to form a smooth black pelt.

Summer wrapped long arms about his waist. "You know," she said with a cheeky smile, "I think I love you."

A smile lit in the depths of his eyes. "Remind me of that later tonight." He turned her around neatly, draped an arm about her neck. "Now," he said, "let's go cheer him up."

Nicholas lifted the piece of meat from the grill. From his *Kiss the Cook* apron, he removed a bottle of jerk seasoning. He shook it vigorously, then poured the pungent contents in a generous layer all over the chicken.

"Mmm, smells great," Summer said.

Gavin went over to the grill to take a look. "We should take a piece for Mom later this evening."

Nicholas wiped his hands on a rag. "Yeah," he said without much enthusiasm. Summer felt a sudden rush of queasiness, and used this as the perfect opportunity to excuse herself. Gavin needed to have a few words in private with his brother, and she needed to take another dosing of Tums. Of late, her stomach had been giving her quite a bit of trouble.

"I'll be back in a little bit," she said, and walked rapidly indoors.

After his wife had left, Gavin leaned on the whitewashed rails, and stared out at the peaceful blue of the Caribbean. Nicholas came to lean beside him.

"Great day for sailing," Gavin said after a moment.

Nicholas shielded his eyes. "Yeah, we should take the boat out tomorrow."

Gavin nodded, and then got straight to the heart of the matter. "Look, Nick," he said. "You've got to put this thing between yourself and Mom to rest. There's no point to it."

Nicholas shrugged. "There's no 'thing.' I just don't have the patience you have."

"Umm-hmm," Gavin said in a noncommittal way. "So, what is going on? Harry's been gone a week, but he'll be back in a few."

Nicholas chuckled. "Harry's good enough company . . . but what I need is the comfort of a woman."

Gavin rested a hand on his brother's back. "Well, that's never been a problem for you before. You're young, good-looking . . . rich. Go out and get yourself one . . . just don't knock her up."

Nicholas drew in a deep breath and let it back out slowly. "That's the thing," he said. "You know I've never had a problem getting girls . . . I've had to work to keep them off me most of the time." He sighed. "I don't know. Maybe they're all just too easy. There's no challenge to the chase anymore."

Gavin scratched the side of this head with a thoughtful finger. "What kind of woman do you want?" He looked behind him to make sure his wife was not within hearing distance. "One like Summer? Bossy . . . feisty . . . a pistol in bed?"

Nicholas chuckled ruefully. "Thing is, I don't know what I want anymore. Maybe I'm having a mid-life crisis."

"At thirty-two, you're a bit too young to be worrying about that," Gavin said, laughing. Then, with a glint of hidden knowledge in his eyes, he asked:

"What about that curvy little number who . . . ah . . . you met at the wedding?"

"That one?" Nicholas straightened. "I really don't need that kind of stress in my life right now. She might be OK in bed, but she's. . . ."

"Take her to bed then," Gavin interrupted. "Get it out of your system. You don't have to marry the girl. You know that."

"Hmm," Nicholas said, and a shade of interest crept into his voice. "I haven't had a single woman all year, that could be why I'm so messed up . . . and this chick is a wild one. . . ."

Gavin slapped his back. "Well, that's all there is to it then. I know you're trying to do the right thing. But you can't just up and quit cold turkey. What you're going through now is simple withdrawal. Bed the girl. OK?"

Nicholas grinned. "OK." His brother always had a way of cutting through all of the nonsense. He was blunt. To the point. But Gavin always got to the heart of things. Nicholas hadn't wanted to admit it to himself, but that was exactly what he needed. He needed to finish with Amanda Drake what they had begun at the wedding. This time, though, if anyone were to be handcuffed, the nut job would be the one on the receiving end, that was certain.

Gavin cracked a beer, handed the can to Nicholas, then selected another for himself. He took a deep swig, grimaced. "I had a look at the pendant Summer has. Her initials were printed on the back of that one, too."

Nicholas swallowed a healthy gulp of golden beer. "Have you said anything to her about it yet?"

Gavin shook his head. "No . . . I've had a P.I. looking into Janet's background for a while now. I won't say anything to Summer until I know for sure, one way or the other."

Nicholas nodded. "It's gonna blow her mind. Can you imagine? Those two can't stand each other."

"Yeah," Gavin agreed, "it's gonna be a big old mess, if things show—"

The clatter of footsteps behind them made them both turn.

"Lunch," Summer said, smiling. In her hands she carried a large bowl of nicely chilled potato salad. Bringing up the rear was the housekeeper, who was pushing a trolley filled with an assortment of steaming dishes.

Nicholas cleared a spot on the circular table, removing foil, silver tongs, and other utensils. "Right here, my love," he said.

Summer placed the salad in the middle of the table, and then went to the pool's edge to clap her hands briskly. "Come on, Amber, time for lunch."

"A little longer, Auntie?" was the plaintive request.

"No," Summer said, "right now."

The little girl swam like a fish, gliding underwater for a good stretch before popping up again by the half-moon-shaped stairs. Summer held out a large beach towel.

"Come on," she said. And Amber clambered up the stairs to be patted dry, then draped in the towel.

"Can I go back in after I eat, Auntie?"

"Maybe later this evening," Summer said with a smile. She walked Amber over to a chair, and placed her gently in the seat. Gavin pulled out a chair for Summer, and she sat.

"You've got to try this jerk chicken," Nicholas said, sawing off a succulent chunk of breast. He popped a sliver into his mouth and chewed with obvious enjoyment. "It's some of the best I've done yet."

Summer reached for the chicken. "You always say that," she teased.

Nicholas winked. "That's because each time is better than the last."

"I like a modest man, don't you?" Gavin said, chuckling.

Summer placed a pinch into her mouth. "Umm-mm," she said, "but he's so right. I can taste the onions, the garlic . . . pepper, and it's so soft and good!"

"Thank you . . . thank you," Nicholas said, then raised a hand to declare, "No . . . no applause now, please."

Amber bounced in her seat. "Silly Dada," she said.

Summer picked up a small plate. "Will you try a little slice of chicken, Amber, darling?"

The little girl shook her head and gave the chicken her four-year-old version of a completely horrified look. "Was that chicken alive before, Auntie Sumsum?"

"Yes," Summer agreed, already knowing what was coming next.

"Well . . . who killed it?"

"I don't know, darling."

"Why do we have to eat the chickens?"

Summer looked at Nicholas, then Gavin. "Because . . . well, because we have to eat if we don't want to become sick."

"But it's cruel to eat chickens, Auntie."

Summer put down the chicken fork. "What about some nice potato salad then? Yes?" She placed a portion of that on the plate. "And some carrots?"

When the plate was filled with a good assortment

of fruits and vegetables, Summer put it before the little girl. She folded a napkin around the neck of Amber's swimsuit and said, "Now, eat everything on your plate."

Gavin shook his head in bemused fascination. "I never realized she didn't eat any meat at all. How long has this been going on?"

"She's never really been fond of meat . . . ever," Nicholas said. "She'll eat everything else. Fish from time to time, but . . . no chicken or beef."

Summer quickly dished a plate for Nicholas, then one for her husband. "It is strange for such a little child to decide to go completely vegetarian. But as long as she has a balanced diet . . . it shouldn't be a problem. And she may grow out of it yet."

"Hmm," Gavin agreed, and bent his head to dig into his meal. They ate in companionable silence for a good stretch. Mrs. Carydice reappeared at some point during the meal to remove their plates and to ask if they wanted dessert. Both Nicholas and Gavin immediately accepted the offer of thickly iced chocolate cake, but Summer patted her stomach and declared, "None for me, thanks."

Amber, who was still working her way quite diligently through her plate of food, said with great anxiety, "I'm 'most finished, Auntie . . . can I have some?"

"Have you had enough then?"

Amber nodded vigorously. "Yes, Auntie," she said sweetly.

Summer scooped up a spoonful of potato salad and put it into her mouth. "OK, I'll finish the rest of this for you."

Amber clapped her hands. "Dada," she said, suddenly switching streams, "can I go feed the kitty?"

Nicholas leaned forward to wipe a smudge of

food from the side of her face. "Didn't we feed her just a little while ago?"

"Yes . . . but she needs lunch, too."

Gavin hid a chuckle behind a hand.

Nicholas smiled. "Go on then. Ask Mrs. Carydice to give you a few scraps. But . . . don't run . . . walk," he said as she bounded from the chair.

"That child never slows down," Summer said. "She must get that from you, Nicky."

Gavin leaned forward to tear a strip of chicken from the half-eaten bird. "Isn't that the truth. When he was a little kid he used to . . ." But what he had been about to say was suddenly interrupted by a loud "Oh, no!" and then an attendant crash.

Almost as one, they were out of their chairs and running for the patio door. Nicholas made it into the house first.

"Amber?" he called, and his eyes hunted the sleekly furnished dining room, and the area just beyond. Mrs. Carydice was down on the floor, sopping up a quickly spreading pool of water. Above her, the aquarium lay on its side. Amber stood close by, her eyes rounded in petrified wonder. Beside her was the completely drenched kitten, which, despite its half-drowned appearance, looked decidedly pleased with itself. Nicholas released a breath. Thank God Amber was OK. All manner of thoughts had swept through him when he had heard that crash.

"What happened?" he asked Mrs. Carydice.

The housekeeper looked up from her busywork on the floor. "She was feeding de cat with de aquarium fish."

Nicholas looked around him. *God.* And those were some very expensive fish, flown in especially from the States, too.

Gavin was behind him now. "What happened?"

Nicholas turned to his brother. "I told her to stay away from those fish. She's fed most of them to the cat. The rest . . ." And he pointed to the tipped-over aquarium.

Gavin turned away a moment as a reluctant smile tugged at the corners of his lips. He didn't much care about the fish, those could be replaced, but the child could have been badly hurt by the falling aquarium. She had to learn that when she was told not to do something, it was not a request.

"Come here, Amber," Gavin said now.

Summer touched her husband's arm and whispered, "Don't spank her, honey."

The little girl looked at her father for help, but Nicholas shook his head. "I can't help you."

The little face crumpled and before she had even begun to move, there were tears streaming down her face. Gavin stooped to her level.

"Why are you crying?" he asked.

"The . . . the . . . kitty . . . was hungry," she said, sobbing.

He held her about the waist. "Didn't I tell you not to touch the fish?"

She nodded. "Yes, Uncle."

"Did you think I meant it?"

She nodded again. "I won't touch again . . . Uncle? Never . . . ever. I pwomise."

"No, you won't," Gavin said. "Now, because you disobeyed me . . . you will have no chocolate cake . . . and if anything like this happens again, you will get a spanking. Do you understand me?"

The little head nodded. "Yes, Uncle."

Gavin brushed a couple of tears away with the flat of a thumb. "Now, stop crying. . . ."

Amber gave one final hiccupping sob. "You still love me, Uncle?"

Gavin picked her up while Nicholas and Summer bent to help with the cleaning. "Should I love you even when you're a bad girl?" he asked with a glint of humor in his eyes.

Amber held his face between her two little hands. "But I love *you* even when you're a bad uncle. . . ."

Gavin smiled at the earnest chubby-cheeked face. She was so like Nicholas. Even when she was at her worst, he couldn't stay annoyed with her for long. One day when she was fully grown, she was going to have them all jumping through hoops.

"Give Uncle a kiss," he said. And she obliged him with two kisses, one on either side of his face.

Nicholas uncurled from his stooped position. In his cupped hands he held what remained of the tank of fish.

"I don't think these're gonna make it."

Gavin nodded to the kitchen. "Put them in a bowl of water. See if they'll come out of it."

Nicholas looked at his daughter, who was now resting comfortably with her head snuggled beneath his brother's chin. He shook his head. "If I was anything like this when I was younger, I don't know how you put up with me."

Gavin chuckled. "Oh, you were much worse."

Nicholas shuddered. "God protect us when she's a teenager. I remember some of the things I did."

Gavin hugged the little body in his arms. "You're not going to give us any trouble, are you, Amber, darling? You're going to be a good girl. Not like Daddy."

The little head nodded. "Dada was a bad boy."

Summer looked at Nicholas with a grin. "Dada is still a bad boy."

* * *

Later that evening, after the heat of the day had burned off, they all walked across to the cottage that stood a little stretch up the beach. It was a burnt-orange evening, and the ocean punched and slapped at the shoreline like a giant hand, tossing up fistfuls of spray as it skidded recklessly across the sand. Gavin and Summer walked with arms about each other; Nicholas, with Amber perched atop his shoulders, chased each wave as it came in. The little girl shrieked in delight as Nicholas ran out after the retreating foam, only to turn when the water reared up in defiance, and race back in with a wave on his heels.

"Dada . . . Dada . . . run faster. Faster," she yelled as the water made up the distance with amazing speed. Nicholas did a little impromptu dance in the warm silky water as it caught him, and Amber laughed heartily and clapped her hands in delight.

"Again, Dada . . . again."

And so it was as they wound their way up the beach toward the cottage. A gentle wind pulled in a friendly manner at their clothes as they got closer to the cozy little place. In the glorious orange-pink glow of sunset, the house appeared like an idyllic spot indeed, the face of it almost completely covered with an abundance of creeping roses.

Nicholas squinted at the house now. "I've never seen it look this beautiful. Almost doesn't seem real with all those white and gold roses."

Summer nodded. "With the sun behind it like this . . . it would make a gorgeous painting. Don't you think, honey?" She turned to her husband with innocent eyes.

Gavin smiled. "I was thinking the exact same thing. What do you think, Nick?"

Nicholas laughed. "It might at that."

They all tramped up the wooden stairs leading from the beach to the wraparound veranda, their footsteps heavy on the wood now after crunching through the sand. Mrs. Robbins, ever vigilant, appeared on the portico before they had cleared the top stair. She beamed a smile, and waved.

"Oh, she's going to be so pleased."

Nicholas took a filling breath. *Pleased? He very seriously doubted it.* He lifted Amber from his shoulders.

"Be a very good girl now, Amber," he said. "You know Nana doesn't like it when you touch things. OK?"

The child nodded. "OK, Dada. But do we have to stay long?"

"Nana likes it when we visit her, so we will stay as long as she wants, OK?"

The little head bobbed in agreement, and Nicholas held on to her hand tightly as they walked through the veranda door.

Ester Champagne looked up as they all entered. She sat in a comfortable white settee, a giant ball of wool on her lap. Nicholas hung back as Gavin and Summer went forward to greet her.

Gavin bent to kiss his mother's cheek. "Hello, Mom," he said. "How're you feeling?"

Ester looked up at her eldest son. "Those damn birds," she said. "If I catch one of them I'll cut its tongue out."

Nicholas covered Amber's ears, but it was too late; the child was already whispering, "Dada, why does Nana want to kill the birds?"

"Hush," Nicholas said.

Gavin knelt beside the chair. "What birds, Mom?"

"Sssh!" Ester Champagne held up a hand. "Listen. Listen to them," she said. "Screaming. All day long they're screaming. It's almost enough to drive you crazy."

A frown creased the smooth skin of Nicholas's brow. *It was a little too late for that.*

"They're just seagulls, Mom," Gavin was saying with great patience. "They're friendly little birds. You'll get accustomed to them after a while."

Ester peered around her son at Summer. "So, you've come back to finish the job, have you?"

Summer exchanged a glance with Nicholas. "Pardon me, Mom?"

Ester switched her attention to Gavin. "That cat-eyed girl is trying to kill me," she said in a low tone. "She's always bringing me food."

Gavin patted his mother's hand. "This is Summer, Mom. You remember her? She's my wife . . . she's the one responsible for this beautiful cottage. She decorated it. Remember?"

Ester pulled her hand away. "Watch her," she said. "She'll be coming after you next. Mark my words."

Summer gave Nicholas a little push. "Go on," she said. "You'll have to give her the jerk chicken yourself. She'll not take it from me."

Nicholas swallowed hard before going forward. "Hello, Mom," he said, not bothering to press the obligatory kiss to her cheek as Gavin had just done. "I brought you some chicken . . . jerk chicken."

Ester peered for a long unblinking moment at the tall man standing before her. "Oh, yes," she finally said, "you're the one who can't keep his zipper up. So, you've finally decided to come and see me."

"I've come before, Mother," Nicholas said, and there was barely concealed irritation in his voice now.

Ester blinked. "Well, not enough. Not enough." Then she changed direction with stunning speed. "Where're the other two?" she asked.

"Mik and Rob are away at college, but they'll both be here next weekend," Gavin said.

Nicholas retreated to stand close to the veranda door. This was a weekly ordeal that he could just as well not go through at all. He pitied his mother for her condition, but what more could he do? He did not feel close to her. He probably would never feel close to her. It scared him to think that whatever it was that was wrong with her might also be lurking somewhere in his genes, just waiting to erupt into uncontrollable life at some nebulous point in the future. He turned his back as he heard Gavin say, "Amber, come say hello to Nana."

Summer came to stand beside him. "It's OK, Nicky," she said. "Just give her some time. Don't blame her too much for what she says."

Nicholas looked down at her. "I'm not like Gavin," he said. "I can't deal with this."

Summer patted him on the back. "Never mind."

Mrs. Robbins bustled in just then with a large silver tray. "Tea," she said brightly.

"Ah, good." Gavin smiled, and they all went to sit around the small center table.

"I wouldn't do that," Ester said, shaking her head as the nurse disappeared again and they all prepared to drink deeply from the pretty gilt-tipped teacups.

Gavin's eyebrows came together to form a straight line. "Why not, Mom?"

Ester put down her ball of wool, and with a diamond-bright gleam in her eyes, she leaned forward to inform the gathering at large that since Nurse Robbins was currently suffering from the stomach flu, they would all be well advised not to have any of the tea.

Understandably, teacups clattered again into the accompanying saucers, and shortly thereafter, a chorus of hasty good-byes was said.

TWELVE

Amanda gave another glance at the directions lying beside her on the passenger seat. According to her map she should be very nearly there. Gavin Pagne had told her to use the coast road that ran between Montego Bay and Ocho Rios. He had also said that the turnoff that led to the Champagne estate was hard to miss. There would be a large wooden sign running between two trees; the sign would have white lettering saying: *Champagne Cove*.

Her brow wrinkled as she slowed the car to a crawl, and peered out the window. She made eye contact with a passing woman who walked the border of the road with a basket of goods balanced impossibly atop her head.

"Excuse me. Do you know where the Champagne estate is?"

The woman lifted a hand to steady her basket. "Champagne? Oh . . . it fur'der down dat side, man."

Amanda squinted at the curving road. "How far? A mile?"

"Jus' follow de road little bit. You can't miss it. Awright?"

Amanda gave the woman a nod and a smile. "Thank you," she said.

The battered Volkswagen bug sputtered a bit as

Amanda eased her foot down on the gas pedal. She gave the gas gauge a hurried glance. It had been a while since she had seen a station, but she was still doing quite well. It was just below a half a tank. More than enough to get her to where she needed to go.

The road weaved and curved, grew bumpy, and just as suddenly evened out again. Tall, spindly coconut palms grew in clusters in certain places, and large leafy green trees of some unknown parentage cast dappled patterns of shadow and light across the road. Between the thick growths of bush and tree, she could see the occasional snatch of glittering blue, and her heart picked up a notch. Was the estate right on the ocean then? How lovely if that were to be the case. There was nothing more wonderful than sitting on a beach, listening to the folding and frothing of the waves against the sand; nothing better, too, than painting until the sky was all orange, silver, and then a smooth velvety black.

She had jumped at the job offer when Gavin Pagne had called just days before. He had been polite and to the point. His wife, herself a professional designer, was in the process of decorating their newly built house, and needed to have a set of specially done paintings. He was familiar with Amanda's work, and thought she might be able to produce the sort of artwork that would suit his wife's tastes. Amanda had assured him immediately that she could do the job, for although her art exhibition had gone quite well, she had not made nearly enough money to live on. The fact that Nicholas Champagne might be close at hand had absolutely nothing to do with her hasty acceptance of the commission, though. She was to do most of her work at the manor house anyway, and chances were very good that she might never even see him. Most families that she was acquainted with did not live in each other's back pockets. So, although Nicholas Champagne might drop by his brother's house from time to time, she did not expect to see very much of him at all. Besides, they had said everything that needed to be said to each other at the exhibition. He had been rude. She had been cutting. She had walked off and left him standing in the middle of the floor. He had left her exhibition in the middle of the proceedings. In short, there was absolutely no reason under the sun why she should turn down a perfectly good job just because Nicholas Champagne was a relative of her new employer. If he did put in an appearance, she would keep out of his way, and he, understandably, would keep out of hers.

Amanda shifted into a lower gear now as the road curved yet again and then went into a little climb. As the car crested the top of the hill, spread out before her like a shimmering band of blue silk was the Caribbean Sea. And it was some of the most beautiful water she had yet seen. A strange blend of navy and turquoise green, rolling away from the coastline, stretching out magnificently toward the smooth horizon. And the air, surely the purest air to be had on earth was right here. Right in this very spot. Beautiful. Just beautiful was what it was.

An unconscious smile curved the corners of her mouth. How much this time in Jamaica had changed her. It had somehow brought her back to her essential self, to that softer part of her that had been all but covered up by the scabs of life. She was purer here. Better.

Her eyes hunted now for the sign. Neatly groomed coconut palms stood guard at a gaping entrance just ahead. Stretched between them was the sign, *Champagne Cove*, just as Gavin Pagne had said. Amanda slowed the car, and turned unto the crunchy drive. Coconut palms lined the pink gravel on both sides, all the way up the neatly manicured driveway. The grass was low-cropped and lush, and here and there on the rolling green, Amanda could see clusters of flowering hibiscus trees. It was a gorgeous place, and huge. Simply huge was what it was.

She pulled to a stop in the circular courtyard and cut the car's engine. Just behind, a glorious waterfall cascaded into a rock pond. The entire place whispered of wealth and privilege, and for a brief moment Amanda felt a stab of envy. How nice it would be to live in this manner. She had struggled every day of her life. She had bounced around the entire continental United States as a child, being passed from relative to relative when she became too much of an inconvenience or too much of a handful. By the time she was sixteen years old, she had lived in ten different states, and had attended at least as many schools. Her memories of childhood had become a blur of faces, towns, and schools. She had gotten into college by some miracle, given her choppy academic past, but once in, with the stability of continuance, she had blossomed, grown. Her artistic abilities had been recognized, and praised. And she had known then that this was the manner in which she would make her life, her living. But she did long sometimes for someone to care for her. A mother. Father. Anybody. But she had no one. No one at all. She had learned early in life that if she were going to survive, she would have to learn to take care of herself. So, that place around her heart that had been born soft and pure had hardened. At the prompting of her roommate Sheila, she had allowed herself to drift into a sordid kind of life, a life where she scammed wealthy men for money. It had been something she had become very good at. She went out with them, allowed them to spend huge amounts of money on her, and then at some opportune moment, she dumped them. Marriage had never been her objective. That had been one level she had never allowed herself to sink to, thinking somehow that to marry a man she didn't love, just for his possessions, was infinitely worse than dating him for just a little while.

She squinted up at the big house now. It would have been nice to be born to all of this, though. Not to have to worry about money ever again; to be free to really stretch out and enjoy the many vagaries of her life. But it was not to be for her. And so she continued making the best of things. She had long since given up on hope. She lived each day that came with a bright determination, but she didn't hope anymore.

Amanda closed the window quickly, gathered her things, and stepped from the car. She shielded her eyes against the sun. The house was a rambling three-story, populated by quaint little window boxes from which a profusion of roses grew. A nice place indeed, she mused as she began to climb the stairs. She placed her shoulder bag at her feet and looked around for the bell. It took her a minute to realize that the huge brass knocker on the door was to be used as a substitute.

She pounded on the wood for a good few minutes before deciding that there was probably no one at home. She was just about to return to her car to wait when a voice behind her asked: "Are you the artist lady we've been expecting?"

Amanda turned to greet the speaker, a polite smile stretching her lips.

"Yes," she said, coming back down the steps, "I'm Amanda Drake. I'm here to see Gavin . . . Champagne . . . Pagne, I mean."

The woman nodded. "We've been expecting you. But you're at the wrong house."

Amanda's brows furrowed. *Wrong house?* But it did say Champagne Cove on the sign out front. "Isn't this where the Champagnes live?" she asked, puzzled.

The woman bent to hoist the little girl at her side. "Yes, ma'am," she said, "but you want the other house. That's where Mrs. Champagne lives. Come, me will show you."

"Thank you." Amanda smiled. "Hello, pretty," she said to the child, who had been staring at her with an expression of open curiosity on her face.

"Hello," was the response. Then: "My name's not Pretty."

"No?" Amanda said, still smiling. "What is it then?"

The black eyes looked her over in a rather adult manner, and apparently found her to be lacking in some regard. "My Dada says I'm not to talk to stwangers," she said after giving Amanda a thorough head-to-toe assessment.

Amanda suppressed the desire to chuckle; *Nicholas Champagne's daughter, no doubt . . . and Sheila's.* She should have recognized the child from the wedding, but at the time, she'd had other more pressing things on her mind.

"Your daddy's right. You shouldn't talk to strangers," she agreed.

They were now walking up a nicely cobbled path that wound its way through a multitude of fruit trees. The property was more expansive than she had originally realized. Behind the first house was a large backyard that seemed to blend smoothly with a fruit orchard, which in turn opened up to reveal another even larger house and acreage of land.

"Oh," Amanda said, genuinely surprised by it all, "this is lovely."

The woman nodded. "Yes. It's a really beautiful place . . . and the Champagnes are just de nicest people. Dem really down to earth . . . you know?" And as though just realizing that she hadn't properly introduced herself, she said: "I'm de house-keeper, Mrs. Carydice, in case you'd been wondering."

They were almost to the house now, and the artist in Amanda appreciated the smooth clean lines of it. Done in glorious ultramodern style, it was a sprawling two-story with a veranda that ran the entire circumference of the bottom floor. Nicely spaced lightly tinted windows on the second level hovered above several smaller jutting patios. Rose-bushes clustered around the stairs on either side. And just behind the house itself, the cobalt-blue ocean.

Amanda took a deep gulp of sea air. It was crisp and wonderful and filling. The soft scent of ocean salt. The gusty winds that rippled fond fingers through her short cap of curls. She could live here forever and not experience even a pang of home-sickness for the States.

The screen door opened just as they mounted the first stair, and Amanda looked up. Summer Champagne. She had seen her before at the wedding, of course, but now, with her flowing ebony hair down about her shoulders, her beauty was a vibrant, golden perfection. A guarded expression entered Amanda's eyes. Summer was tall and slender, and *God*, Amanda had never been overly fond of women who possessed her particular brand of good looks.

But she would at least try to get on with the lady
of the house, even if she did turn out to be as conceited as her appearance suggested she might be.

"Welcome." Summer beamed, and she came clat-
tering down the stairs in a pair of high-heeled sandals.

The little girl, who had been as quiet as a mouse
since her initial conversation, came into shrieking
life now. "Auntie," she bellowed, "we bwought you
someone."

"So I see." Summer pressed a kiss to the child's
face, then said to Amanda: "I'm so glad you're finally here. Let me help you with your bag." And
she whipped the carry case from Amanda before
she could even think to object. She gave Amanda a
bronzed hazel look. "How was the drive up from
MoBay?"

Amanda made her lips smile. "Not bad. The drive
along the coast was great."

Summer hooked an arm through Amanda's.
"Then I guess you must be starved. All that ocean
air always makes me hungry."

And she pulled Amanda into the house. "You're
going to be staying with us. Did Gavin tell you?"

"Well . . . not exactly. He did say something
about accommodations being provided . . . but I
wasn't sure where."

Summer smiled. "My husband is sometimes a
man of very few words. You mustn't let him intimi-
date you, by the way. He's really a big sweetheart,
but some people find him a bit overpowering."

Amanda nodded. "Don't worry about that. I
don't scare easy."

Summer handed the bag she'd been carrying to
the housekeeper. "Would you put this in Amanda's
room, Mrs. Carydice . . . and Amber could do with

a little snack. We'll fix a little something for ourselves."

Amanda followed her through a glorious sunken sitting room decorated in shades of white and aqua. She was immediately impressed by the wonderful way the colors blended with the light, the ocean, the trees; even the air seemed to sit in gorgeous contentment in the room. There was a huge stone fireplace at one end, faced with chunky uneven rock. And the patio swept out and down a few stairs to a large black-bottomed pool, Jacuzzi, and barbeque area. The walls, though, the walls were completely bare. Hence the reason she was now here.

"Your husband told me you're a professional designer," Amanda said now.

"Um-hmm," Summer agreed, and she sat her guest at a shiny black-top island that divided the kitchen in two, then went about pulling open cupboards and removing glasses, plates, forks.

"I'm originally from L.A.," Summer went on. "Came down here on a special job . . . long story really . . . Nicky hired me to refurbish the cottage up the beach . . . without Gavin even knowing about it." She turned from the cupboards for a second, hair swishing about her shoulders, eyes gleaming with hidden fun. "That Nicky," she said, "he chose me, you know?"

Amanda blinked. *Nicholas Champagne had chosen her?* Whatever could she mean?

Summer observed the immediate flushing of Amanda Drake's cheeks, and she turned back to the cupboards to hide a smile. The poor girl was quite smitten with Nicky. *Good. Very good indeed.* She would see what could be done to help things along.

Summer charged on. "I'm sure you're wondering what I mean by that. . . ."

Uncharacteristically, Amanda found herself stumbling into speech. "Oh, no . . . I would guess you meant that . . . that he hired you because he liked your work?"

"Wrong." Summer tossed the comment over her shoulder. "He hired me because *he* decided that I would be the one to tame his brother."

Despite herself, Amanda leaned forward, interested. "Had he met you before then?"

"Not really. We both went to UCLA . . . but he didn't really know me then. He just saw a picture of me in a portfolio, and decided on me. Kinda like picking me out of a lineup, I guess."

Amanda laughed. "That's crazy."

Summer was back at the center island now, laying down things. "You're telling me," she said. "You don't know the half of it. When Gavin found out I'd been hired . . . he told me that he was putting me on the first plane back to LA . . . can you imagine? After I'd flown all that way?"

"You didn't leave, though?" Amanda asked as she helped arrange the utensils.

Summer went across to the fridge and began to remove a collection of multicolored Tupperware. Her head poked out of the fridge to grin at Amanda. "Go back? Are you kidding? I told him I was here to do a job and I intended to do it. And if he wanted to fight me on it . . . I would sue him for breach of contract, and any of a variety of other reasons."

Amanda snorted. "You didn't say all that?"

Summer put down the containers. "I did," she said with dancing eyes. "But that was after I bit

Gavin on the shoulder, and bashed him in the head with my shoe."

Amanda was speechless for a moment, and then the laughter bubbled out of her. "You can't be serious? You bit him?"

Summer sat. "That's right I bit him . . . Nicky's fault again. What would you do if someone climbed into your bed in the middle of the night, smacked you on the backside, and told you in no uncertain terms to get out? I thought I was being attacked, for heaven's sake."

Amanda wiped a tear from the corner of her eye. "Oh, my God . . . you're crazy," she said.

Summer ladled a healthy portion of potato salad and carrots unto a plate. "Do you like jerk chicken?" she asked. "Even if you don't really like it . . . you've got to try this." She tore off a strip of the chicken and chewed with obvious enjoyment. "Nicky's specialty."

"Looks delicious," Amanda agreed. "So what did poor Gavin do with you after everything was sorted out?"

Summer sampled a forkful of potato salad, chewed with eyes slightly slitted. "The only thing he could do. He let me stay and finish the job. Halfway into it, though," she said, leaning forward with a conspiratorial whisper, "I had decided that he was the man I wanted to marry. And marry him I would."

Amanda choked on a swallow of food. *What audacity. What absolute nerve. She might actually come to really like this woman.* Summer leaned forward to give her back a pat.

"You didn't tell him that, though?" Amanda asked after she had recovered from her spate of coughing.

Summer grinned. "Oh, no. You know you can never tell them things like that. The poor things would run screaming into the sea. But Nicky was on my side. That helped tremendously, believe me. They're very close . . . Gavin and Nicky."

"Hmm," Amanda said through a mouthful of wonderful chicken. "Does he live in the first house I saw?"

Summer nodded. "They all lived there originally when I showed up. Gavin, Nicky, Mik, Rob. This house wasn't here at all. It's completely new. Built just for Gavin and me. Now Nicky lives there alone with little Amber when Mik and Rob are away at school."

"Wow," Amanda said, "it must be nice to have all this. And right on the ocean too."

Summer leaned forward to gesture with a chicken bone. "All this would have meant nothing at all to me had I married the first guy I'd been engaged to . . . and lived right here with him."

"Oh," Amanda said, not knowing if she had somehow blundered onto sensitive ground. "I didn't mean. . . ."

Summer gripped Amanda's arm in a warm and very friendly manner. "No, really," she said, "possessions mean nothing at all if you marry for the wrong reasons."

Amanda nodded. Now that she firmly believed.

Summer smiled at her. "Take me, for example. I used to be a very . . ." She sighed. "Not materialistic really," she said. "But . . . I knew what I wanted out of life, and no one, but no one, was going to stand in my way. So, I chose a guy whom I didn't care for at all . . . just because I thought that together we could have all those material things I thought I needed to be happy. I never would've met

Gavin had I gone ahead with that. . . . I can't even
imagine my life now without him. Sometimes you've
just got to surrender yourself to fate. . . . God
knows what's best for you, even when you don't."

Black eyes locked with golden brown, and in that
glance a friendship was sealed.

"So what happened to change things?" Amanda
was curious, and very seriously impressed with how
candid and open Summer Champagne appeared to
be.

"Gavin happened. Nicky happened. Mik and Rob
happened. I came to Jamaica empty . . . and this
family of Champagne men . . . they filled me up . . .
made me whole again."

Amanda turned away for a second, for she felt
the sudden unbelievable prick of tears at her eyes.
How could it be? How could it be? They were so
similar in type. In experience. In feeling. She, too,
had arrived in Jamaica empty. She, too, had been
searching so very long for that important something
else that she sensed was out there. Family. Roots.
Belonging. Not love, though. She didn't have any
belief in that.

"It's hard to believe," Amanda said now, "that a
family . . . any family could do all that."

Summer poured them both frosted glasses of pink
lemonade. "Take it from me, girl . . . it's the God's
truth. Before I came here to Jamaica, my life had
completely fallen apart. In just one short week, I
had lost my job . . . my fiancé . . . and found out
that not only was I adopted, but that my parents'
only biological child had been abducted . . . taken
away from them."

Amanda gasped. "Oh, my God. Not really?"

Summer nodded. "It took me a while to recover
from all that. It was such a horrible thing to go

through, you know. I mean, people lose jobs . . . and so what really? You can always get another. But adopted? That really blew my mind. And my only sister . . . abducted? God. You just can't imagine how all that shook me."

Amanda gripped her hand. "So, did they . . . I mean, was she ever found? Your sister?"

A glint of sadness came and went in Summer's eyes. "No. Never. My parents accepted after a while that she wasn't coming back, I guess. They spent a lot of money searching for her. A lot of time praying for her." Her shoulders raised and fell in a sigh. "But you know what most of the studies say? Most abducted children don't make it through the first twenty-four hours after they're taken."

Amanda tightened her grip on Summer's hand for there was nothing she could think of to say that could ever be the right thing. There was one thing she knew now though. She had been wrong to judge this woman so hastily. They would be friends. Good ones.

"So," Summer said after a brief moment of silence. "Now that I've totally depressed you . . . would you like to see your room? I gave you one with a great view. You can literally see miles and miles of ocean from the window."

Nicholas jogged up the front stairs to the house, pushed the screen door, and asked: "Whose car is that parked in the courtyard of the front house?"

Summer came forward smiling. "Nicky, darling . . . you're home." And she pressed a kiss to his cheek and wound a soft arm about his waist.

Nicholas looked down at her with an amused glint in his eyes. "What have you done?" he said. "I don't trust you at all when you're like this."

The golden eyes rounded and became a little too innocent. "Like what? Can't I welcome my favorite brother-in-law home if I want to?"

He put her at arm's length, and asked again, "Whose car is that?"

Summer patted him on the back. "Just someone I've hired . . . she'll be staying here with Gavin and me, so you needn't worry about her being in the way."

The hairs at the base of his neck stood straight up. "She? You've hired a woman?"

Summer made a clucking sound with her tongue. "Now Nicky, I know you've completely gone off girls . . . but really, that doesn't extend to whom I hire too, does it?"

Although quite a gusty breeze was now blowing in from the ocean, the air in the room felt suddenly ten degrees warmer. She didn't fool him for a second. She had hired a woman, but not just any woman. She had hired Amanda Drake. He would bet his life on it. Under some perfectly reasonable pretext, she had brought the nut job into the house.

"What have you hired her to do?" he asked, deliberately playing along for a moment.

"Oh, I need some help with the walls," she said, and her eyes glowed at him with the charm Eve must have shown Adam on that infamous day.

His only response was a considered "Um-hmm." Then he went to sit in one of the living room chairs, and began to loosen the tie about his neck. When he was through with the tie and the buttons on his shirt were undone to mid-chest, he said, "And where is your new employee now?"

Summer came to sit beside him. "I like her very much," she said.

His eyebrows raised a fraction. "Really?" How much would she really like this woman if she knew what he did about her? If she really understood the propensity Amanda had for chaining men to beds and cavorting about recklessly with feathers in her teeth, hair, and every other conceivable place? He would take Gavin's advice, of course, and take the woman to his bed as soon as was polite. Sooner if at all possible. But after he had slaked himself with her numerous charms, he would move on, just as he had always done before.

"Nicky," Summer was saying now, "you don't really mind me hiring her . . . do you?"

Nicholas smiled. "Amanda Drake . . . no doubt?"

Summer beamed at him. "Yes. She's a great artist. I've seen some of her work. She does just lovely seascapes . . . and other stuff."

He pinched her chin. "Well, what's done is done. And I'm hazarding a guess that Gavin had a hand in this, too."

"Don't blame him, though, it was entirely my idea."

Nicholas stood. "Well, I'm going to go up to look in on Amber. She taking a nap?"

"Fast asleep." Summer nodded, very pleased with herself. Her eyes followed him as he left the room. She had to admit that he had taken the news very well. Very well indeed. She hadn't known really what to expect. A struggle? Maybe not. In these last several months, she had ceased trying to figure her beautiful brooding brother-in-law out. Generally, he was not a man given to moodiness, but of late, he had been just that. Perhaps with Amanda around, his temper might improve.

She gave the matter no further thought, and instead clattered out to the kitchen, to sit for a nice chat with Mrs. Carydice. Determinedly, she held her mind away from any thought of what might be occurring just upstairs.

THIRTEEN

Amanda bent over the little traveling bag, now fully unzipped and spread like a dismembered thing on the bed. She had not brought many things with her, enough to last her a week or two, but no longer than that. She had figured that by then she should have received her first paycheck, and would be able to get herself whatever else she needed. She busied herself between the bed and the main walk-in closet, hanging things, folding others. When she was through, she re-zipped the bag, and placed it to stand very neatly behind a lovely little fold-up stool in a wooden cabinet designed for this very purpose.

The gusty call of the wind and the crashing of the waves on the sand pulled her across to the window now, and she stood with fingers curled around the white sill. The sky was awash with color. Reds. Golds. A snatch of purple. A bit of blue. Some white, but not very much now. Far out beyond the horizon, the sun hung like a ripe untried plum, fat, sweet, innocent. She closed her eyes, and inhaled it all. The wind was like a warm, living thing. And the scent, the beautiful tropical fragrance got into her pores and lifted her up to some higher level of being.

She sucked in a delicious breath, and thought: Surely this natural extravagance must be something that was completely unique to Jamaica. Never had she thought it possible that a place could ever bring her to tears. But this one, this one did something magical to her soul.

At the knock on the door, she turned. For as long as she was here, she would enjoy this place, enjoy the easy friendship she had almost immediately struck up with Summer Champagne. Her initial impression of Summer had been completely wrong. What a nice person she was. So warm. Friendly. Almost like a sister. Had things been different, she would have liked to have her for a friend at least. But after this job was through she intended to return to the States. To her life there, whatever little there was of it. She had fulfilled her promise to Sheila. Partially anyway.

She pulled back the door with a smile. "I hung my things in the big closet, I hope that's . . ." But the words croaked to a halt in her throat as she looked up into the very eyes that had haunted her dreams for so many steamy nights now.

"Hello," Nicholas said, and there was a pulling smile flickering somewhere in the depths of his eyes.

Amanda's heart gave a great thump, and then started pounding like a wild thing against her ribs. She had not expected to see him this soon. She hadn't had time to prepare for this. She swallowed in a tight clenching movement of her throat.

"Hi . . . ah . . . I didn't know . . . didn't think you'd be here," she said stupidly.

He gave her a slitted black-eyed look. "Well, I live in the first house so, it was only a matter of time. May I come in?"

And he was in and closing the door before she could think of any possible objection as to why he should. He leaned back against the wood with hands in his pockets, and Amanda's eyes ran over him in a hurried sweep. He was still in business dress, although his tie had been abandoned, and his shirt unbuttoned to reveal a length of smooth brown flesh.

She knotted her hands before her. He thought to unnerve her, obviously. He probably had some devious plan in mind, given the current expression on his face. He was probably thinking of a way to handcuff *her* to the bed, in return for what she had so recklessly done to him. She had to put an end to any such crazy ideas he might be having. She was sorry she had handcuffed him. Very, very sorry. But there was nothing she could do now to change that particular reality. It had been a stupid thing to do without actually knowing the man. Maybe, a stupid thing to do period.

"Look," she said, stumbling into speech because he still watched her without uttering a single word. "I know you're still upset about . . . about earlier. But if I'm going to work here, I think we'd—"

"Come here," he said, interrupting her gush of words.

A tide of hot blood rushed to her head. "What?" She had narrowly avoided stammering out the word. If he thought she was interested in beginning some sort of torrid affair with him, he had a shock coming. She had no intention of getting involved with him; not now or ever.

His eyes met hers in a very direct manner, and the smile now was gone. "You heard me," he said. "Come . . . here."

Amanda swallowed. Maybe he wasn't all there. Maybe what she had done had unhinged him in some terrible way, and he intended to do away with her now.

"Your sister-in-law is right downstairs," she croaked. "All I have to do is scream."

His chest rose and fell silently, and she could tell that he was laughing at her. "When I make you scream," he said, "I will be the only person capable of helping you." She took a tight breath. So that was it. He thought she was just aching to jump into bed with him. *Well, that was true.* But she would never admit it to him. She would just have to be convincing. Very convincing.

"I have no intention of going to bed with you," she said, and prayed that her voice not shake when she said it.

He straightened away from the door. "Is that what you think?" And he laughed. "You don't know yourself very well, Amanda Drake. You have every intention of going to bed with me. You know it, and I know it."

She shook her head, and reached down deep for the band of steel she used so well on other men. "You think too much of yourself. I know women generally find you attractive, but please, restrain yourself. I have absolutely no interest in any of your goods."

He walked over and very calmly sat on the end of the bed, leaned back on an elbow so that his shirt pulled open even further. "So, you don't find me even the tiniest bit attractive?"

Amanda cleared her throat. Didn't he know that she was an expert at this game of flirtation? "This is silly," she said, and her voice trembled just a little.

He smiled because he had heard it. And despite her every effort to prevent it happening, Amanda felt a frisson of awareness ripple down the sensitive skin of her back. *He was a magnificent specimen of manhood; there was no debating that.*

"OK," he said. "I believe you." And he patted a spot right next to him. "Come sit down."

She almost wrung her hands in anxiety at that. She didn't want to sit down beside him. She didn't trust him for a second. *She didn't trust herself for a second was actually closer to the truth of it.* If he only guessed, only suspected the things she wanted to do to him. Things that had only just gained a voice inside her. If she ever got started on him now, she would never be able to find the strength to pull herself away this time. But she couldn't do it, no matter how she really felt about things. She couldn't. Strangely, she had been battling for weeks with a warped and twisted kind of jealousy. She couldn't bear the thought that he had lain with Sheila. That his hands had touched her with tenderness; had touched her at all. It tore at her that he would never lie with *her*. What she felt was demented, she knew it. But what could she do? She wanted him so much, but she could not have him. Could never have him. *God.*

"Are you afraid of me?" he was asking, and Amanda stilled the confused tumble of thought rushing through her.

"I've completely forgiven you for that little incident. So you needn't worry about that anymore," he said with a pulling smile. He straightened up and looked about the room. "Summer gave you a nice room. Do you like it?"

His sudden change in direction was almost as startling as what had come before. Amanda's eyes swept the room, glad that he appeared to have abandoned his thoughts of seduction.

"It's lovely," she said, and she really meant it. "It's more like a mini-suite than a room. With the chairs . . . the large walk-in closets. Fireplace. Patio. Even my own bathroom."

"Good," he said. And he stood with hands in pockets again.

A feeling of disappointment swept over Amanda. *Was he leaving so very soon?* She had somehow expected a little more pressure from him. She looked across at the window. "It's a beautiful view, too. I love the ocean."

He walked across to rest on the sill, leaning slightly out of the window so that the wind ruffled his gleaming black curls. Unbidden, she came to stand beside him now, and he looked up. A thrill of something hot and wild rippled through her as their eyes met. *God, she wanted to kiss him so much.* This insanity that he made her feel was ridiculous. Impossible. Frightening.

His index finger reached out to gently stroke the back of her hand, and she knew that she should pull her hand away from him, but God help her, she couldn't do it. Her eyes went to the finger and the wonderful things it was doing. How could a simple touch make her feel so very much? Why? Why did this have to happen to her now?

He turned her palm over and stared at the lines crisscrossing her palm. His thumb ran over the soft skin, and a bead of perspiration slipped down the very center of Amanda's back.

"You're going to have a long and happy life," he said now, tracing one of the lines with the blunt of his thumbnail.

"You mean, it's going to be different from what I've had so far?"

His thumb settled in the middle of her palm. "Umm," he said. "It's going to be much better.

And . . ." He looked up at her. "I see a good man . . . who's going to . . ."

She pulled her hand from his. She didn't want him to say these things to her, even in jest. She knew very well what kind of life she was likely to have. It would be a lonely struggling one. Not unlike the kind of life she had lived until now. There were no good men left; the few that had existed had been snapped up by women much smarter than she was.

"It must be nice to live here all the time," she said with a little crack in her voice. She was completely unaware of the distant sadness that had suddenly filled her eyes. But the man beside her saw it instantly, and it touched him in a deep and profound way. He had come to her room to play with her. To begin the inevitable dance that would end between the sheets of his four-poster bed. But he hadn't expected to feel anything for her. Nothing beyond the strong lust that shook him each time he ran into her. But there was more to this woman. More maybe to what he thought he felt for her.

Nicholas tilted her chin, and she looked at him with that soft, confused look. His thumb traced the little rosebud mouth. Everything about her was so tiny, yet so perfectly formed. She was like a pocket Venus with her brown pixie face and curvy body. He wanted to kiss that mouth of hers over and over again until the feel and taste of her no longer held any mystery for him. He wanted to feel her soft arms about him, begging for that which only he could give her. But he couldn't see her now as strictly an object of desire. Somehow, in some unfathomable way, she had touched that deeper part of him.

"I'm sorry about just now," he said. And the back of a finger stroked slowly down the length of her cheek.

Her nostrils flared, and she struggled for breath. She had thought herself much stronger than this. How she had to fight herself right then, fight herself so that she would not do as the pulsing blood in her veins demanded. It would be so very easy to turn her mouth into his palm, to kiss the gritty skin there, over and over. Why could she not right now? They were in a room, behind closed doors. Who would know? Who would tell? Sheila would never find out. He wouldn't tell her. She wouldn't tell her. It would just be a little kiss. A one-time-only kind of thing, something that she would never let happen ever again. Could fate be this unkind? To prevent her from having this very little thing?

His thumb went beneath her chin to lift it to just that right angle. She could see in his face what he intended, and her hand went up to hold his, and she whispered hoarsely, "No. We can't."

He paused just scant inches away, his beautifully cut mouth deliciously close. Her neck ached with the restraint it took not to close the distance.

"Why not? Are you married?" It was something that had only just occurred to him, and the possibility of it caused a tightening in his chest. *She could not belong to someone else.*

"No. I'm not married. But it's . . . it's . . ." She hunted for a reason she could reveal. Something. Anything. "It's more complicated than you know. . . . I can't explain."

His hand slipped around to stroke the ridge running the length of her back. His voice dipped, and became soft, coaxing. "How could one simple little kiss be that complicated? It's the least complicated thing there is."

She wanted to rest her head against his chest, absorb his warmth, and listen in blissful silence to the beat of his heart. But she turned instead to the window. The night was upon them now, stretching its dark skin far beyond the curve of the horizon. She thought to distract him. He was close behind, his arms now resting on the sill on either side of her.

"Everything's so quiet all of a sudden," she said. "Only the waves. . . ."

"It always gets like this at night." He was even closer. And his cheek was against hers, warm and comforting.

She breathed. "Nick?"

"Umm?"

"Do you always get what you want?"

She felt him smile against her face. "Always. Do you think there's any hope for me?" She turned slowly to face him. The black eyes watched her with a glint of lurking humor. An answering smile tugged at her lips. She would give him what he wanted this time. But not again. It couldn't happen again.

Her hands went to his wrists, and she ran her fingers slowly up his long arms, pausing at his elbows to softly caress the skin there. His hands slid in to hold her, and the feeling was infinitely sweet. Infinitely familiar. He bent to rub his nose against hers. And then, with the tiniest tilt of his head, his lips were on hers. Breath escaped in a long sigh. This was what she had wanted all these many weeks. Had needed all these very lonely nights. How could she have thought to resist him? Kissing was harmless. It hurt no one. No one at all. *But Lord, he was good at this.* He seemed to know exactly where to touch, how to touch, where to kiss. . . . *What a splendid man.*

Her fingers clung to him and the words *Never stop, never, never* drifted like cotton candy through her mind.

How long they stood clinging to each other, she

did not know. How long they would have stood in
that manner, she could only guess at. But the per-
sistent sound would not go away, and when he raised
his mouth a fraction, she whispered a deprived "No.
Not yet."

There was someone at the door. Knocking. And
he straightened away from her with very obvious re-
luctance. Thought was only just returning, and
breath still came in jerky spasms. Amanda straightened the bodice of her blouse. She had not wanted
him to leave her. She had not wanted him to stop.
What would she do next time when he wanted more
of the same? How would she hold him at bay? *How
would she hold herself?*

Nicholas removed himself from her, almost as
though it was the only way he could manage to keep
any distance between them at all. He sat in a chair
facing the door, with the fingers of both hands stee-
pled beneath his chin.

Amanda drew a needed breath, and when she felt
herself to be sufficiently calm, said in a choppy
voice: "Come."

FOURTEEN

The room door opened with some hesitance. Amanda released a silent breath. Thank the heavens above it wasn't Summer. Nicholas's presence in her room might have been a bit difficult to explain away. And as shrewd as she suspected her employer to be, Amanda knew without question that there would be no hiding of anything at all from her.

But it was the housekeeper who stood on the threshold now with a stack of towels in her hands. The woman's eyes darted to Nicholas, then returned to the window where Amanda still stood.

"Oh," she said, "me sorry. Me wasn't sure if you were in or gone fe a walk 'pon de beach." She stretched her arms. "Some extra towels."

Amanda smiled at the poor woman, who was obviously under the impression that she had interrupted something decidedly more intimate than what had just occurred.

"Thank you very much, Mrs. Carydice. These will come in handy." And she went across to take the towels.

"Dinner'll be served in half an hour," the housekeeper added. "Mr. Gavin has just gotten in."

Amanda assured her that she would be down in a few minutes, and with that said, the woman beat a very hasty retreat. Amanda closed the door again, and was sorely tempted to rest her heated forehead upon the cool wood. She found it difficult now to turn and face him. He had not said a single word since he had removed himself from her, and she wondered what it was he now thought. All of her grand protestations had come to nothing, nothing at all. It had taken no more than a single touch from him to transform her into someone she hardly even recognized.

She turned now in a jerky manner, the words rushing from her. "Dinner's almost ready. I guess I'm to eat at the table with . . . with everyone else."

Nicholas came to his feet smoothly, and momentary panic shot through Amanda. *Surely he did not intend to kiss her again?*

"Why wouldn't you eat with everyone else?" he asked.

She wasn't sure what to say. She had not expected to be welcomed as though she were a part of the family. Wasn't she an employee? Wouldn't she be expected to keep her distance from them all?

"I thought . . . maybe, I would be expected to provide my own meals."

He shrugged in a lazy manner, and her eyes were drawn again to the broad expanse of shoulder. *What would it be like to be free to touch him whenever she liked?*

"Unless you prefer not to eat with us," he said. "But I think Summer might be disappointed. You're welcome to do anything you'd like . . . including"— and he approached her now with an expression of devilry in his eyes—"staying overnight at the front house . . . whenever it takes your fancy."

It had been years since she had given into anything as juvenile as blushing, but she felt hot blood rush to her cheeks now. *Had she not been thinking the exact thing?*

"I don't think that would ever be a good idea."

He stood directly before her, not touching, but close enough for her to feel the waves of heat emanating from his body. "Why?"

A simple question. Deserving surely of a simple answer. But what could she say? The mother of your child is a close friend of mine? Our friendship is important, is sometimes the only thing of constancy I have in my life? She asked me to weave my usual brand of magic? To make you fall in love with me, and to then break your heart in my usual callous fashion? But should I ever lie with you in that manner, my heart would be the one in jeopardy?

"It's just not. I don't go in for one-night stands."
She had in another life, but not now. Not now.

He smiled in a manner that made the muscles in her abdomen spasm. "Well, I can promise you that what we share will never be anything nearly as sordid as that."

A towel fell from her grip, and he bent to retrieve it. He replaced it atop the stack in her hands.

"Think about it," he said. "I'll not pressure you. But if you feel the need . . ." And he let his words taper off.

She said not a word as he walked from the room. Instead, she went to the bathroom, placed the towels neatly on a bare shelf, and then went to the shower cubicle to turn on the water full blast. *Cold.*

Dinner was taken outdoors beside the pool at an elegant table set up for this very purpose. The breeze blew in softly from off the ocean, and Amanda marveled again at the fact that there was not the slightest chill in the air. The wind picked at the edges of her little black dress, and she chided herself for not having had the presence of mind to wear a blouse and a pair of pants. Summer was gorgeous in a flowing strapless white jumpsuit that was loose at the waist, and tapered at the legs.

And as soon as Amanda appeared in the doorway, Summer went over to link arms with her.

"Lovely dress," Summer said with beautifully smiling eyes. "Come meet Gavin." Amanda looked across at the man who stood leaning casually on the railing. She had not paid much attention to him at the wedding, but she was struck immediately now by how very big and powerful he appeared. Tall. Trim. Maybe an inch or so shorter than Nicholas, but there was an aura of strength about him. And there was no disputing the fact that he was a Champagne. The beautiful well-cut features were there. The curly black hair, smooth milk-chocolate skin, high cheekbones, and blacker-than-night eyes. Yes, there was no mistaking the family resemblance. Why it was that he did not use the name Champagne was something she had puzzled over. She would have to remember to ask Nicholas about it later.

"Darling," Summer said, pulling Amanda along with her, "this is Amanda." Her hand was immediately swallowed in a very solid grip, and Amanda got the distinct impression that she was being evaluated. The reason for such scrutiny was unclear to her though, since she knew that she had already been offered the job. The shrewd black eyes watched her with an unblinking directness. And she got the immediate impression that this was not a man to cross. He would be a formidable enemy.

"Hello," he said now, "have you settled in OK?"

Amanda smiled. "Yes. The room's lovely. I couldn't be happier."

The skin around his eyes crinkled into smile lines.

"Good," he said. "Summer's taking good care of you then."

And with that said, they settled down to a delicious meal. Mrs. Carydice brought out the first course, which was spicy soup with hard pot-sticker dumplings, chunks of beef, and sweet potatoes. As they ate the wonderful soup, Summer leaned forward to inquire, "Has Nicky told you yet about the cottage?"

Amanda sampled the soup in her spoon. *So, they knew Nicholas had been in her room?* What else did they know?

"No . . . that's the one up the beach you were telling me about, isn't it?"

Summer nodded. She gave her husband a mischievous look. "Should I tell her about the history, honey? About the legend and the gold?"

Gavin gave his wife a tolerant smile, and the affection that radiated between them both struck Amanda. *By God, they loved each other, these two. Really loved each other.* How strange. How wonderful.

"I know you're just itching to tell her," Gavin said.

Summer gave the back of his hand a playful pinch, and then leaned forward. "Well . . ." she said, "it's an old story. One involving runaway slaves, pirates, and hidden gold."

Gavin patted his mouth with a napkin. "Don't forget the curse."

Summer waved a hand at him. "I'm getting to that. I'm getting to that. Let me tell the story my way."

Gavin grinned at Amanda. "Bossy, isn't she? But isn't that why I love her?" Amanda laughed. *Oh, they were wonderful.* This was family. This was what married life should be like. *God, how she wished. How she wished.*

"About the curse," said Summer. "It's said that the cottage belonged to none other than Sir Henry Morgan, the pirate . . . sometime in the seventeenth century, wasn't it, honey?"

Gavin nodded. "That's the story."

"And," Summer continued, "he used the cottage as a storage place for his stolen Spanish gold. He would come and go as he pleased, you see . . . under cover of night, paddling his longboat in from his ship, and straight into the catacombs running beneath the house."

Amanda paused with her spoon halfway to her lips. "Catacombs? Beneath the cottage itself?"

"Umm." Summer nodded. "Nicky will have to show them to you. Might make a great painting. But anyway . . . over the centuries, the cottage changed hands several times. In the sixteenth century it was used as a safe house for runaway plantation slaves . . . because it's so close to the sea, and they could escape without anyone seeing them."

"You're not telling the story right, honey," Gavin said. "You're probably confusing poor Amanda."

Amanda chuckled. "No . . . I think I'm getting the picture. Really."

"Don't listen to him," Summer said. "He never likes the way I tell a story."

"That's because you never tell things in the right order."

Summer grinned. "Anyway . . . where was I?"

"It was used as a safe house," Amanda supplied helpfully.

"Right," Summer said. "In the early twentieth century, though, the cottage was acquired by a Dutchman called Vanderhagen. . . ."

"Or Vanderhaagen," Gavin said. "We're not clear on the name."

"And he was an evil one . . . he dealt in the occult, you know. He was well known on the island for his dabblings. Both of his wives died horribly. One flung herself from the cliffs, and the other set herself ablaze. . . ."

Amanda shuddered. "Horrible."

"But that's not all," Summer said, gripping Amanda's hand. "A few years later, Vander . . . whatever his name was, was found hanging from a beam in the basement of the cottage. Beneath him was a circle of chalk, a black candle, and a pile of kindling."

Amanda's eyebrows rose a bit. "Someone murdered him then?"

Summer broke a bread roll, chewed it with great consideration before saying: "No, it's said he committed suicide. Possessed by the spirits of dead slaves . . . he did away with himself. And he put a curse on the cottage with his dying breath . . . according to local legend, of course."

"There're so many stories like that roaming about," Amanda said, and she proceeded to tell them of her encounter with the bull at Rose Hall.

Summer chortled merrily. "You actually climbed the tree?"

"It wasn't easy," Amanda agreed. "Especially since I'd never climbed one before." She had, of course, neglected to tell them that her underwear had been torn off by a shard of tree trunk.

Gavin threw back his head and guffawed. "Someone was playing a trick on you," he said. "It was probably a papier-mâché bull. They knew you weren't a local, so they decided to have a bit of fun with you."

Amanda smiled. "Well, it certainly looked real at the time . . . and the caretaker who came along later told me that everyone called the bull a Rolling Calf."

Gavin nodded. "A Jamaican superstition. A harbinger of bad luck . . . ill fortune . . . that sort of thing." He leaned forward to pat her hand. "Hope you're not superstitious?"

Amanda assured him that she was not. They told her more about the hidden gold, and of Nicholas's unsuccessful search for the old bounty. And, she agreed with them both that the gold and the curse on the cottage were probably as real as the Rolling Calf she had seen. She leaned forward now to liberally apply warm sweet butter to her roll. This was one of the nicest evenings she had had in a very long while. The housekeeper had been absolutely correct. These Champagnes were definitely not the pretentious kind. They both made her feel like a welcome friend . . . like family almost. And the thought of how nicely they were treating her made her deeply ashamed of her original reason for coming to Jamaica. It was slowly beginning to dawn on her that the stories Sheila had told her could not possibly be true. Not the ones about Gavin. Not the ones about Nicholas. Maybe, not any at all. *What a conundrum.*

Mrs. Carydice bustled in now with a succulent cut of juicy beef, nicely adorned with little cubes of sweet pineapple. She collected their soup plates with swift efficiency, stacking them all on a service trolley standing just behind the seating area.

"Me hope you have enough room fe this," she said, smiling.

Amanda grinned at Summer. "At this rate, I'm going to look like a blob in no time at all."

Gavin shook his head. "You women," he said, "always worrying about your figures."

"If we didn't worry," Summer countered, "you men wouldn't pay us any attention, and you know that's true."

Gavin carved healthy slices of beef for everyone before saying, "I don't care what you look like. I love you . . . for you."

Summer's eyebrows arched. "Thank you, honey," she said, "but I'm sure if I blew up to, say . . . four, five hundred pounds, you'd have something entirely different to say."

"I'd just roll you in and out of bed in the mornings," Gavin said with an overly solemn expression on his face.

Amanda held on to the chuckle bubbling in her chest, and her black eyes danced merrily between the two. *God, they were hilarious.* She'd not suspected for one second that they would be like this.

Summer laughed. "My husband has been working a little too hard, as you can plainly see," she said, turning to Amanda. "So he is understandably a little delirious."

They continued joking back and forth through the peas and rice and beef course. Halfway through the meal, the realization settled in that Nicholas was not going to be putting in an appearance. And Amanda asked as casually as she could manage, "Wasn't Nicholas going to be stopping by for dinner?"

Gavin exchanged a look with his wife before saying with an equal degree of casualness, "We never know when he's going to pop in. He took Amber back to the front house to put her to bed. He may be back later." Then, with innocent black eyes, he inquired, "So, you two have met then?"

Amanda swallowed an entire chunk of beef without chewing, and the meat very nearly lodged in her throat. Water welled in both eyes, and she reached a blind hand for her glass of red sorrel drink, gulped a goodly quantity before saying in a voice that croaked around the edges, "Yes . . . yes, we met . . . earlier."

Summer propped her elbows on the table, and leaned in to dissect. "Earlier? Before today, you mean?"

Gavin hid a smile behind a hand. "Let Amanda eat in peace, darling," he said. "You've been asking her so many questions, she very nearly choked a minute ago."

"Oh . . . that's . . . that's OK," Amanda assured Summer with great haste. "We met . . . at . . . at your wedding actually."

"Oh, really?" Summer moved her leg to avoid the nudging of her husband's knee beneath the table.

"Yes," Amanda agreed. Her eyes were flushed a gentle pink now. "Just briefly. And then again a week or so ago . . . at an art show in Montego Bay."

Summer smiled. "And what do you think of our Nicky?"

Gavin cleared his throat. "Time for dessert, isn't it? Where's Mrs. Carydice? Mrs. Carydice?" And he spun in his seat to stare at the patio door.

"Honey," Summer said, "I can't hear what Amanda's saying."

Amanda shuffled a bit in her chair. "Well, he seems nice. I mean, I don't know him very well at all. . . ."

"He's very cute, though, isn't he?"

"Mrs. Carydice?" Gavin bellowed.

The housekeeper hustled through the doorway,

wiping her hands on the apron hanging from her waist.

"I think we're ready for dessert," Gavin said, and he stood to begin stacking the dishes.

Summer smiled, and there was a glint of mischief in her eyes. "I'm not finished yet, honey."

"Weren't you just telling me that you didn't want to blow up to six, seven hundred pounds?"

"Five hundred is what I said."

Amanda rose to help with the stacking of the plates. She was very glad of the interruption. She most definitely did not want to answer Summer's last question as to the beauty of Nicholas Champagne, for she was completely certain that that bit of information would find its way right back to the man in question.

"You know," Amanda said after everything was nicely stacked, "I really don't think I'm up to any dessert tonight. In fact, if you don't mind, I think I'll go off to bed a little early . . . so I can get an early start tomorrow."

Gavin gave her a satiny black-eyed smile. "Good idea, I think. You'll want to spend the day tomorrow having a look around the property, and gathering your thoughts . . . ideas for the paintings."

"Well," Summer said, and she stood to give Amanda a hug, "looks like I'm outvoted here. We'll talk again tomorrow then."

Amanda nodded. "Thank you so much for dinner. It was wonderful."

As soon as she was out of sight, Summer said to her husband, "I like her. Don't you?"

Gavin leaned over to press a quick kiss to her lips. "I don't know how it is that you and Nicky are so very much alike. You can't force things, you know.

You have to let them happen naturally, if they're going to happen at all."

Summer came across, sat on his lap, and held his dear face between her hands. She placed a kiss on both cheeks, and very gently said, "OK, Daddy."

The black eyes met hers. "You're . . . you're not?"

Her eyes glowed. "I am. Completely and totally pregnant."

FIFTEEN

Nicholas was up with the dawn. He had spent an extremely restless night, thrashing around in bed. For no good reason at all, he had found it almost impossible to get to sleep. After leaving Amanda Drake he had gone for a long windy walk on the beach, walking all the way past his mother's cottage to the very edge of the next property. Across acres and acres of sand and shells, pools and shallows, rocky caves and thrusting coral. His mind had been a roiling restless thing. What to do, what to do about the *nut job* Amanda Drake was the question. He wanted her, and would have her. But how could he do this without hurting her? He didn't want to hurt her when it was all over and time for him to leave. *He liked her, strangely.* There was a quality about her. Something he couldn't exactly define. *A goodness, maybe?* Although she was obviously wildly promiscuous, there was still something decent about her. She was like a jaded rose that had somehow fallen out of bloom in the peak of its season.

It was a dilemma he had never before faced. There was that certain quality of hard fragility about her. Like beautiful glass that had been put through the smelter's fire. But surely the kind of glass that would break and splinter into a thousand pieces if dropped carelessly to the ground.

He frowned at the spreading light. Why did things have to be this complex? Why did the softer emotions ever have to become involved? He had resisted such emotional entanglement for years. Why should this woman, of all people, cause his mind to go in that direction? With little effort on his part, she could become his pocket Venus. *His woman.* But did he want her for more than just a tumble? Could she still his reckless spirit; bring peace to him at last?

He tapped another cigarette from the box lying on the sill, lit it, and took a deep considering drag. It was crazy how much he wanted her. Any number of women would have jumped at the chance had they been invited to his bed, but she had turned him down. Nicely, but turned him down nevertheless, contrary woman that she was. Why would she say no to him, when she knew very well that this thing between them was like nothing else? Her very skin knew the touch of his hand, and he craved the soft feel of her mouth beneath his.

She would not deny him for much longer, though. *He would have her.* But if she desired it, he would pursue her gently. He would charm her, romance her, and dance her. And when she finally consented to lie with him, he would show her pleasures unlike any she had ever known before.

He turned from the window now, half dressed and sleekly magnificent. "Amber?"

There was a small pause; then the little voice said sweetly: "Yes, Dada?"

"Are you finished brushing your teeth?"

He had left her for just a little while, so that he might enjoy his cigarette by the window. But for a good several minutes now, there had been nothing but silence coming from the bathroom area. The kind of busy silence that automatically made him worry.

"Dada . . . I'll brush after. I'm shaving now."

A fond smile twisted the corners of his mouth. *What a sweet, sweet child she was. Shaving indeed. How absolutely adorable.*

He crushed the stub between his fingers, and lit up another cigarette. "Will you be OK on your own for a few more minutes?"

"Yes, Dada," was the immediate response.

"Good. Dada will be in in a minute to bathe you then, OK?"

"OK."

Nicholas dragged hard, and let his mind ramble again to the manor house. The nut job was probably still asleep. It was barely seven. She would sleep on her side, he knew. Curled up in a tight little ball, her tiny toes wrapped about each other like so many fingers. Would she snore? Would that gorgeous little mouth part while she slept?

The sound of a disturbed meow caught his attention for a moment.

"Amber?"

"Yes, Dada?"

"What're you doing?"

"Nothing, Dada."

Nicholas ground the cigarette head into the burnt ashtray, and let the final wisp of blue smoke drift out of his nostrils. With slitted eyes, he turned from the morning sun.

"OK, Amber, love, Dada has left you alone for long enough."

He went to the pink-and-white closet Summer had designed for his daughter, and looked around at the rows and rows of hanging garments.

"What would you like to wear today, Amber?"

There was no reply, so he settled on the closest item at hand: a lovely little red and blue sailor suit, with cut-off shorts, a floppy collar, and red socks with lacy trim.

"How about this one, love?" He walked to the bathroom, and poked his head around the entrance. She sat on the floor with her back to him, and around her, in an ever-widening circle wash . . .

"Black?"

The pretty outfit fell out of his grasp. *Oh God, she couldn't have. She wouldn't have.* His knees felt a trifle shaky, and for a second he was afraid to move. Afraid to actually see what it was she had done.

"Amber?" There was a tremble in his voice. "What are you doing . . . to the cat?"

She turned, smiling angelically. In her hands she held something very small and very pink.

"Look, Dada . . . look at Ruggles."

"Oh, no!" He covered his mouth and turned away from the sight of it. *Oh, God. Oh, God. Oh, God!* It was like a scene from that old movie *The Bad Seed.* The child was demented. She had been put on the face of the earth to try his patience. To wear him down. To drive him stark staring crazy! He had to be calm. Maybe, maybe there was a reason. Maybe there was logic behind the whole thing. There had to be. There just had to be.

"Amber . . . child . . . are you possessed? Why in the name of heaven have you shaved the cat?" There was not a single speck of hair on the poor wriggling thing. Not even a speck.

Amber stroked the little quivering pink body. "I've shaved Ruggles, Dada."

Nicholas ran a hand through his hair. "I know you've shaved him, sweetheart . . . the question is why? Why have you done this thing?"

She put the kitten on the floor. "Because he's a boy."

"What?" And Nicholas stooped to pick up the cat. He turned it this way and that. Well, she had done a very thorough job of it. That much was certain. And how she had managed to get all of the fur off without even nicking the skin was another matter entirely.

"What do you mean . . . he's a boy?"

She gave him an exasperated four-year-old sigh. "Remember, Dada . . . you said boys shave." She pointed to the pink thing. "Ruggles is a boy."

Nicholas groaned. He had told her that boys and not girls shaved. But how could he possibly have known that she would have interpreted the information in this horrific manner?

He stooped to put the cat back on the ground, and then he held his daughter's shoulders.

"Amber. Ruggles is a boy, but he's a boy cat. Boy cats don't shave. Do you understand me? Only boys . . . men . . . humans shave. Dogs and cats don't shave. Animals don't shave."

The black eyes staring directly into his appeared a trifle disappointed. "But why, Dada? Why can't they shave too?"

"Because . . . well, because they don't like it. They really, really don't like it. And you wouldn't want to do something to Ruggles that he doesn't like, now would you?"

She shook her head, but was not entirely convinced yet. "But you like it, Dada?"

"Yes . . . no, I don't like it either."

"Then how come you do it every day?"

"Look . . ." Nicholas said, and for the life of him he couldn't think of a better way to explain it. "Look, listen to me now. Ruggles is a cat. OK? Do not . . . under any circumstances . . ." And he lifted his hand to count off on his fingers what it was she could not do to the cat. "Shave Ruggles, bathe Ruggles, pluck his eyelashes out . . . put lipstick on Ruggles . . . take him swimming, or anything else. You understand me?"

The little face frowned. "Well, what can I do to him then?"

Nicholas looked at the ceiling and muttered, "God help me, please. Can you tell me what to do? Can you tell me what I'm going to do with this child?"

Across the lawns at the manor house, Amanda had experienced her waking moments in a much more peaceful manner. She too had woken early and, surprisingly, given her steamy encounter with Nicholas Champagne, she had slept well. The great food and conversation of the night before had sent her off to sleep in a warm haze of contentment. She had snuggled beneath the thick covers for a while, just listening to the beautiful ebb and flow of the tides. Slowly, softly, the incessant rhythm had lulled her to sleep. And her dreams, her dreams had been filled with warm thoughts of black eyes and long sinewy limbs. In these wonderful meanderings, she had been able to taste, touch, and sample every glorious inch of him. There had been no restraints. Nothing at all to consider. It had been wonderful. *Delicious.*

She walked now with hat in hand, trailing the bleached straw in the lacy break of a foam-capped wave. She wore a sleeveless white vest, and a pair of ragged denim shorts. Her feet were bare and completely unadorned, save for the solitary toe ring of platinum gold, which she wore on her right foot.

Overhead, a rush of wild parrots, with thick and colorful feathers, swooped and glided raucously through the morning air, and Amanda turned to look until they were no more than distant specks in the sky. Her brow furrowed in thought. Wouldn't that be a beautiful thing to capture? The sun rising, golden and splendid, the breezy blue ocean, the birds flying off to some unknown destination. It would surely make a wonderful painting.

She stopped to dip a foot into a glinting pool that huddled between a cluster of rocks, but drew back startled by the sight of several scurrying white crabs. She dropped her hat on the sand to capture one of them, and then knelt to peer beneath the straw at her prize.

"Hello there," she said to the strangely knotted white thing that stood frozen with claws in the air.

"Hello." The voice just behind caused her to spin about, and a hand rose to shade her eyes against the brilliant morning sun.

He stood there in a pair of faded denims and a white sleeveless vest, his thumbs hooked carelessly through the loops of his pants.

"Oh," she said, and the blood rose beneath her skin. "I didn't hear you . . . where'd you come from?"

Nicholas came to lean against one of the jutting boulders. "I took the shortcut . . . and you were far too busy with the crabs to notice me." He gave her a glinting smile. "You look very beautiful today."

Amanda cast a hurried eye at her skinny vest and ragged shorts. There was nothing even remotely beautiful about them, and he knew it.

"You're wearing the same colors I am," she said.

He gave her a lazy look. "Strange coincidence, isn't it? Can it have a deeper meaning, I wonder?"

Amanda rocked back on her heels. He was going to launch right back into the chase, she could sense it. She straightened to face him, and took some time dusting the sand from her hands.

"Why aren't you at work today? It is Wednesday, isn't it?"

His shoulders moved in a shrug. "I took the day off. Decided I preferred spending the day with you than in some stuffy office in town."

She let the crab go, picked up the straw hat, and replaced it on her head. "I've heard all about the Champagne offices, and I don't think you could call them 'stuffy.' "

He smiled. "Oh, yeah? What have you heard about us?" And his eyes swept over her in a manner that made her regret her early morning choice of short shorts.

"Champagne Shipping covers more than half a block in downtown Ocho Rios. And you in particular run the operation with an iron hand. All the secretaries and everybody there hates you."

He threw back his head, laughed, and Amanda found herself smiling too. What she had just said was not true, as far as she knew. She had very little information at all about Champagne Shipping. And she certainly didn't know if he mistreated his employees or not. But she had felt the need to tease him, just to see how he might react.

"I think you've got your facts a little mixed, Mandy, love. Gavin is the one who strikes fear into the hearts of living mortals. I, on the other hand, inspire nothing but love and devotion."

"I like Gavin," she said. "He and Summer are great together."

"Umm. Yes. I know. But what a struggle that was."

She bent to pick up a delicately whorled pink and white shell. "What do you mean . . . struggle?" She put the shell to her ear, and listened with pleasure to the rushing sound of the ocean.

"You mean, Summer hasn't told you all about it yet? Well, she will, believe me," he said without waiting for her to make a response. "Gavin was definitely who she needed, and she . . . she was what the doctor ordered."

"So . . . you got them together?" And her eyes hunted the sand for a minute. "I need something to put these shells in."

"I did." And before she could even think to stop him, he was removing his pristine white vest, and handing it to her with the careless comment: "Here, why don't you use this?"

She grabbed the vest from his outstretched hand, and muttered something that even she in calmer moments would have been hard pressed to decipher. *Had she not seen his chest before in the semidarkness of the hotel suite?* By God, what was the matter with her? But was it not even more beautiful than she remembered? All those rippling lines, and curving muscles. Flesh and bone, yes, but what spectacular flesh. What wonderful bones.

"So, do you like me?"

She'd been staring, and he had caught her at it. Her eyes darted to his. "You're . . . in very good shape. I would guess most women like you."

"But not you?"

She dropped the vest to the sand, and began filling the cloth with shells in a hurried, confused manner.

"What does it really matter if I do or don't? Nothing can ever come of it . . . nothing." And she wiped a hand across her cheek, leaving behind a trail of sand and salt. Nicholas sat beside her in the sand, and gently, he rubbed a thumb across the area. And as the finger stroked, and dipped, her breath paused and began again in hurried, uneven bursts.

She was getting soft. That's what it was. *Soft. Soft. Soft.* No man had ever had this effect on her before. No man. Why this one? Why this one? A philanderer. A ladies' man. That's what he was. That's all he could ever be. She knew his type. She knew him as well as she knew herself. Oh, God, he was turning her head. *No, please. No kiss. No kiss.* But his skin was so divine. So warm. So smooth. She couldn't fight him now. Just one more kiss then. One more, and then that would be it.

His mouth was on hers, and her fingers went up to hold the broad, strong shoulders. What feeling. What sensation. Was the roaring in her ears the ocean, or was it the blood pouring like molten lava through her veins?

With every vestige of strength she possessed, she tore her mouth away from his, and laid it like a fluttering and broken thing upon the warmth of his shoulder. His hand came up to stroke the tender flesh at the nape of her neck. Breaths came, breaths went, and the lightly stroking finger calmed her. But still, she did not want to move. Did not want to talk. *Could they not stay exactly as they were forever?*

Nicholas looked down at the bent head. At the shining cap of soft black hair. This thing he felt for her was almost unnatural. The taste of her, the very taste of her was like nothing he had ever had before in his life. She was soft and warm, and tender and right. She fit every curve of his body. As key to lock. As flesh to bone. *God, what was this thing?*

He buried his face in the sweet fragrant curve of her neck. *He had to have her. He had to have her.* Maybe then, he'd be able to get his focus back.

"Mandy?" The sound was husky against her skin.

She turned slowly, and her eyes were as blisteringly hot as his. "We can't, Nicky. I can't."

He didn't understand. He wanted her. She wanted him, didn't she? They were both adults, well able to deal with the consequences of their actions.

"Why not?"

She pulled away from him, sucked in a deep needed breath. "Because . . . well, because it wouldn't be good for either of us. Afterwards, I mean."

"Are you afraid you'll lose your commission here? Because you don't have to worry. Gavin . . . wouldn't do that."

She sighed. OK, let him believe she was afraid of losing her job. That might make it easier.

"You have to forget this, Nicky. Forget me. I'm no good . . . no good for you. Besides, you only want me because . . . I haven't fallen into your bed on the first offer."

He said nothing for several minutes, and she experienced a plunging sense of sorrow. He knew that what she had just said was right. That *was* the only reason why he was pursuing her. He wasn't accustomed to being rejected.

"So." And his eyes were more serious than she'd ever seen them. "We can only be friends then?"

She held his hand, and his fingers felt good and hard, and solid. "Don't be upset about it." Her lips twisted in a travesty of a smile. "You'll just have to think of me as the one who got away."

"All right," he said, and Amanda felt her heart freeze and die in her chest. "You win." The smile was back, and he was extending a hand to help her up. "We'll be friends then."

She blinked sorrowful eyes at him. "Yes. It's the best thing."

There was a broad swatch of sand running the entire length of her legs, and he bent to help her with it, his hand dusting her in long sweeping strokes. She stood very still, knowing that this would probably be the last time that he would touch her in this way.

When he was through, he said with dark simmering eyes, "Are we going to be close friends . . . do you think?"

He was after something. She could see it in his eyes now. "Good friends, as long as you behave yourself."

He ran a finger from the round of her shoulder all the way down the length of her arm. "What would you say to one more kiss between friends?"

Amanda smiled at that. "You know what happens every time we do."

He gave her a long considering look. "You mean . . . you actually feel something?"

"You know I do."

Happiness. It was happiness she saw in him now. The shining black eyes, the dimple she had never noticed before on one side of his face.

"You're not going to keep me as a friend," he said.

She didn't understand him, but he was happy, and suddenly, she was happy, too. "What do you mean?"

He took her by the hand, interlaced his fingers with hers, and smiled down at her. "Never mind about that now. Has Summer told you all about the legend of the cottage?"

She looked up at him, and a deeper contentment took her. *He was holding her hand.* There was nothing wrong with that. Nothing at all. They were friends now. Friends.

"Yes," she said, "she told me all about the curse and the hidden gold."

"Well." He smiled, and his eyes were filled with wicked fun. "Now's as good a time as any to go check it out. Would you like to put a friendly arm around my waist?"

SIXTEEN

It was close to three before Amanda was able to coax Nicholas to go back to the manor house. They had picked up a picnic basket from Nurse Robbins, said a quick hello to the elder Mrs. Champagne, who had appeared none too pleased to see Amanda in tow, then taken themselves off to the catacombs beneath the cottage.

They had spent the early afternoon gorging on crackers and cheese, and paddling about in the wonderful blue-green waters of the subterranean lagoon. At one point, Nicholas had stretched out on a flat little ledge overlooking the water, offered her a hand, and said, "Come lie next to me. It's nice and warm here."

It was then that Amanda had decided it a good thing indeed to try to make it back to the house with all due haste. She couldn't trust herself with him; of that much she was certain. During their time together, she had twice convinced herself that it might very well be the best thing to allow him to have his way with her. *Twice she had come very close to ripping the clothes from his back, and having her way with him.* Only barely, on each occasion, had she managed to talk herself back from the precipice. She had made up her mind then that there was only one thing she could do. Hide. She had to avoid him for the duration of her time at the Champagne Manor. He had not taken her offer of friendship with any serious intent. So there was nothing else she could do. *There was really, but that was not an option to be considered.*

So, at a few minutes before three, she had said, "Nicky, I promised Summer I'd be back early this afternoon. Think she wants to talk with me about some of the other paintings she wants me to do."

He had looked at her then with glinting eyes, but followed her without protest, back up through the tunnel, and into the basement of the cottage.

The walk back down the beach had passed surprisingly quickly, given the distance, and before long, Amanda was dusting the sand from her feet at the foot of the stairs and saying, "Gavin's home early. And he doesn't sound very happy."

Nicholas looked up at the closed screen door, sighed, and proclaimed, "It must be Amber. I wonder what she's done now." He stepped around her, and trod lightly up the stairs.

"Nicky," Amanda hissed at him before he could make it to the door. "Here . . . put on your vest. Don't go in like that."

He looked down at his bronzed chest and said, "Ah. That's right. We don't want to give them the wrong impression."

He came back down, accepted the vest, and yanked it over his head. Then he was away from her and into the house without another word.

Amanda gathered the small collection of shells in her hands, made very sure that her feet carried no more sand, and then went up too. Inside, she could hear more clearly. Gavin was on the phone, and he was livid. Amanda stood in the foyer for a moment, not knowing what to do. Should she go back out?

Or should she try to tiptoe up to her room and pretend that she had heard nothing?

Summer came rushing into the room, just as Amanda had decided that she would go back out.

"I'm sorry about this," Summer said. "It's Rob . . . Gavin's cousin. He raised him, you know."

Amanda nodded. She felt sorry for the poor kid, whatever it was he had done. Gavin was giving it to him with both barrels fully loaded.

"What's happened?" she asked.

Summer pressed her lips together, then said, "He's either being expelled or suspended from the university. We're not sure which one . . . yet."

"Oh," Amanda said. "I'm sorry, I shouldn't have asked."

Summer waved a hand. "Oh, no . . . no, it would've come out eventually anyway. Rob . . . along with a few other kids . . . apparently set up some sort of hidden camera system in the private apartments of the dean and several other professors. Then they proceeded to feed those images live . . . on the Internet. They called the site RobTV.com of all things."

Amanda gasped. "Oh, no."

Summer lowered herself into a chair. "Exactly. Apparently, the site was the most popular one on campus . . . with thousands of hits a day. It was also gaining in popularity on various UWI campuses across the Caribbean."

Amanda stood uncertainly for a moment more, then sank onto the sofa with her shells cradled in her lap. She wrinkled her nose. "Do you think Gavin wants me sitting here . . . getting an earful?"

Summer held up a hand. "Ssh," she said, "let's listen."

And Amanda obliged her by going silent. They

both heard Gavin's voice rise to a full-fledged bellow: "Drinking at fifteen and coming home falling down drunk . . . now this! What were you thinking, Rob? Can you tell me that?"

There was a snatch of silence as Rob obviously attempted to explain what it was he had been thinking as he broadcast intimate pictures of college officials on the Internet.

Then came Gavin's strident voice again, biting into the quiet. "You thought . . . what?"

Again the silence, then: "Did I send you to college for that? Answer me!" The bellow tore through the house, and Summer lifted a hand to nibble anxiously upon a well-manicured nail.

"I've never seen him so upset," she whispered to Amanda.

Amanda sucked in a tight breath and knotted her hands together in her lap. She could almost feel sorry for Rob Champagne. Any lesser mortal would surely be in tears at this point, after so ferocious a chewing out.

"How old is Rob?" Amanda asked quietly.

Summer was now on her second nail, and Amanda felt compelled to lean across to hold her hand.

"He's nineteen," Summer said, interlacing her fingers with Amanda's. "He had a minor . . . drinking episode four years ago. But that's all done with. He was doing so well at college. I can't believe he did this . . . I just can't believe it."

Amanda patted her hand. "Teenagers do crazy things sometimes," she said. "I shudder when I think back on some of the things I did in my time."

The sound of the phone crashing into the cradle brought Amanda to her feet. "I'd . . . I'd better go up," she said. She was definitely not looking forward to running into Gavin Pagne while he was in the throes of his current upset.

She turned to go, and barely managed to suppress a shriek as something resembling a pink rat ran quickly by. "Oh, my God," she said, drawing back and raining shells all over the floor. "What *is* that thing?"

Summer's voice was somber. "Oh, that's the cat," she said. "Amber shaved him this morning. Never a dull moment in this family."

Despite the current mood in the house, Amanda giggled. "I'm sorry," she said when Summer looked up at her. "It's . . . I know it's not funny. Is the poor thing OK? I mean—" And Amanda clamped down hard on the humor bubbling in her chest.

An unwilling smile twisted the corners of Summer's mouth, and for a moment she, too, struggled. "Don't make me laugh," she said to Amanda. "This is serious."

"Oh, was the cat hurt?"

Summer took a breath, composed herself. "No. No, Ruggles is fine. His fur will grow back in. I meant about Rob."

"Well, I'm going up," Amanda said. "Fill me in on the details later. And, don't worry, it'll be OK." She had no idea what had prompted her to utter such wonderful reassurances. By the looks of things, it would be quite a while before things were again OK.

Amanda walked from the room, took a quick look around the corner, and then hurried up the stairs to her room. Once inside the air-conditioned suite, she leaned back against the door, and let out a breath. Thank the Lord above she had not run into Gavin or Nicholas on her way up. She didn't feel right at all about eavesdropping on a problem of this magnitude. Summer might think it OK, but her husband might be of an entirely different opinion.

She pushed away from the door now, and went to the bathroom to put down her shells. She hadn't noticed before, but they had a decidedly fishy smell to them. She placed them in a smooth ceramic bowl on the side of the sink, poured a good quantity of liquid soap on them, ran the hot-water tap at full blast, and when the water was good and steamy, settled the bowl beneath the deluge. Then she stood for a moment more looking at her face in the mirror. She turned her face this way and that, examining her jawline, and pulling the skin down beneath her eyes to inspect the delicate pink of the flesh there. Yes, she was healthy. No doubt about it. And she did look younger than her twenty-six years, too. So, these current completely unexplainable feelings that she was having for Nicholas Champagne could not be explained away by illness.

She made a wry face at herself, and almost jumped out of her skin at the sound of a little voice saying directly behind her, "You're really ugly."

She turned. *Little Amber.* She sank to a knee so that she was eyeball to eyeball with the child. "I remember you," she said.

The little girl pulled back half a step, and gave her a blistering look. "I don't like you," she said. "And my Dada doesn't like you either."

Amanda sank back on her heels. *Well, what now?* What had she done to so antagonize the child?

"Why don't you like me?" Amanda asked.

The little face worked for a second. "Because I just don't," she finally said.

Amanda pulled her bottom lip between her teeth and nibbled on the skin for a bit. "Well," she said slowly, "I was going to show you all of my lovely paints and brushes and stuff . . . but since you don't like me . . ." She let her words taper off.

The black eyes blinked, and the child tilted her chin up a bit. "I hate paints," she said. "Besides, my Dada'll buy paints for me if I ask him."

Amanda uncurled, and stood looking down at the child. She was the tiniest bit spoiled, it would seem. But maybe it was all right for a child of this age to be just that little bit spoiled. Who knows what challenges and worries life might throw her way once she was an adult? This would probably be one of the few times in her entire life when she would be truly carefree.

Amanda extended her hand. "Would you like to come have a look at some of my paintings?"

Amber snatched her hand away, and hid it behind her back. "No," she said. But as Amanda left the bathroom, she followed. Amanda smiled. *What a child.* She had obviously inherited her fair share of contrariness from her father.

Amanda went across to the closet, and removed the very large, and very sleek leather-bound, zipper-enclosed portfolio.

She brought it back to the bed, and sat. Amber sat beside her, saying not a word, but obviously highly interested in whatever it was she had hidden behind the leather. Amanda unzipped and laid the two leather halves against her bare knees.

"Oh," the child gasped. "That's Dada."

Amanda's heart thudded for a second in her chest. She had completely forgotten about the sketch she had done.

"That's a man who looks like your daddy," she said, and wrinkled her nose at the lie.

The little head went forward to further inspect

the drawing. "No," she said after a good minute spent staring at it, "that's Dada."

Amanda hustled the sketch to the bottom of the pile, and pointed at a beautiful print of a stormy seascape she had done only just recently. "Look at that one," she said. "And look at the boat. . . ."

The child looked up at her with serious black eyes. "My Dada has a boat."

Amanda flipped to another print. "Does he?"

Amber nodded. "Yeth. It's a big, big boat. . . ." And she spread her arms as wide as she could make them.

"And what do you and Dada do on the boat?"

Amber considered this carefully, and then lifted her hand to count off on her fingers, much as her father often did with her. "Fwishing . . . eating . . . and other stuff."

Amanda chuckled at her adorable lisp. And before long, they were both chatting it up like a couple of magpies.

"Dada says not to put lipstick on Ruggles?" Amber was saying hopefully now.

Amanda wrapped an arm about the child and pulled her into a tight squeeze. "No, darling. You can't put lipstick on a cat."

"Not even a little bit?"

Amanda shook her head. "Cats don't like lipstick, sweetheart." And she fought against the urge to laugh.

Amber was leaning both elbows on her now, her black eyes inspecting her. "Your hair isn't long like Aunty Sumsum."

"You don't like my hair then?"

A little hand went up to play with the short snappy curls that just barely kissed the tips of

Amanda's ears. "Can I ask Dada to make mine like yours?"

Amanda looked down at the soft curly black hair that had been braided into two hanging pigtails.

"I don't think your daddy would like it if you cut off all of your lovely hair, Amber, love."

"I'll ask him." And before Amanda could utter a single word of caution, the child had jumped down from the bed, and dashed from the room yelling for her father at the top of her lungs.

Amanda sat for a moment without moving. Why was fate conspiring against her? She had thought to avoid Nicholas Champagne for the remainder of the evening, and now here it was, none other than his own daughter was summoning him to her suite. She zipped the leather case back up with hands that were not quite steady. And just as she thought, within only minutes, there was the sound of heavy footsteps on the stairs.

Amanda tucked a leg beneath her, and waited for him. She felt him in the hallway, even before he filled her doorway. His daughter was not with him. He lingered there for a moment smiling at her. And she wished for the umpteenth time that things were different between them.

"Amber tells me that she wants her hair cut like yours."

Amanda pulled her leg even tighter beneath her. "It wasn't my idea."

He stepped into the room, closed the door behind him, and turned the key in the lock. Amanda felt her throat go dry. *Oh, no, please, not another session of kissing.* She wouldn't be able to restrain herself this time. Not after such a long and taxing day.

She rushed into speech. "How're things downstairs . . . with poor Rob, I mean?"

"We're going up to the Mona campus to bring the idiot home."

And he began peeling off his vest. Amanda gripped the sheets on both sides of her. *Control. That's all she needed. Just a little bit of control.*

"What're you doing?" she croaked when his hands, almost without pause, went to the fastenings on his jeans.

"I need a shower," he said. "I'll use yours, if you don't mind." He strode away from her, leaving his vest lying in a crumpled heap on the floor. She removed herself from the bed only when she heard the sound of the shower.

Muttering, she stooped to retrieve the discarded vest. *What was he, crazy or something?* How could he just stalk into her room, and with barely a single greeting, begin to take his clothes off before her? Did he think she was made of steel?

"Mandy?"

She folded the vest across an arm. "Yes?" *What did he want now?* Probably wanted her to go fetch him some fresh clothes or some such thing.

"Would you come in here for a minute, love?"

Amanda gritted her teeth. Must he continually refer to her in such a heated manner? *Love indeed.* She was not his *love.* He saw her as a little bit of flesh. Nothing else. She went to the lip of the door, and took a quick breath of the steamy air. *God in heaven, his scent was all over the place.*

"I'm here," she said.

She heard the shower door slide back. "Where are you?"

"Out here. Right by the door." If he thought for even one second that she was going in there, he had another think coming.

"I need my back soaped. There's a spot right in

the middle I can't quite reach." Her mouth sagged open. *His back soaped? He was crazy. Crazy as a loon. She was not going in there to soap his back, for God's sake. What did he think this was?*

"Look," she said with thick traces of panic in her voice. "I . . . this isn't. . . ."

"Oh, come on, Mandy, my love. Help me out. I'll even keep my eyes closed." *It wasn't his eyes she was worried about. It was hers. Her eyes, and her hands moving all over that glorious, glorious body. Didn't he understand? How could he not know what it did to her?*

She swallowed. *Well, OK. If he could stand it, then she could, too.* Her legs trembled just a little as she entered the bathroom.

"Where's the soap?" she asked in a voice that did not resemble hers in the slightest.

"In here, sweetheart."

She gritted her teeth. There he was, humming away merrily, and she was in the process of having a nervous collapse.

"Are you sure you can't get to that spot on your back without my help?"

The shower door opened. *And there he stood, elastic briefs barely covering him, completely wet and, God, so unbelievably fine.* Her eyes locked with his, and the entire world seemed to grow quiet and dim. She heard him say, "Here's the soap." And she knew that, somehow, she moved toward him to take it. But how she moved, she had no idea. She touched his fingers as she grabbed for the bar, and silver electricity rattled her from head to toe in one searing bolt.

"Turn around," she requested.

And he did, presenting her with the wonderful length of his back. So long, so rippling, so smooth. The steam of the shower was all about them now, and Amanda wondered for an erratic moment what he would do if she leaned forward and bit him right on his cute little backside.

She touched the sleek bar to the middle of his back. He made a little sound as her fingers began to move, and Amanda closed her eyes and prayed for strength. But it would seem that even God was not in her corner right then, for as her fingers dipped and glided, they developed a will, a stubbornness of their very own. They clung mindlessly to the textured muscles, massaging, probing, caressing in tiny, delicious, and ever-widening circles.

Nicholas bit back a groan. And he bent his head against the steamy tiles. *Jesus Christ. How could just her touch alone do this to him?* Why had he asked her to soap his back? To undo her resistance to him? Yes, that had been it. To unravel the fight in her. But it was he who was being unraveled. What magic did she possess that made her know exactly how to touch him?

In the foggy steam, his fingers curled against the shower tiles, and with jaw clenched hard, he reached for the cold-water tap, steeled himself, and then turned it to full blast.

Amanda recoiled from the sting of icy water. "What are you doing?"

He turned, and Amanda's eyes widened. "Oh," she said.

"Yes," he grated. "Definitely not a friendly response."

Amanda dropped the cake of soap into his palm and almost ran from the bathroom. She went to stand out on the little flower-rimmed balcony, and for long minutes, she stood with arms wrapped about her, just breathing. In. Out. In. Out. Just breathing, not thinking, not thinking at all. But slowly, traitorously, like so many dark shadows, the thoughts sneaked back. She couldn't go to bed with him. She couldn't. If she did, it would destroy the tenuous hold she had on things. She would begin to want more from him. She would begin to hope again, and perchance to dream? It was all too bad. Just too bad that she had to meet him now, after the years had softened her. She should have met him six years before, when she was still going through her wild child stage. She would have been able to handle him then. But why now? Why?

She looked up at the heavens, and closed her eyes. There was no such thing as love. No such thing really. At least not between men and women who were unrelated to each other by blood. It was just lust. Biology. Mating for procreation. Chemicals. Hormones. Something.

"Praying for my immortal soul?"

Her eyes flicked open. "Oh . . . you're finished."

He stood beside her now, hair wet and gleaming, chest bare, towel hanging from about his neck.

"You're cold," he said, looking down at the rash of goose bumps on her arms. "Let me. . . ." And his arms were about her, softly rubbing the entire length of *her* arms before she could even think to move. She held herself stiffly, not allowing even a single hair the luxury of relaxation.

"Why're you fighting me, Mandy?" His breath was husky against her neck.

She shivered. "I'm . . . I'm not."

"You are. With every tiny inch of you . . . you are."

She turned to face him, eyes glowing like cut diamonds. "Do this for me . . . please. You have to stop this. You have to."

Nicholas leaned closer. "Don't you think you could ever love me?"

The breath paused in her lungs. *Oh, now that wasn't fair. He was playing dirty now.*

"I don't believe in that kind of love, and you don't either."

"Don't you think Gavin and Summer are in love?"

Now why did he have to bring that up?

"Maybe they're an exception. There're always exceptions."

He smiled, because he knew he had her with that. "We could be an exception, too."

"No. No, we couldn't."

"Why?" The husky vibration rattled along her spine, spreading warm fingers up her neck, and puddling somewhere near the base of her brain.

"Because . . . this is just a game to you. I've played enough in my lifetime to know the difference."

He straightened away from her, pulled the towel from about his neck, and rubbed his hair for a good long stretch.

When he was finally through, he said, "I have to think about what you're asking. I've never had that kind of relationship, you know?"

Amanda sucked in a breath. *What was he talking about now?* Did he think she'd been asking him to make a commitment of some sort to her?

"What . . . what?" She was inarticulate again.

"You want me to be your man. Yours exclusively?"

Amanda was almost wild with desperation. "No . . . no, that's not what I meant at all. I was saying that . . . that this . . . this thing between us is not serious. So, to talk of love and that sort of thing is crazy. I mean, especially since it's all fake anyway."

He took her hand and pressed the flat of her palm to his chest. "Feel." The thudding was so intense that the vibrations sent a ripple of answering tremors through her.

"Is that real?" he asked.

She sucked in her bottom lip, let it back out. "It's just biology."

He leaned down to kiss her softly on the mouth. "And this?"

Tears of need pricked the backs of her eyes. "Chemistry," she muttered, and stood on tiptoe to grab his mouth again.

SEVENTEEN

Janet Carr adjusted the fit of her skirt and walked slowly up the wooden front stairs. She took a breath before reaching forward to ring the bell. She was only doing this because the nice old couple had asked her to. They had mistakenly assumed, though, that she and Summer had been friends at some point in time. That she would actually want to spend any time whatsoever around the gold-eyed witch. Wormed her way into the Champagne family is what the witch had done. Teach Summer to cook, they had begged in their letter to Janet. Teach her to cook so that her husband would not stray from her. So that he would grow fat and content with her.

A frown creased the skin between Janet's eyes. She had no idea why it was she felt compelled to do as the letter had asked. But the witch's parents had asked it, so she would at least try to be friendly. She rang once, and then again.

"Can I help you?" An older woman was standing in the doorway, with a little girl holding on to her hand.

Janet smiled. The housekeeper. How nice. How cozy. All this should have been hers. "Hello, Amber."

The little girl looked up at her with her father's black, intelligent eyes. "Hello," she said.

Janet mussed the little head, and then transferred her attention again to the housekeeper. "Are the Champagnes home?" It galled her even now to refer to the harpy as a *Champagne*. But she would do what needed to be done. Say what needed to be said.

"Mr. Gavin and his brother have just gone out. Mrs. Champagne is at home."

Janet beamed. "Good." *Perfect. Just perfect.* "Will you tell her that Janet Carr is here?"

The housekeeper nodded. "Will you wait a minute, ma'am?"

Janet waited with foot tapping on the metal runner stretched across the base of the screen door. She heard the fall of soft footsteps long before she actually saw her, and she straightened. She would try to be nice even if it killed her.

Summer pulled back the mesh door, and Janet gave her a simmering look. *God Almighty, how she disliked this woman.* With her long and lanky self, and peculiar devil eyes.

"Hello, Janet," Summer said, and there was at least an inch of solid frost in the depths of her eyes.

Janet smiled. "May I come in? I'd like to talk about a little matter."

Summer took a filling breath. She could be rude and refuse to let Janet in, but she was bigger than that. Besides, as Nicholas had quite rightly said, she no longer needed to worry about this woman. Not to the same degree anyway.

"Sure. Come on in. Amanda and I were just hanging out by the pool. We can talk out there."

Janet followed her through the sumptuous sitting room, and out through the French doors. Her eyes flicked from left to right, taking in the many plump sofas, the soft luxurious carpeting, and the lacquered dinettes. It was truly a gorgeous house.

Whatever else Summer *Stevens* was, she was certainly a great little decorator. *But it didn't take much brains for that.* She had a body, too; a tight little frame. That was undoubtedly the thing that had gotten her into Gavin Pagne's good graces. The body.

"This all your doing?" Janet asked now.

Summer gave a tight nod. "Yes. It's not finished yet, of course. There's still a lot of work to be done."

They were outside now, and walking beside the enormous navy pool. Amanda saw them coming, and shifted her legs from the lounger, closed her book, and sat up. She hadn't known Summer for very long, but she knew her well enough to instantly recognize the expression of icy reserve on her face.

"Amanda . . . this is Janet Carr. A . . . friend of the family."

Janet extended a hand. "Yes. I remember you from the wedding. How are you?"

Amanda's eyebrows lifted a bit. "Fine. Thank you." *There was fire here. Fire beneath the surface of things. Was this one of Gavin's old girlfriends?*

"Have a seat." Summer indicated a softly padded deck chair.

Janet arranged herself elegantly on the chair, crossing her long, smooth, well-taken-care-of legs before her.

Summer exchanged a quick glance with Amanda before saying as pleasantly as she could, "So, what was it you wanted to talk to me about?"

Amanda looked at the other woman, and the hairs on the back of her neck began to rise slowly. *This Janet Carr, whoever she was, was here to make a bit of trouble. That much was certain.*

Janet opened her neat little handbag, and removed a white envelope. "As you know, I received a letter from your parents," she began.

Summer gritted her teeth, and nodded. "Um-hmm."

Janet unfurled the paper. "Among other things . . . they have asked me to promise to patch up our friendship."

Summer blinked. *Friendship?* The woman was insane. Stark, raving crazy was what she was. There had never been a friendship. There had been nothing but instant hatred between them both, and she knew it.

"Oh," Summer said sweetly, "how nice of you to come all the way over here just to tell me that."

Janet tinkled the little bell-like laugh that grated on Summer's very last nerve.

"We should be friends again," Janet said. "I mean, there is no reason why we shouldn't . . . is there?"

Amanda sucked in a breath and waited. Summer smiled nicely. "No. No reason at all. But I really wasn't aware that you didn't consider me your friend all along."

Amanda opened her book and began flipping the pages in rapid succession. *Warfare. Open warfare was only minutes away.* Where was Nicky? Both he and Gavin had been gone for hours. Surely they should be on their way back with Rob by now.

Janet pursed her lips, and considered the woman seated before her. *This usurper, this pretender was smarter than she appeared.* "I've always thought of you warmly, Summer," she said now, leaning forward to emphasize her point. "But I thought somehow that you didn't care for me . . . very much."

Amanda glanced anxiously at the door. *Lord in heaven, what would she do if a full-scale conflict broke out between the two?* She couldn't very well stop them if they decided to go at it. She was all of five foot three, and 105 pounds soaking wet. They were both, what, six, seven feet?

"Why don't we have something to drink?" Amanda broke in before Summer could say a word. "Punch?" she asked Janet. "Would that be . . . I mean . . . would you like that?"

Janet nodded. "Fine with me."

Amanda swallowed. "Right. Summer . . . can you show me where everything is . . . I think Mrs. Carydice might be a bit busy in there . . . what with bathing Amber and all that."

Once they were both in the kitchen, Amanda peered back out the window at the woman seated by the pool. "Who in the world is that?" she whispered to Summer.

Summer opened up an overhead cupboard, and began slapping glasses onto the counter. "That," she said, "is the spawn of Satan. Beelzebub's little helper. One of the Devil's minions." She wrenched open the fridge, peered around blindly for a moment, then grabbed a pitcher of something or the other.

Amanda stilled her hand. "That's not punch," she said.

Summer yanked the container out. "Looks OK to me."

Amanda chuckled. "See . . . it says prune juice."

Summer clunked a couple of ice cubes into a glass. "Perfect for her," she said, making a face. "Prunella De'vil."

Amanda grabbed her hand, and led her across to sit. "Who is she really? One of Gavin's exes?"

Summer rolled her eyes. "God, no. He was *never* interested in her. And I can't tell you the number of times he told her so. But every time he would send her away, she would come right back again.

Kinda like a bad penny or something. She's made my life a living nightmare these past four years I've lived in Jamaica. Always turning up with cakes, pies, puddings . . . all sorts of mess."

Amanda laughed despite herself. Summer was so dramatic. "Listen," she said, "you can beat this girl at her own game. You think she's still after Gavin?"

Summer nodded. "Wouldn't surprise me a bit if she were."

"Um-hmm," Amanda said, and there was a thoughtful light in her eyes now. "OK. Tell you what . . . first things first. Let's find out what her game is. Once we know that, we'll figure out what to do. OK? Just remember one thing, though. . . ."

"What?"

"Don't be too nice. If she comes at you, give it right back to her. She'll respect you for it. I've met her type before."

Summer grinned at Amanda. "I'm scared of you, girl," she said. "I'll know never to get on *your* bad side."

Amanda grinned back. "Oh, I've played a game or two in my time." She went to the fridge, and removed a pitcher of red sorrel drink. "She thinks she can outplay you . . . see. That's why she keeps coming back. Even though you're married now, she doesn't see the game as being over . . . you know?"

Amanda poured three glasses of drink. "So, Summer, dear heart. What we have to do is simple. We have to convince her that the play *is* at an end. And we can decide to do that nicely . . . or not."

Summer's eyebrows flicked upwards. "I didn't manage to do that in four long years . . . how could I do that now?"

Amanda put an arm about her. "My child, my child," she said, "*you* have a lot to learn."

Summer giggled. "You know," she said, "you're just like Nicky. It's really uncanny. That's exactly like something he would say."

They both emerged laughing after a bit more time spent arranging a nice little snack platter. Amanda carried the drinks on an ornate silver tray, while Summer wheeled a little cart packed with sandwiches.

Janet watched them both with slitted eyes. She didn't trust the little one at all. Not even for a second. She recognized a schemer when she saw one. *Who did she have an eye on? Nicholas? That was a joke.* He was definitely one Champagne man who had his head screwed on right. He would never be swayed by the simple charms of the flesh. He would partake of them, of course. But if the girl was thinking of anything more permanent than a couple nights of steamy passion, she would be severely disappointed. *Severely.*

"Snacks," Amanda said once they were close enough. She placed the tray on one of the little round tables. And while Summer busied herself with setting the wheel brake on the cart, Amanda handed Janet a glass, and then bustled around the sandwich platter.

"Let's see," she said, "we've got chicken salad sandwiches, cheese, roast beef . . . what's this one, Summer?"

"Curry goat."

"Curry goat," Amanda continued, "vegetarian. So, what would you like?"

Janet patted her stomach, "I've got to keep an eye on my weight," she said, eyeing the soft swell about Summer's stomach that she was only just beginning to notice.

Summer gave her an icy smile. "Well, thank good-

ness I don't for a while." She gave her own stomach
a pat. "I'm expecting, you see."

Janet's mouth sagged open, and Amanda barely
managed to turn the laugh that swelled in her chest
into a session of rather hacking coughs.

"Sorry," she said after a moment, "something
went down the wrong way." Then she bent close to
Summer and whispered. "Congratulations. Does everybody know?"

Summer shook her head and whispered back.
"Not yet."

Janet chomped on a vegetarian sandwich for long
minutes without saying a single word. Her mind was
working fiercely. *A baby. Just imagine that.* This creature was going to produce the heir to the Champagne fortune. She hadn't thought that Summer
would be this quick about it, though. But then
again, it *was* the only intelligent thing to do. How
else could she ensure that her position in the family
remained secure? If Gavin ever divorced her, the
little Champagne heir would continue to be her
meal ticket. *Smart move, Summer Stevens. Very smart.*

"Well," Janet said after a little bit, "I'm really
happy for you. Are you going to hold a party or
something to celebrate the event?"

Summer gave Amanda a little sideways glance.
"We haven't decided yet."

Janet plucked another sandwich from the tray and
said in a considering manner, "I'd love to hold a
shower for you. If you'd like?"

Amanda swallowed an entire lump of sandwich
without the benefit of chewing. The woman had
guts. She had to give her that. It was as clear as glass
that she was not thrilled by the news of Summer's
pregnancy, and here she was, as boldly as you please,

offering up her services as the shower-giver. *What nerve.*

Summer took a sip of sorrel punch. The entire situation suddenly struck her as truly amusing. *Poor Janet. Poor lonely, demented woman.* Did she really think that she could fool her with this pseudo-offer of friendship? After all she had gone through with her in the past several years?

"It would be too much to ask," said Summer. "We're probably not going to do anything too spectacular anyway . . . what with the wedding and everything . . . you know, everyone's kinda burnt out on parties."

Janet leaned forward to grip Summer's arm. "Let me do this for you." She smiled. "My way of saying I'm sorry for . . . whatever harsh words might have passed between us before."

"Do you have a large circle of friends?" Amanda asked now with a slightly cocked eyebrow.

Janet gave her a pert little stare before saying, "It would be mostly Summer's friends at the shower . . . not mine."

"Oh, I didn't mean the shower . . . I was thinking of . . . you know, in general. Do you have many friends?"

Summer nudged Amanda with a leg and did her best not to collapse into laughter.

"I don't see what that has to do with anything," Janet sniffed.

Amanda leaned back, bringing her legs up to rest on the lounger. "A lot actually. You'd probably have a much happier life . . . with friends to hang out with."

Janet blinked rapidly. "I didn't say I had no friends."

"Well, I'd be surprised if you did have any at all.

Your entire demeanor is not one that inspires warm bosom friendships."

Summer placed a hand across her mouth as Janet opened and closed hers much as a recently landed fish would.

"How . . . how dare you!" She stood in a flourish. "You don't even know me." And she turned blistering eyes on Summer. "I'll talk to you later about the shower. Don't get up, I'll find my own way out." And without a single word more, she clipped smartly across the concrete, and disappeared into the house.

Once she was out of sight, Summer collapsed in her chair. "Oh, my God . . . I can't believe you actually said all that."

Amanda sat up. "Why not? She needed to hear it. Somebody should've told her all that years ago. She has some very serious personality problems."

Summer chortled. "I wonder what she really came for. She seemed to be working up to something, but I couldn't figure out what exactly."

Amanda nibbled on a cheese sandwich. "I wouldn't waste any time worrying over it. So, are you going to let her throw the shower?"

"What?" Summer said. "No. Of course not. She'd probably put strychnine in the food."

"Hmm," Amanda said.

Summer cocked an eyebrow. "Hmm? What do you mean 'Hmm'?"

"Maybe you should. If she wants to throw the shower, let her throw the shower. This might actually help her realize that Gavin is now off-limits."

"Well . . ." Summer said, wrinkling her nose, "I . . . don't know. I really have no interest at all in hanging out with her, to tell you the truth. The woman gives me the heebie-jeebies."

Amanda leaned closer. "She doesn't expect you to accept, you know. If you were to say yes, she would be in such a state of confusion. She wouldn't know what to do with herself. Can you imagine? Her throwing a shower party for . . . who?"

Summer chuckled. "Well, as long as she doesn't poison the food . . . maybe it might be fun . . . for us anyway, to see her try to squirm out of it."

"Umm," Amanda agreed, and was about to elaborate when the sound of car doors slamming shut halted the words on her lips.

"They're back," Summer said, and she got to her feet and hustled into the house.

Amanda worried at her lip for a second. It was incredible how much a part of this family she already felt. With each passing day, they sucked her in a bit more, and a bit more. Their problems were slowly becoming her problems. *Was that what family did?* She was even worried now about Rob, and him she'd never even met.

Her heart soared at the sound of approaching voices. They were all coming out. Nicholas appeared first, and Amanda stepped firmly on the thrill that rippled through her as his eyes held hers from across the distance. She mustn't begin to build silly romantic fantasies around him. He was a good-looking man. She was a healthy red-blooded woman who was in Jamaica, seated by a pool in a beautiful windswept villa. What he made her feel was not real. It was just situational.

"There you are," Nicholas said, smiling. Behind him was a lanky teenager she very vaguely remembered. He was a budding beauty himself, she mused, with his dark flashing eyes and that very Champagne look about him.

Nicholas wrapped an arm about the boy's shoulders. "This," he said, "is Rob. You've never met before . . . I don't think?"

Amanda felt a rush of sympathy as she smiled at the poor kid. "Hi. Nice to meet you." Rob took her hand and muttered a greeting. He appeared so severely subdued that Amanda knew that the confrontation must have been a spectacular one once Gavin had arrived on campus.

Amanda went to the cart. "Can I fix you a plate to eat?" The boy nodded.

"You, Nick?"

"Thank you, love."

Amanda busied herself over the two plates, handing a nicely stacked one to Rob, and then another to Nicholas. She poured punch, and offered that too.

A shadow loomed for a moment in the doorway. "Rob," Gavin called, "I want to talk to you."

The boy bolted up from his seat without delay.

"Take the plate," Nicholas said.

When he had gone, Amanda couldn't help asking, "Was it bad?"

Nicholas sampled a sandwich. "He got off easy. Gavin managed to convince the dean to only suspend him for the rest of the year." He took a swig of drink. "The last time I got a hiding from Gavin over something like this, I was sixteen . . . not too much younger than Rob is now."

Amanda's brows rose. "Gavin raised you, too? He doesn't look much older than you are."

"Ten years or so. But . . . it was almost as though the age difference was at least double that. He was forced to become an adult because of . . . the situation. He raised us all, you see. Rob . . . from the time he was a baby . . . his mother died. Gavin's been more than just a brother to us all . . . in many ways, he's our father. . . ."

"Oh." Amanda swallowed. She'd had no idea. No idea at all. What an absolutely amazing man Gavin Pagne was. What an absolutely amazing family they all were.

"I . . . I didn't know. Did he change his name because of the . . . the situation?" She had no idea at all what situation he'd been referring to, but she would certainly find out about that later.

"His legal name is Champagne. But over the years . . . it was shortened to Pagne . . . because Champagne sounded kind of . . . show-business-y."

He fiddled around in his pocket. "You're full of questions tonight. I thought you didn't want to know anything about me. . . ."

"I never said that."

He pulled out an envelope and offered it to her. "This came for you this afternoon, and I forgot to give it to you."

"For me? Are you sure?" No one knew where she was. No one, except *Sheila*, of course.

Amanda accepted the envelope with fingers that shook just a bit. Had Sheila written her name and return address in the usual place on the top of it? Had Nicholas noticed it, and was he now playing some perverse game with her?

"Thank you," she mumbled, and immediately shoved the envelope in the pocket of her shorts.

Nicholas bit into another sandwich, chewed, and then offered the uneaten portion to Amanda. "Piece?"

"No. Thanks. I've already had my fill."

Nicholas polished off the remaining sandwiches on his plate, gulped down the punch, and stood. "Well," he grated, "I think I've gotten in your hair for long enough. I'll leave you to your reading. Good night."

And with that, he left her. Only when he was safely in the kitchen did he turn again to peer back out through the window slots at her. A smile curved his lips. *He would get Amanda Drake yet.* She was still fighting, but slowly, slowly, the struggle was ebbing out of her. She wouldn't resist him for much longer. Of that he was certain.

"What are you smiling at, you wicked thing?"

Nicholas turned. "Ah," he said, beaming, "my favorite girl."

Summer chuckled. "That's not the way I see it."

Nicholas leaned back against the counter. "You mean the nut job out there?"

Summer frowned. "The what did you call her?"

Nicholas pinched her cheek. "Just a little joke."

"I hope you're treating her well," Summer said, wagging a finger at him. "She's a really nice girl."

"She's not allowing me anywhere near her so far . . . so . . ." His shoulders lifted in a shrug.

Summer grinned at him. "Finally . . . someone who is immune to your charm. I almost don't believe it."

His brows lifted. "You think she's immune?"

"No." Summer was in the fridge now, pushing plates around, and making a general racket. She emerged with a leg of chicken and some potato salad. She waved the leg at Nicholas before taking a very hefty bite. "She likes you . . . I know that much. It's as plain as day if you've even one solitary eye to see. There's something else going on, I think. She's holding you off for some . . . reason." She bit again, also pausing to sample the potato salad. "Do you want me to find out what?"

Nicholas's eyes ran over her. "You know," he said,

and a considering tone sneaked into his voice, "you're beginning to gain a bit of weight there, Summer, my love."

"It's all right." She patted her stomach. "Don't you notice anything?"

Nicholas folded his arms. "You've put on a few pounds about the middle. That I can see."

"Ah-hah . . . and?"

"And, you've been eating entirely too much potato salad."

"That's all you can think of?"

"Actually . . . no. In the last few weeks, you've also had too much jerk chicken, sandwiches, peas and rice, ice cream, pickles. . . ." He paused in midstream. "Wait a second . . . wait one solitary second. Are you trying to tell me that . . . are you . . . ?"

Summer nodded, eyes gleaming. "Yep. I most certainly am. You're going to be an uncle, my boy."

Nicholas threw back his head and laughed, and then he picked her up and spun her about the kitchen.

The noise brought Gavin in. "What on earth is going on in here? Nick . . . put her down, she's . . ."

"I know." Nicholas said, grinning. "She just told me." He settled Summer carefully on the floor, then went across to envelop his brother in a bear hug. "What is it? Do we know yet?"

Gavin smiled. "It's too soon to know. But . . . I don't think we want to know. Do we, Summer?"

"I don't know . . . maybe later on . . ."

Nicholas rubbed his hands together. "A party . . . we've got to throw a party. A big announcement in the papers . . ."

"You'll never guess who wants to throw a party for us . . . a shower really."

Both pairs of eyes turned in her direction. Summer smiled. "Janet Carr."

EIGHTEEN

The next several weeks passed in a glorious jumble. Every morning Amanda was up before seven. She would go down, make herself a quick breakfast of hot wheat cereal, toast, and juice. Then she'd be off to the beach or the orchard to sit for hours on end, sketching. On these days, with the sound of the ocean ever present, and the wind rushing in, in such a friendly and sweet way, she found that perfect contentment could almost be hers. Almost. For it was also at these moments of complete peace, complete quiet that her mind would turn to Nicholas Champagne. She would find herself thinking more and more about him, wondering what it was he might be doing right then. She had done a pretty good job of avoiding him, though. She had learned his schedule well, and always endeavored to be somewhere far away from the house whenever she knew that he was likely to be by. She could tell that Summer was puzzling over her behavior, too. On more than one occasion, she had been forced to give evasive answers to the woman she was coming to love more and more like a sister every day. But it was the only thing she could think of to do now. Things had gone too far for a confession of any sort. As close a family as they were, she knew that once she revealed her original reason for coming to Jamaica, she would be asked, very nicely, to leave. And she didn't want to leave them all just yet. Not just yet. They had become her family. And she wanted them. She wanted them for a little longer.

It was true that Sheila's vitriolic letter had left her a bit shaken, but she had torn it to shreds immediately after reading it, and simply filed her comments away for later reflection. Sheila had been upset that she had not done as they had planned. But the arrangement that they had made seemed a part of a different life now. *Had she ever really been that bitter, that angry, that unscrupulous a person?*

"Amanda?"

A rustle of leaves crunching underfoot. "So this is where you've been hiding."

Amanda looked up at Summer with a little smile. Nicholas was at home today, she knew, and she hadn't wanted to bump into him by accident. She had seen him several times in the last week, of course, but always at a distance. A safe distance.

"Thought I'd finish my orchard sketches today," Amanda said, looking at Summer with an expression that was entirely too innocent to be believed. Summer sat on the ground beside her, pulled her legs up, and rested her back against the solid bulk of the Mango tree trunk. Her stomach was still quite small, but day by day, the size of it was becoming more and more noticeable.

"Poor Nicky," she said now.

Amanda's ears pricked up. *Poor Nicky?* What was the matter? What had happened?

"What?" she asked, through lips that had gone a bit dry.

"He's been feeling off-color all week."

He had? She hadn't been aware of it. The poor darling man.

"What's the matter with him?"

"We don't know exactly. He's gone off his food." Summer turned glowing golden eyes and gave Amanda a direct look. "Won't eat, you know."

Amanda put down the coal-tipped pencil. "Shouldn't he go to the doctor then? You mean he hasn't eaten anything at all in days?" *Why had no one mentioned this before?* How could they do this? How could they keep her in the dark like this, when Nicholas needed her? Was sick and needed her?

"Is he . . . is he at the manor house . . . or . . . ?"

Summer sighed deeply. "He's at home . . . his home. He hasn't come to see us in days, though. We've been taking care of Amber . . . as you know."

"You mean, no one's gone to make sure he's OK?"

Summer shrugged. "Mrs. Carydice sees him every day. Takes him his meals. But . . ."

Amanda was panicked now. "You haven't gone . . . or Gavin . . . or Rob? Just to check?"

"I would've gone myself yesterday . . . but I wasn't feeling very well." She gave her stomach a little pat. "The youngster in here is acting up again."

"Oh, yes," Amanda agreed immediately. In her heightened concern, she had very nearly forgotten that Summer was pregnant. She chewed on a nail. "I think someone . . . from the family should go and make sure he's all right."

"Rob's at the office with Gavin . . . so that leaves only . . . us."

Amanda was already on her feet, dusting the dirt and leaves from the back of her pants. She glanced at her watch. *It was nearly five, and what if he had died of starvation or something by now?* What if Mrs.

Carydice only thought he was sleeping, when he was really stone cold dead?

Amanda's heart thudded in her chest, and a rash of cold sweat broke out across her brow.

"Let's go now," she said. "Let's go right now."

Summer struggled to get up, and Amanda extended a hand to heave her to her feet. "Being pregnant really makes you lose your center of gravity somehow," Summer said once she was up and standing.

"Come on," Amanda said. "We don't have time to be hanging about talking about centers of gravity and all that stuff. Nicky could be . . . could be really sick up there."

Summer wrinkled her nose. "I'm not sure if it's that serious. And besides, I think we should stop and get some food for him first . . . from the house."

It took them five minutes to get back to the manor house. Five minutes too many as far as Amanda was concerned. It seemed to her that Summer was entirely too unconcerned about Nicholas's welfare. Something she would have pointed out, had she not been in such a state of terrible worry.

"You know," Summer said as they reached the front stairs of the house, "you left your sketch pad and pencils in the orchard. Should you go back for them?"

Amanda gave her the kind of look that made Summer struggle to maintain an appropriately serious countenance. "OK," Summer said when she had finally managed to get herself under control, "get them later then."

Amanda bounded up the stairs taking them two at a time. She was in the kitchen, cutting breads and slabs of cheese and meat, by the time Summer had managed to make it to the door.

"There's soup on the stove," she said to Summer. "Pour some into a thermos, while I fix some lemonade . . . and don't take too long about it."

Summer saluted. "Yes, ma'am."

Amanda neither noticed nor even realized that she was ordering her boss about, and in her own house. In the space of time it had taken them to walk from the orchard to the house, she had imagined and discarded at least a dozen possible horrors that she thought had probably befallen Nicholas in the past hours. She was now convinced that since he was possibly dehydrated, not to mention on the brink of emaciation, he had probably staggered from his bed in a daze of starved confusion, fallen down the stairs, and broken his neck.

She sliced and juiced lemons with maniacal speed. "Are you finished there?"

Summer bit back a chuckle. "Not yet. I need to get a bag to put everything in . . . and some flowers. What do you think? Roses?"

Amanda's brows lifted. *Roses? Had she completely lost her mind?* How could she possibly be thinking of flowers at a time like this?

She poured in the sugar, lemon juice, and water in one gush, and stirred like a madwoman, sloshing drink here, there, and just about everywhere on the counter. Summer was back with the bag and two beautiful long-stemmed roses by the time the lemonade was done. Amanda almost ripped it from her grasp. She had put the sandwiches in a long Tupperware container, and the drink in another flask.

"You'll need cups," Summer said. "I'll get them."

Amanda shoved everything into the haversack as

Summer handed them to her. Tupperware. Forks. Cups. Flasks. Napkins. *Napkins? What for?*

"OK . . . OK. That's enough. Let's go. Let's go."

Summer sat on a stool. "I have to rest for a minute."

Amanda shrugged on the haversack. "Come on. You can rest once we get there. Exercise is good for you and the baby anyway." And she yanked Summer along with her.

"Wait a minute, you're forgetting the roses."

"Forget the roses. He can't eat them."

"Take the roses."

Amanda darted back into the kitchen and snatched the flowers from the table. *Damn roses. Who needed them?*

They very nearly ran the distance to the main house with Amanda in front the entire way, yelling to Summer, "Come on. Come on. God. Why are you going so slowly? He could be dying in there."

She had, of course, completely forgotten to ask whether or not Summer had spoken to Nicholas on the phone that day, or any day this week. She was just desperate. Desperate to see him. To make absolutely sure that he was all right. And then to insist that he eat something.

They were at the main house now, standing in front of the lovely faux-marble-slab stairs, and Summer was half bent over, panting: "Let me get my breath back. Let me just get my breath back."

Amanda took the stairs at a bound. She turned the handle, then turned back to say, "It's locked. You have the key, right?"

Summer was all innocence. "Key? No . . . I don't have the key. Knock and see if he'll come down."

Amanda gave her a look of complete exasperation. How could he come down, in the name of heaven, if he was lying at the bottom of the hall stairs with a broken neck? She rattled the handle again, and then pounded on the door. "Nick? Can you hear me? Nick?"

She sucked in a breath. *He was dead. She just knew it.* He was stone cold dead, and that was why he wasn't answering. Oh, God in heaven, why had she turned him away? Why had she said no to him? Why must everything in her life always, always be too late?

"There must be another way in. Maybe a back entrance?"

Summer shook her head. "Nope. Just the front."

"Well, maybe a window might be open on the ground floor. Let's have a look." And she was off, bounding down the stairs, and walking around to peer in and then rattle every available window.

"Should I go back to the manor house for the key?" was Summer's helpful suggestion.

Amanda waved it away. "No . . . no. That'll take too long. Where's his bedroom window?"

Summer pointed at a small window on the second floor under which a sturdy metal trellis ran. "That's his window. And it's open."

Amanda gave the spot a long considering look. Then she turned to Summer to say, "It's not that high."

Summer put a hand on her arm. "You're not thinking of climbing that?"

"Why not? It's not that high. Even if I fell . . . I wouldn't hurt myself . . . with all of the bushes underneath. Besides, it looks like a really easy climb. And I'd be able to get right into his bedroom window, too."

"Well, I'm not climbing it," Summer said with a definite shake of her head.

"No," Amanda agreed. "Too risky for you. Just give me a leg up . . . I'll be OK. Once I get to the top, I'll let you know that he's OK."

Amanda tested the bottom slat of the trellis. "See . . . exactly as I thought. It's nice and firm. No metal rot or anything. Just like a ladder really."

"Here," Summer said, "put the roses in your mouth . . . bite down on the stems . . . but not so hard that you crush them."

"I really don't think"—Amanda began.

But Summer shushed her with, "Take the roses. The flowers will cheer him up. Trust me."

Amanda held the stems in her mouth while Summer steadied her from behind. "Are you OK?" Summer asked.

"Yes," Amanda said.

"Sure you're not going to fall?"

"Sure."

Summer stood back with a hand held across her eyes. The sun was going down, but it was still bright enough to cause a bit of a glare.

"You're doing good," she called to Amanda. "Just don't look down."

"I'm not," Amanda mumbled. The darn roses had all kinds of thorns, and they were beginning to prick the sides of her mouth. In a moment, she would let go of the horrible things.

"OK . . . you're almost there. Almost. Keep going."

Amanda climbed, slowly, carefully, rung by rung, slat by slat. Inching closer and closer to the window. It hadn't seemed this high from the ground. But all in all, it wasn't so very bad. She was almost there. She could see the window ledge now. Almost touch it. OK. Good. She could touch it now.

Summer clapped her hands down below. "You did it."

Amanda hooked an arm around the top slat of the trellis, and then inched slowly across to the open window. Her head just barely crested the top of the sill. The room was in darkness, but she could just make out a bed, and . . . yes, there was someone lying in it.

Her heart went cold then, and shards of panic raced through her. Why was he lying there so still and silent? Oh, God. *He was dead.* She gripped the sill, and scrabbled around for a moment as she tried to pull herself up and over. There was no way that she was going to fall now. Absolutely no way.

In the room, Nicholas came awake slowly. He had come home a bit early because he'd stayed very late at the office the night before, working out the legal angles of a new and possibly very lucrative venture for Champagne Industries. He'd also not been sleeping exceedingly well in the past weeks. Insomnia had never been a problem before, but of late, he found that he struggled to get even a few hours of good solid sleep. And when he did sleep, his dreams were filled with Amanda Drake. Touching her, kissing her, loving her. *God, it was almost too much to bear.* The woman was driving him crazy, avoiding him as she had the past weeks. And for no good reason, too. No good reason whatsoever.

He turned on his side to adjust the pillow more comfortably, and that was when he heard the soft scuffling sounds just outside the window. He lay very still in the darkening room, listening. Yes, there was no doubt about it; there was someone attempting to get into the house through his bedroom window. And not only that, his accomplice was on the ground cheering him on. With great stealth, he removed the body pillow from its usual position against the headboard, shoved it beneath the blankets, and then crawled from the bed. He was only half dressed, but that did not matter. A plan of action was slowly but very clearly beginning to come into focus in his head. He would grab the guy as soon as he came through the window. The element of surprise would be on his side, so even if the man turned out to be a huge bodybuilder type, he would be able to overpower him without much difficulty. And chances were, the intruder would not have any weapons at hand either, since he would not be expecting the sudden attack.

Just outside the window, Amanda shifted her weight yet again in an attempt to throw her leg over the windowsill. *God, the roses were just tearing her mouth to shreds.* She placed her chin on the whitewashed ledge, and released one of the flowers so that it fell softly to the carpeting inside.

In the darkness, Nicholas saw the object fall, and he pressed himself against the wall. *So, the man had come equipped with some sort of weapon.* It was long and narrow, he could see that. But it would do the man no good. No good at all.

Amanda managed to hitch her heel on the underbelly of the ledge, and that gave her the leverage she needed. With a mighty heave, she was up, and straddling the wooden window. She was just turning her head again to look at the still form lying in the bed, when something grabbed her from behind and yanked her from her perch.

"Didn't expect to find anyone home . . . did you . . . ?"

She was rolled to the ground, and the air left her lungs in a giant gush as he sat atop her.

"You're soft, boy . . . soft . . . not cut out for this kind of thing, are you?"

Relief washed over Amanda then. It was Nick. Nick. Nick. He was still very much alive, it would seem. She tried to talk as he wrestled her arms back against the carpeting, but the rose in her mouth prevented coherent speech.

"Nick," she muttered. And then there was light, glorious, golden light. And there she lay on her back, with rose in mouth, and Nicholas firmly astride.

His eyes locked with hers, and for a moment, there was nothing in his but blank incomprehension. Then, he removed his leg from its stranglehold across her chest, threw back his head, and laughed. Amanda removed the rose, and sat up with great care.

"You . . ." she said, and paused to take a breath. "You almost killed me." She shrugged out of the backpack, and said with a touch of ire, "Well, at least you're feeling well enough to laugh . . . I'm glad you think all this is so funny."

Nicholas gave her a gleaming look, and then collapsed into guffaws again. When he finally managed to get himself back under control, he said, "God Almighty . . . this I've definitely never seen before. Climbing through my window with a rose between your teeth. Don't you think it would've been a bit easier to use the conventional means of entry?"

"Oh, shut up," Amanda said. Then: "You don't look sick at all to me. So, why aren't you eating?"

Nicholas scratched the side of his head. "What?"

"Eating. I said, why aren't you eating?"

Nicholas rolled to his feet, and extended a hand to help her up. "Look," he said, "you might have hit your head or something when I wrestled you to the carpet. Your brain seems to be a bit scrambled. Come on over to the bed and sit down for a moment."

Amanda pursed her lips. "My brain is not scrambled. You're sick and haven't been eating . . . not for days . . . Summer told me."

A wicked light came into glorious life in the depths of his eyes. "Oh . . . yes . . . that," he said now. "No, I haven't been eating . . . food . . . just the thought of it makes me sick."

"Um-hmm," Amanda said slowly, "you may be mentally sick . . . physically, I'm not so sure." She was beginning to suspect that maybe, just maybe, he had not been ill at all. *That Summer.* No wonder she hadn't appeared overly concerned about him. No wonder she had insisted throughout the whole thing that Amanda take the roses.

"I have a really, really bad feeling right here. . . ." And he took her hand and pressed it to the flat of his gut.

"You're going to have a really, really bad feeling right there too . . . in a second," she said, tapping a finger against his temple.

Nicholas gave her a suitably mournful look. "Heartless woman. Here I am on my deathbed . . . and you treat me so shamefully. . . ."

Amanda did her level best not to smile, but the humor of the entire thing was beginning to get to her, and she just couldn't prevent her lips from twitching, and then blooming into a full-blown grin.

"You are such an idiot," she said, laughter spilling from her eyes. But she was glad, glad that he was all right. Glad that he was still alive. "Just cut it out now. You know you're not even sick."

He went to lie on the bed, his head resting on a

palm. "Come on over here, and say that to me again. My hearing's all messed up, too. . . ."

Amanda chuckled. "I'm not coming over there because I don't want to give you any ideas. I'll throw you your food from here, though, if you open your mouth."

Nicholas laughed. "Darling Mandy. Why do you torture me like this? I've missed you so much. You won't believe how much."

She zipped open the haversack. "You're only saying that now because I come bearing gifts."

He pulled himself up to sit cross-legged on the bed. "What have you brought me? I'm so excited I can't wait."

"Shut up," Amanda said, giggling. "Why are you so silly?"

In response, he sucked in his cheeks and rolled his eyes. "I . . . I don't know, ma'am."

"OK," Amanda said, "you'd better behave . . . or you'll get no food at all. Here's what I have . . . are you listening?"

"Yes . . . baby."

"Stop looking at me like that. I've got soup . . . some lovely sweet-potato-and-chunky-meat soup. And all kinds of sandwiches. . . ."

"Ah-hah-hhh."

"Yes, and I also made you some lemonade . . . ice cold."

"Did you do that for me?"

"I did."

"Thank you."

"You're welcome."

"Come over here and check my pulse."

Amanda shook her head. "I give up. You're too much for me."

He wiggled his eyebrows. "Don't make me beg."

Amanda went across to the bed and sat. She was beginning to think that the only way out of everything would be to go to bed with him. She would be forced to deal with her feelings afterwards, of course, but she was certain that once he had lain with her, he would slowly but surely lose interest in the pursuit of her. And maybe, and she was thinking about things very clearly now, that was the very thing that she feared the most. Not becoming too attached to him. Not any attendant damage that reality might do to her friendship with Sheila. Not any other consideration at all. Just that, and that alone. She didn't want to lose him. But if she slept with him, she would.

He was smiling at her in such a very infectious way, and she looked at him now with affection brimming in her eyes. *Darling Nicky.* It had taken this to bring her to her senses; the thought of him being ill, helpless, possibly even dead, had scared her in a manner that nothing else ever had before. She reached out a hand to stroke the side of his face, and he turned his head to softly kiss her palm. In that moment, as she looked at his black head bent so slightly against her, a terrifying notion struck her. *Could it be that she loved this man? But how could that be? She didn't even believe in the whole love tangle. Loving until death do us part was a fantasy. It wasn't real. Didn't exist. It was lust. Just lust that people felt. Surely?*

He looked up at her, and the residual traces of shock caused by the sudden impact of realization were still there in her eyes.

"I bought you something," he said with a little lift of his eyebrows.

"Bought *me* . . . something?"

He kissed her palm again before saying, "Umm."

"Food?"

He shook his head. "No, not food. Wait here." And he was away from her and out of the room.

Amanda got up and took a quick peek out the window. Just as she had thought, Summer was nowhere in sight. She lifted a hand to shield her eyes from the glory of the setting sun. What a beauty it was. What absolute perfection there was in this simple yet inevitable act. The red-and-gold, blue-and-silver sky, the body of ocean getting darker and darker by degree, an arc of birds heading home to some lovely secluded spot, the wind rolling in off the ocean, gentle and tinged with the essence of evening salt and soft fragrant hibiscus. There was a magic to it all. An inscrutable cosmic magic.

A kiss on the side of her face, and his arms were about her, turning her gently from the magnificent sky. He held a long black velvet box in his hand, and Amanda looked at it without comprehension. He handed it to her with a smile.

"Open it," he said when she still stood there, not moving, not smiling, not doing anything at all.

Her fingers trembled. *Oh, but she couldn't accept this from him. Whatever it was. It wouldn't be right. Would it?*

She looked up at him, and inexplicably, there were tears swimming in her eyes.

"Nicky." She struggled with the words, with the feelings. "You don't have to buy me things . . . I . . ." Her voice croaked a bit, and she cleared her throat.

"Darling," Nicholas said, "why don't you open the box first before you tell me what I don't have to do?"

Amanda pulled the velvet lid back, and the tip of her tongue darted out to moisten her lips. The flash of diamonds lying against soft cloth stilled the breath in her lungs. Nicholas reached in to lift out the bracelet, and then spent a moment fastening it about her wrist.

"White diamonds," he said. "I thought they might suit you."

Amanda gaped at the finely wrought band of diamonds and gold entwining her wrist. "You got this for me?"

He nodded. "And if you're good . . . I'll get you the earrings to match." He was smiling at her again. "Don't I get a thank-you?"

Amanda rested her hands lightly on his arms, balanced herself on tiptoe. His lips were on hers before she could even gather sufficient breath. He kissed her mouth once, twice, three times. Warm satisfying little kisses that lasted longer and longer each time. . . . A silver tear trickled down the flat of her face. It was this, this that she had known all along. It was this unstoppable thing that she had been trying to hold at bay. But she couldn't anymore. The dam had broken. Her strength was all gone.

Her hands lifted to gently stroke the back of his neck, and she matched him, caress for caress, kiss for kiss. She could see it now; she was his equal in every respect. His mirror image. His very self.

Nicholas broke contact for just a moment with the soft, sweet lips, to feather a line of kisses down the bridge of her pert little nose, to smooth away the tears with the velvet stroke of his tongue. She was his. How could she not know it? How could she not feel it?

"Mandy?"

Warm breath on his face, then a broken, "Yes?"

"Stay with me . . . ?"

She pulled his mouth back, and kissed him slowly. *Yes, she would stay. She would stay.*

NINETEEN

Nicholas lifted her into his arms, and took her across to his bed. He rested her gently on the flat of it, and then came to kneel above her. Amanda smiled at him. "Do you know what they used to call me in college?"

"Amanda the terrible?"

She wound her legs about his waist. "Sunshine."

He laughed. "You are a wicked one, Amanda Drake." He spread her arms on either side of her head, and did nothing but look at her for long, very warm minutes.

"You're beautiful."

She linked her toes behind him. "So are you . . . my sweet."

He lowered himself to her slowly, and she watched him come to her. He kissed the round of her forehead. "No handcuffs tonight?"

"None."

"No feathers in the bag?"

"I've a rose . . . will that do?"

He rested on his elbows just inches from her, his eyes sooty black and flickering with wicked delight. "What shall we do first?"

She put her fingers in his hair, and with the touch of gossamer, massaged his scalp. "Anything you want, baby."

He stroked a finger across her eyebrow. "I've waited so long for you that I don't even know how to begin. . . ."

She smiled. "Well, let me show you." Her fingers went to the drawstring at his waist, pulling fabric aside, bending to kiss hot flesh with the flat of her tongue. But his hand came down to stop her.

"Mandy?"

She looked up at him with surprise in her eyes. "Umm?"

"Lie with me."

She was puzzled. "But . . . isn't that what we're doing?"

"I mean lie beside me. I want to hold you. Just hold you right now." He was down on his side beside her now, his black eyes burning their imprint on her mind, her very soul. God, it would tear her apart when it came time to leave. How she would miss seeing him. Talking to him. Touching him.

He was lying on his side now, watching her. "Tell me about yourself."

Amanda rested her head on his chest. "You are a very strange man . . . do you know that?"

His fingers stroked the curls back from her face. "I love your face," he said, and there was a flicker of something deep and intangible in his eyes.

She touched the tip of his nose with a finger. "It's just an ordinary face. Nothing at all special about it."

He shook his head. "No . . . that's not true. It's a very special face. Why did you hide from me these past weeks?"

She sighed. "I was afraid of you . . . of this. I knew that if I saw you every day, there would be no preventing this. . . ."

"Sex," he said, "such a complicated yet simple thing."

"Umm," she agreed.

"So tell me . . . have you had a happy life so far?"

She blinked at him. No man before had ever cared enough to ask such a question. She swallowed, and thought on how she might answer without revealing too much.

"It's been a hard life."

"Not happy at all?"

She rested her head on his chest again. "I don't know . . . I guess there must have been times over the years when I was happy. But I was mostly lonely, you know?" And she lifted her head to look at him. "I never had a family . . . really. I was passed around a lot as a kid."

"What happened to your folks?" He ran a hand slowly down the ridge of her back, up again, then down. . . . The rhythm was so soft and soothing, it was almost hypnotic, and Amanda closed her eyes.

"I don't know what happened to my folks. . . . Maybe they didn't want me. No one would ever say." Her eyes sprang back open. "Can you imagine that? Not being willing to tell a child where they came from . . . nothing."

His brows wrinkled. "Sometimes no knowledge is a good thing. At least you can create some warm and fuzzy fantasy of your parents. I have cold reality to deal with."

She propped herself on an arm. "You mean your mom?"

He nodded, and the expression in his eyes hardened. "I almost wish I hadn't found out about her . . . about her condition. For years I thought she had just abandoned us . . . Gavin shielded us all from the truth." His shoulders moved in a shrug.

"Now that I know . . . I don't even . . . I just want it to go away. I don't want to deal with it."

"Nicky," Amanda said, and her eyes were earnest. "She's your mother, and whether or not she's ill . . . she'll always be your mother. Do you know how lucky you are to have her?" She sat up. "I can't tell you the number of nights I prayed for someone . . . anyone. To love me. To care about me. And you . . . you have it all. Your brothers . . . your cousin Rob. Summer. Amber. And a mother, too?" She shook her head. "You're just not seeing it. You have a lot to be thankful for."

His eyes were turbid now. "She doesn't care about me."

"How much time do you spend with her?"

He shrugged. "It doesn't make a difference. She's . . ." And he finally allowed himself to say the word. "She's crazy."

Amanda held his face. "You're the crazy one. Take it from me . . . I know. Don't let this precious time with her slip by. Life is so short . . . so very short. You know? Even if she isn't perfect. Cherish her. Spend time with her. Find something about her to love. Because it's there. You just have to be willing to spend the time looking for it."

He lay back on an arm. "When did you become so wise, Mandy, my love? Was it during or after your 'Sunshine' college days?"

She clambered out of bed and went to fetch the food. She snapped open the Tupperware container, poured them each a cup of ice-cold lemonade, then returned to sit cross-legged on the bed.

"I've done a lot of stupid things in my life," she said, and leaned forward to offer him a cheese sandwich. She munched on hers for a bit. "I regret each and every single one of my escapades in college.

Looking back on them now . . . I don't even remember why I did what I did. I don't recognize the
person I was then. But"—and there was a smile in
her eyes now—"that girl is gone for good. When I
return to the U.S. in a couple months or so, I'll
be . . ."

"When you what?"

Surprise flickered in her eyes at the vehemence
of the question. "What do you mean . . . 'When you
what?' I can't stay here forever."

He was sitting up now and looking at her with a
very peculiar expression on his face. "Why can't you
stay here in Jamaica? With me?"

Her heart gave a massive thump, then lay as still
as a slab of granite. *Did he want a long-term relationship
with her? Something that would last a little longer than
just a few nights?*

"You want me to stay here with you?"

He swallowed the drink in his cup, wiped his
mouth with the back of a hand. "Do you have a
better offer?"

She studied the tiny nails on her right foot for
an inordinately long period of time. *Did she dare accept what it was she was being offered? What would Sheila
do if she found out? And did she even care anymore?*

"What does the silence mean? No?"

She looked up at him. "How long are we talking?"

He smiled. "As long as it lasts?"

TWENTY

Summer was waiting for her with gleaming eyes when Amanda returned the next morning. The night spent with Nicholas had been like none other she had ever spent before. They had talked and talked until the wee hours of the morning. About everything and nothing. His life. Hers. Politics. Religion. *Babies*.

Finally, at about three o'clock, they had fallen asleep, exhausted. There had been no sex. There would be more than enough time for that later. They'd been content just to hold each other for right then. And never had she ever experienced such peaceful, happy sleep. With his arms about her, her head nestled into the space right beneath his chin, the crash of the waves in the background, she had been nothing short of blissful.

They had both come awake at just before seven, and had lain there for a good long while wrapped in golden contentment. Then, Nicholas had tilted her chin up, smiled at her, and said, "Get all the rest you can today, my love . . . 'cause tonight you're gonna need it."

She was still chuckling at the thought of that when she opened the front door with her key, and ran straight into Summer.

"So . . ." Summer said with a beaming smile, "where were *you* all night?"

Amanda closed the door and said, "I shouldn't even speak to you, you know. How could you do that to me?"

Summer chuckled. "I know. It was wicked. But I had to do something. You and Nicky are such hard-heads. I couldn't stand to see him moping around. . . . you ducking and hiding at the sound of a single footfall." She spread her hands expressively. "It couldn't go on. My nerves couldn't take a second more of it. So . . . give me details . . .details. . . ."

Amanda grinned. "You know I can't kiss and tell."

Summer made a face at her. "Determined to spoil my fun, aren't you? OK, no matter." And her eyes fell upon the glint of ice about Amanda's wrist. Her eyebrows lifted. "Somebody must've been a really good girl." And she turned the bracelet on Amanda's wrist. "This is gorgeous."

Amanda nodded. "I couldn't stop him."

Summer wrapped an arm about her. "I wouldn't stop him either." Then she switched subjects with lightning quickness. "You know, that Janet Carr person called again."

Amanda followed her into the kitchen, and sat on a stool. "She came by again, you mean?"

"No. Phoned. About the shower she wants to give. The woman is psycho, I tell you. She said that she's already got a list of people she wants to invite . . . and food . . . and other stuff. I really can't figure her out."

"Is she invited to the party Nicky's throwing for you and Gavin?"

Summer went to the stove and fiddled around for a moment with a large lidded pot. She ladled a steaming amount of Cream of Wheat into two deep bowls, drizzled maple syrup, and topped everything off with a dollop of whipped cream and a cherry. She handed Amanda a bowl, then sat.

"I don't want her here," she said after stuffing several spoonfuls into her mouth. "But . . . it's going to be hard to keep her away. She's so . . . so . . . I don't know what. Peculiar? Yes, peculiar is a good word."

"Maybe it's Nicky she wants," Amanda said now.

Summer gave her a darting glance. "Nicky? No . . . no, I really don't think so. They've never shown any interest whatsoever in each other. It's been Gavin all along." She leaned forward. "Actually, a couple of years ago, she and Nicky were hardly even speaking. Mostly from her end, to be honest, though. He accidentally spilled an entire glass of red punch all over her, at a fair we went to one day. . . ."

Amanda chuckled. "Knowing Nicky, there was nothing accidental about it, I'm sure. And—"

But she was suddenly interrupted by a little voice saying, "Auntie . . . ?"

They both turned. Amber stood in the doorway rubbing a tiny fist against an eye. "I had a bad dweam. . . ."

Summer went to her immediately. "Come here, sweetheart. Tell Auntie what happened." She put the child on her knee, and the little girl snuggled against her breast. Summer kissed the top of her head. "Tell Auntie. Was it a scary dream?"

The little head nodded. "A bad woman took me . . . and Dada was there, but he couldn't find me. . . ."

Summer rocked her, making comforting sounds.

"It was just a nightmare, sweetie. You're safe now. Safe with Auntie Sumsum. . . ."

"Summer?" The bellow came from somewhere in the environs of the sitting room, and Summer rolled her eyes and said, "I'll be right back. He's probably lost his socks again."

She put the child on her feet and said, "Stay with Aunty Mandy, OK?"

Amanda stretched out a hand, and after a moment's hesitation, Amber offered her little one. After Summer had gone, Amanda lifted the child onto a stool and said, "So, what would you like for breakfast, little Amber?"

The little black eyes regarded her with very serious intent. "Where's my Dada? He didn't come to kiss me g'morning today."

Amanda bent to her level. "Can I kiss you good morning today, and have Dada kiss you later today?"

Amber wrinkled her nose, and gave a very definite shake of her head. "I only like Dada to kiss me g'morning." Then she gave Amanda a very suspicious look and asked, "Are you really my auntie?"

Amanda hid a smile. It was going to be a difficult morning, it seemed, and mainly because the poor little mite had not seen her father yet.

"No, I'm not your real auntie . . . but I could be close to a real auntie if you'd like?" Amber thought carefully on that suggestion while Amanda went to the fridge.

"Would you like cereal . . . ?" she asked after a moment of looking.

"Hate cereal."

"OK. What about some nice grilled cheese?"

"Hate grilled cheese."

Amanda straightened. "What do you think you'd like then, darling?"

"I want my Dada."

Amanda went back to sit on a stool before her. "How about if we go see Dada at work? How about that?"

"At work?" And suddenly her face was wreathed in smiles, and she was bouncing on her stool.

"Careful," Amanda said. "Don't fall off."

In downtown Ocho Rios, Nicholas stood before the large plate-glass window in his office, a slight frown creasing the skin between his eyes. In the distance the blue shimmer of ocean was just visible between the buildings. He bent his head to take a sip of black coffee, and then turned back to his desk.

"Mary?" he said, lifting the phone. "Can you get Harry Britton on the phone?"

"Certainly, sir." The efficient voice of his secretary.

Within less than a minute, Mary Francis was buzzing again to say, "Harry Britton, sir."

Nicholas picked up the phone. "Harry. You got that information about Janet?" He listened for a bit. Then he said, "And you're coming back out this weekend?" He smiled. "Great. Bring Alana and Damian, too . . . and the kids . . . if they can get away. They'll be company for Amber. Oh, they can't? Right . . . ah-hah. . . ." There was a knock on the door, and his secretary looked in. "Amanda Drake and a little person to see you," she whispered. Nicholas covered the mouthpiece. "Send her in."

Amanda smiled at his secretary. She was really rather impressed with everything. The office building took up what seemed like half an entire block. And what she'd seen so far of the interior left her in no doubt that Champagne Industries was a very elegant and efficiently run business.

"You can go right in," said the secretary.

Amber gripped Amanda's hand tightly and said, "This is where Dada works. . . . I remember."

"That's right, honey." Amanda lifted her, propped her securely against her waist, and entered the huge wood-paneled office. Her heart battered against her ribs at the sight of him. Sitting there behind his desk, so handsome, so powerful.

"Dada," Amber shrieked as soon as she caught sight of him. And she was wriggling out of Amanda's grasp, and running across the carpeting.

Nicholas scooped her up, and kissed her soundly. "Dada had to come to work early today . . . that's why he didn't come to see you this morning. Do you forgive me?"

His daughter kissed him on both cheeks, and then announced, "I've got a new auntie."

Nicholas put her in his chair, and looked across the room at where Amanda still stood a bit uncertainly. His eyes smiled at her. "And why are you standing all the way over there, Amanda, my sweet? Don't you have a kiss for me, too?"

"Oh, Dada," Amber chimed in from the chair, "grown-ups shouldn't kiss."

Nicholas chuckled. "No?"

"Nope."

"Well, do you mind if I give Auntie a kiss on the cheek?"

The child wrinkled her nose. "Well, maybe just this once."

Amanda grinned at him, and offered him her

cheek. He kissed it slowly and said, "Come into the bathroom with me."

"No way, buster," she said. "You're just going to have to wait until tonight."

He gave her a very mournful look. "That's too far off. I can't wait that long."

The door to the suite pushed back at almost that very instant, and Summer appeared.

"Can't wait that long for what?" she asked.

Nicholas groaned. "Don't tell her, whatever you do," he said in a stage whisper to Amanda.

Summer beamed at him. "We thought we'd stop in to say hello. We're going to spend the entire day shopping."

Nicholas gave her blossoming stomach a glance. "By the looks of things, it's not a moment too soon either."

Summer batted him with the rolled-up *Gleaner* newspaper in her hand. "Oh, shut up," she said. "Amanda's never had Ackee and salt fish, so we're going to stop in at that nice little restaurant on the corner and have lunch there first. Wanna come?"

Nicholas looked at his watch. "Well," he said, "it is almost eleven-thirty. Why not?"

Summer smiled. "You're so easy," she said.

Nicholas winked at her. "I'm not turning down a free meal . . . are you kidding?"

"You're paying," Amanda said.

And Summer nodded her approval. "Of course you're paying."

Nicholas shook his head. "I'm beginning to think you women only want me for my money."

They both cackled at that, and Summer patted his back and whispered in his ear, "Some want you for your body too."

On the way down, they dropped in on Gavin. His

office was just slightly larger, but had the same general layout. He was in the middle of a conference call with the Los Angeles office, but he waved them all into a chair with a smile.

"Be finished with this in a minute," he said.

They all sat. Nicholas on the edge of his brother's desk; Summer, Amanda, and Amber in the soft leather seats facing Gavin.

Gavin was off the phone in only moments.

Nicholas uncurled from his perch on the desk. "We're going to eat."

Summer smiled at her husband. "Come on, honey, you can take a break now, can't you? Besides, I need you."

Gavin looked at his brother. "They want us to pay, huh?"

Nicholas nodded. "I don't think we'd better fight them on this one." He picked up his daughter and pinched a cheek. "We're outnumbered. Right, chubby cheeks?"

Summer got to her feet with a smile. "All right then. What about Rob? Should we take him along, too?"

"No," Gavin said. "He has to follow the same rules the junior employees do. Lunch is at twelve-thirty."

They went down in the private elevator, but not before stopping in to say hello to Rob, who was hard at work in the warehouse going through a stack of shipping invoices.

"Everything OK here?" Gavin asked.

Rob, whose cheerful personality was firmly back in place, waved a hand and said, "Yeah, man."

Out on the street, Summer asked her husband, "How's he doing really?"

Gavin put an arm about her. "He's OK. He's got

to learn that in the adult world there are consequences for your actions. He could've been prose-
cuted for that little stunt he pulled . . . not to
mention expelled. Working in the warehouse will
give him a good taste of what real life is like."

The restaurant was at the end of the next block,
and Amanda absorbed everything as they walked.
The European-model cars, the light bustle of busi-
nesspeople on the sidewalks, the Rastas with their
thick locks and drooping green, black, and gold
Kangols. The warm sunshine, the subtle fragrance
shimmering in the air that was somehow completely
indefinable, and completely Jamaican. Life here was
like raw knobby silk, Amanda realized. It was soft,
and gritty, but capable of being spun into something
sleek and wonderful with just a little know-how and
patience.

"America seems like an entire world away," she
said to Nicholas now. And he looked down at her
with a mysterious light flickering in the depths of
his eyes.

"Think you'd like to live here?" he asked.

Amanda looked up at him, and she felt the
strange, almost magnetic pull of the blacker-than-
night eyes. "For more than just a vacation, you
mean?"

"You don't think you could?"

"I . . . I don't know. I haven't really thought
about it."

They were at the restaurant now, and Nicholas
put Amber down. "Dada . . . Dada . . ." the child
said, pointing. "There's that lady. . . ."

Nicholas shushed her with: "Don't point, Amber."

Summer drew in a breath and said, "We just can't
seem to get away from her at all. Every place we go,
she's there, just waiting to jump out of the shadows.

It's almost as though she's got us hooked up to a bug or something. Honey . . ." She turned to her husband now. "Let's go somewhere else."

But it was already too late. They had been seen. Janet stood. "Oh, this is lovely. Come eat over here," she beckoned.

Nicholas chuckled at the expression on Summer's face. "Come on," he said. "How bad could it be?"

"Don't ask," Summer hissed beneath her breath.

Janet was upon them before they could even make it to the table.

"Are you eating alone?" Gavin asked.

Janet was all smiles. "Yes," she said, offering her cheek for a kiss from Gavin, and then Nicholas. "Wasn't that lucky?"

Amanda pinched Summer in the side. "Don't say it . . . don't. . . ."

"I thought you were the outspoken one," Summer whispered back.

"Hello, Summer . . . and what was your friend's name again?" Janet said with a flickering glance cast at Summer's stomach.

Summer gritted her teeth. "Amanda," she said, just barely managing to return the smile. Gavin pulled out a chair for her, and she sat.

"Behave now, darling," he whispered in her ear.

A waiter came over almost immediately, and they all placed their orders, with Amber declaring quite loudly, "I want coconut biscuits, Dada . . . the really, really big ones."

"After you eat your food," Nicholas said with a little smile.

As soon as they were alone again, Janet leaned forward and said with great enthusiasm, "The plans for the shower are coming along nicely. And Gavin," she said, turning to place a light hand on his arm,

"I know it's not customary for men to show up at these things, but . . . we can bend the rules every so often. If you'd like to come, it. . . ."

"He doesn't have the time," Summer interrupted.

Janet shrugged. "Well . . . the invitation's open. If you do find the time."

Nicholas plunged into the gaping conversational hole. "Harry Britton's coming back in this weekend."

Janet's brows lifted. "Harry? Really . . ."

Amanda exchanged a meaningful look with Summer.

"Yes," Nicholas was saying, "we're having . . . ahh—" And the words he had been about to say stalled in his throat.

Amanda coughed into her napkin to hide the almost overwhelming desire she had right then to break into gales of uncontrollable laughter. Beneath the table, she had seen Summer give Nicholas a swift kick in the shins.

"We're having . . . what?" Janet asked with brightly curious eyes.

"We're having a . . . sort of . . . conference," Nicholas continued.

"Well," Gavin said, rubbing his hands together in a rather relieved manner as a trio of waiters appeared carrying steaming trays, raised above their shoulders in the manner that was now fashionable. "Here's lunch."

Janet forgot about that particular conversational thread for the moment, and focused her attention on her plate of okra and stewed fish.

The remainder of lunch passed quickly. And Amanda found herself really enjoying the Ackee and salt fish, which had been served with liberal quan-

tities of soft sweet roast breadfruit and several hunks
of hard dough bread on the side.

"Eat it together with the breadfruit," Summer instructed. And she leaned forward to show Amanda
exactly what she meant.

"It's delicious," Amanda agreed after a couple of
chews. "It looks like scrambled eggs, but tastes totally different."

"So, Janet," Nicholas said, "how old were you
again when you came to live in Jamaica?"

Gavin looked across at his wife, and then transferred his gaze to the woman who was in the process
of patting her mouth very delicately with a white
linen napkin.

"I don't remember how old I was . . . young. Very
young, I think . . . maybe less than five."

"Ah," Nicholas said, and he dug into his food for
a bit before saying, "So, your aunt brought you here
to Ochi to live. Do you have any Jamaican relatives?"

Janet's brow wrinkled. "No . . . no relatives. We
have relations, of course, in the States. Maybe one
of these days I'll look them up."

"Um-hmm. Never had any brothers or sisters,
though . . . as far as you can remember?"

Summer shot Nicholas a puzzled look. *What was
this?* Polite conversation was one thing, but deathly
boring, completely inconsequential conversation
was something else entirely.

"Nicky, I'm sure Janet doesn't want to rehash old
history. What's the matter with you?" Summer said
now.

"Oh, I don't mind," Janet demurred. "It's been
a long time since I've thought about it. My memories of the States are really foggy. I don't remember
anything clearly . . . before Jamaica. But I'm pretty
sure I don't have any siblings." She laughed. "Can't

be absolutely sure, though. Isn't that strange? And my aunt would never tell me anything at all about my parents. I always wondered, though . . . how could they give me up to my aunt, just like that . . . and never even visit me . . . write me? I don't even know if they're still alive. For years I wondered. But now . . . I don't really care to know."

Amanda leaned forward. "That's not as strange as you might think. I was bounced around quite a bit as a child, and my relatives would give me no information on my parents either."

Janet nodded. And soon, they were chatting up a storm, dissecting the merits of family life and whatnot, with Summer observing the entire interplay with an increasingly dark expression on her face.

"Summer's adopted," Gavin said helpfully at one point.

Janet gave her a look. "Oh. I didn't know that."

"Yes," Summer said, shooting her husband a "wait until we get home" look. "My parents' biological daughter was abducted. . . ."

Janet paused with a forkful of okra halfway to her mouth. "Oh, no," she said, "I'm sorry to hear that. . . . I really liked your parents. That's such a shame really. But more and more children are falling victim to child predators these days. . . ."

Summer smeared a warm, soft roll with sweet butter, then bit into the bread and chewed. "It was a long time ago. But we . . . they don't think she was taken by a . . . well, by a stranger."

"No?" Janet said.

"No." There was a trace of butter on her mouth, and Gavin patted it away with a napkin. "Thank you, honey," Summer said, smiling at her husband. "Anyway," she continued, "this is a really depressing topic for lunchtime conversation. Do you mind if we talk about something else?"

Nicholas exchanged a look with his brother, and held up a hand to signal the waiter over. They were out on the sidewalk again, saying good-bye, when Amanda broke in. "You know, Janet, Summer and I are going shopping. Would you like to come along?"

Janet accepted immediately. "Shopping? Really? I'd love to."

Summer gaped at Amanda, and Gavin took the opportunity to give his wife a quick kiss on the cheek. "See you later, sweet. I've got to get back to the office."

Nicholas mussed Amber's head. "And don't you give your aunties any trouble. OK, little one?"

Amber gave him an outraged stare. "But, Dada, I never give any trouble."

Nicholas smiled. "Right. See you later?" he said to Amanda.

And she nodded, and tried really hard not to feel too happy about things. "Later then."

TWENTY-ONE

Shopping turned into an afternoon affair. They browsed the open-air craft markets, where Amanda picked up some nice hand-carved statuettes, after much haggling with the vendors, and stopped to buy bags of spicy hot and lightly golden Jamaican patties.

"These," Summer told her as she hesitated over the wonderfully flaky pastries, "are to die for. The meat'll literally melt in your mouth."

"It's true," Janet agreed, and the first really genuine smile passed between the two.

Amanda left them alone together and drifted across to the other end of the market to examine a rack of funky-looking handbags. She bought a couple of those, making a mental note that should she still be in Jamaica near the end of the year, they might make for great Christmas presents. Then it was on to shopping for what turned out to be an unbelievable amount of baby clothes, shoes, bottles, nipples, and just about every other conceivable necessity for a new baby.

Amber helped them dig through sales bins and discount racks, running back and forth along the aisles every so often to inquire, "This one, Auntie? This one?" Janet, too, got into the spirit of things, and insisted that the clothes Amber had chosen be placed on her credit card. Summer immediately objected to that, but Amanda's whispered "Let her" brought things to a satisfactory close.

At the end of several hours of very thorough shopping, they all staggered back to the car, and collapsed in the seats.

Summer kicked off her shoes, and wiggled her toes. "I think my ankles are broken."

Janet, who was seated beside her in the front seat, took a look at her feet and said: "They're swollen. I don't think you should drive."

Amanda opened her patty bag, and offered it around. "You drive then, Jan," she said. Summer's eyes flashed to the rearview mirror, and Amanda nodded at her.

"Well, let's have a bite to eat first . . . before we try any driving at all," Summer said. "Amber, love . . . would you like to try a patty?"

"They're scrumptious," Amanda coaxed. "Here," she said, offering a bit of hers, "try this piece. A little crust."

Amber chewed tentatively.

"Like it?" Amanda asked.

The little head nodded, and Amanda offered another larger piece.

Summer blotted her head with a handkerchief. "What we need is something to drink. Oh, there's a water coconut vendor. Let's call him over." And she proceeded to bellow out the window, until the man was forced to come over just to put an end to all of the shouting.

"Yes, ma'am?" he said, leaning down to rest on the lip of the window.

"Four water coconuts, please."

The vendor returned with four neatly cut coconuts, and handed them into the car one by one. After he had pocketed the money, he said to Summer, "You know, ma'am, fe a nice-lookin' 'oman like yourself, ouno mouth really a little too loud." He tapped the side of the car with the flat of his palm, and gave her a parting: "Walk little easy dere, dawta. Awright?"

After he'd gone, Amanda asked: "What did he say?"

Summer rolled her eyes, and Janet said with a laugh, "He thinks it's . . . unladylike to holler at people."

"I don't holler," Summer said with the beginnings of a grin.

Amanda chuckled. "Yeah, right."

They all laughed heartily at that, and Janet chimed in: "Summer just knows how to get things done. You've got to in this life. God knows."

They sipped on the chilled water for a bit, watching the many vendors go about their business, some carting products into and out of vans. Others packing up their stalls, and loading produce into big wicker baskets.

"I saw a woman balancing one of those on her head when I was coming in to Ochi a while back," Amanda said, pointing at the basket.

Janet nodded. "Most of the female vendors carry their wares that way. It's a traditional African thing, you know. Besides, it's easier than trying to carry the basket in your hands if you don't have a car or something."

"Umm," Summer agreed. "It's not as hard as it looks once you get the right balance going."

Amanda sat back against the cool leather seats. "I could never do that. My neck isn't strong enough."

Janet turned around. "Yes," she said, "you're just a little too short, Amanda."

"Hey." It was Amanda's turn to pretend outrage. "I may be short, but I'm sturdy."

"She may be likkle bit but she talawa," Summer chuckled.

"None of that patois now," Amanda said. "I know you're saying something nasty about me."

"It means the same thing you just said," Janet said, grinning.

And for the next several minutes, Summer and Janet joked back and forth in a manner that brought a pleased smile to Amanda's face. When they were through with their impromptu meal, Amanda asked, "How'd you get into town, Jan?"

Janet turned, and there was the beginning of something very like gratitude in her eyes.

"I . . . took the bus. My car's in the shop."

"Well," Summer said without hesitation, "we'll just have to drop you home then. My ankles feel much better now."

"Oh, I can drive you home," Janet offered. "I can take the bus back from your place."

"I've got the perfect solution, Summer," Amanda said. "Janet can drive us home . . . then we can have Nicky drive her back when he gets in. How about that?"

With that agreed, they switched seats, and Summer relaxed in the passenger-side seat of the big black jeep. She reached across to touch Janet's arm. "Thank you," she said simply. And Janet blinked rapidly, and cleared her throat in a gruff way.

"It's nothing," she said. "No sense in us all getting into an accident."

* * *

Nicholas dressed with particular care that evening, lingering over his selection of clothing in a manner he had never really done before. He chose a loose-fitting white knit shirt with buttons running halfway down the front, and a pair of tapered black pants that perfectly complemented the selection. He combed his gleaming black curls into sleek ebony waves, and spent a great deal of time shaving his face and jaw. When he was through, he gave himself a final look, and decided that he would probably do.

He went to the phone next and called the captain of the little yacht moored in the harbor. "Everything ready, Mr. Tolbert?"

Everything was ready, the captain assured him. Nicholas thanked him, collected the satiny box of long-stemmed roses from where it sat waiting on the bureau, and ran lightly down the stairs.

Across the orchard at the manor house, Amanda was involved in a slightly more chaotic scene. Summer sat on the lip of her bed, and spread around her was a virtual mountain of clothing.

"But I can't wear this one," Amanda said, emerging from the bathroom yet again in a lovely dress that literally swam on her tiny frame.

"Hmm," Summer said. "You know, you're really a little thing."

Amanda sighed. "I know. But what can I do? I've nothing nice to wear."

Summer's brow wrinkled. "Well, what about that nice little black dress you wore to dinner one night?"

"That?"

"Why not? It has a nice elegant cut."

"But it's as old as the hills."

"Why didn't you buy a dress or something today when we were out?"

Amanda went to the closet, and pushed around the meager offerings that hung from a smattering of hangers. "I got so caught up in shopping for the baby that I forgot about myself." She pulled out the dress, and held it up to the light. It wasn't that bad. But not that spectacular either.

Summer took it from her and gave it a good going-over. "You know what it needs?" she said after a moment of consideration. "A wrap. Something to jazz it up a bit." She held up a finger. "And I think I have just the thing." She leaned out the door. "Gavin?"

Her husband appeared in very short order. "Don't tell me to get another stack of things from your closet . . . please. I never realized how much stuff you actually have. There're enough things in your closets to clothe an entire nation."

Summer smiled at him and wiggled her eyebrows. "Oh, come on, honey. We have to help Amanda look her best. Would you get me some of the wraps and scarves? They're. . . ."

Gavin held up a hand. "I think I know where they are." And he was gone from the room. Amanda chuckled. "Poor thing. Men really hate this sort of thing, don't they?"

Gavin was back in just a few moments, with a pile of gauzy cloths over an arm.

"OK," he said, holding up a shimmering wrap, and speaking in a horrible falsetto. "For your personal consideration, madam, we have here a lovely piece of rat hide." He spun the cloth. "Do you see how it flows? It would be *just* wonderful on that black thing you're thinking of wearing."

Summer and Amanda chuckled.

"Not that one, sir," Summer said. "Let's try the white."

Gavin held up another. "This one, madam?" And he handed over an interesting-looking see-through cloth.

"Wrap it around your neck and just let it hang," said Summer.

Amanda did as instructed, but the cloth, instead of flowing nicely and adding a touch of elegance to the ensemble, just lay there and did nothing at all.

The sound of the front door opening and closing had Amanda gasping, "Oh, no. I'm not even ready yet."

"Go down and keep Nicky entertained Gavin," Summer said. "Hurry. And don't let him come up here, whatever you do."

Gavin released a long-suffering sigh and left the room.

Summer locked the door behind him. "Go on. Get into the dress while I see if I can find a nice wrap."

Amanda took a quick look at her face in the mirror. *God. She looked just terrible. Was her face actually breaking out?*

She pulled on her sheer black nylons, then clambered into the black dress, which somehow seemed to fit a lot more snugly than it did when she had just arrived at Champagne Cove. The zipper in the back lolled open, and Summer came into the bathroom to yank it closed. She held Amanda by the shoulders and turned her around.

"Wow," she said. "How'd you get a figure like this one?"

Amanda wrinkled her nose. "I think I've gained

a few pounds or something. This dress never fit me like this before."

"A few pounds in all the right places," Summer said, smiling. "OK. Makeup now." She had brought in cases and cases of powder, foundation, creams, and other concoctions.

She took a good look at the shape of Amanda's face, turning it this way and that.

"You've got some golden undertones . . . so . . ." And she began opening up an alarming number of powders and creams.

"Summer . . ." Amanda said, trying to intervene. But she was shushed.

"Let me work. Let me work. OK. Close your eyes."

Amanda did as instructed, and prayed that she wouldn't look like something fit for a Halloween horror show by the time Summer was through with her.

"Suck your cheeks in," said Summer.

And again, Amanda felt the feather-soft brush dancing against her face, over her cheekbones, her forehead, and her eyelids.

Summer worked quickly, wielding her powders and creams with exquisite skill. In less than five minutes, she was stepping back to say: "OK. Open your eyes."

Amanda cracked her eyelids with great trepidation. She took a fearful glance in the mirror, blinked, and looked again. The face looking back at her was simply . . .

"Gorgeous," Summer said with a beaming smile.

"Incredible," Amanda said. "You're amazing . . . how'd you do all this?"

"Come on now. It's not as if you had a face like a bent-up tire iron."

Amanda laughed. "Summer Champagne," she said. "I love you." And she gave Summer a giant hug.

Downstairs Gavin was at the little bar out on the pool deck. Nicholas sprawled in a chair, sipping a glass of rum and Coke.

"Amber asleep?" he asked.

Gavin came back with his scotch and soda. "Mrs. Carydice put her to bed about an hour ago."

Nicholas sloshed his drink around in his glass. "So . . . what'd you think of the nut job?"

Gavin laughed. "Nut job? Amanda? That's one woman who has her head on straight."

"Summer seems to like her."

Gavin took a swig of his drink. "And you know what that means. I'm never going to hear the end of it if you play around with her . . . and then dump her in a couple of months."

Nicholas downed the remaining swallows of drink, grimaced, and said, "Well, what does she want me to do? Marry the girl?"

The sound of footsteps in the entryway brought them both to their feet. Amanda appeared first, with Summer almost directly behind her.

Gavin shot a lightning glance at his brother, and a little secretive smile twisted his lips. Nicholas went forward slowly, and there was a fiery gleam in his eyes.

"Mandy Drake," he said. "I'm almost speechless. . . ." He kissed her on both cheeks, and then whispered softly so that only she might hear him, "I hope you've got some feathers in that bag of yours tonight."

Amanda felt her cheeks burn. She did just happen to have her feathers, and a couple of other items, too. She aimed to ensure that he would never forget this night as long as he lived. There would undoubtedly be other women after her, but always, always he would remember her. On his deathbed, hers would be the name he muttered. The name he would remember.

"Why won't you tell me where we're going?" she asked now.

He held her wrist and looked in satisfaction at the diamonds glinting there. *His diamonds.* "Don't you like surprises?"

He went back to his chair, and returned with a box of soft white roses.

"For you," he said with a devilish smile.

Amanda swallowed and whispered a thank-you through a scratchy-sounding throat.

Gavin and Summer, who had both disappeared back into the house, returned now to say: "The car's here."

Amanda's eyebrows lifted. "Car?"

Nicholas smiled and took her by the hand. "Mandy, my love. This is gonna be a night for the record books."

They were through the house and down the front stairs before she could say too much at all in response to that. And waiting in the drive was one of the largest white stretch limousines she had ever laid eyes on. She turned then, to make eye contact with Summer, who stood at the door. And a smile of utter glee passed between them both.

The driver stood at the open door, and handed both Amanda and Nicholas into the soft leather interior of the car. A long black bottle inside a bucket of crushed ice sat at the ready atop a satiny leather bar. Beside it were two fluted glasses.

Amanda drew in a breath. *Was this how he romanced*

all of his women? God in heaven, who would have the strength to resist all this? And why would anyone want to?

He was pouring the golden champagne, and handing a glass to her. She accepted it with fingers that shook just a little. With a soft jolt, the car was on its way, and Nicholas clinked his glass to hers and said, "To us."

TWENTY-TWO

The drive to the docking area was over in less than five minutes, and before she knew what was happening, they were pulling to a stop and Nicholas was leaning over to say, "We're here."

Amanda took a quick glance through the tinted windows. *Well, this was certainly unusual. Were they going to dine right on the wharf then?*

The door was open now, and the driver was reaching in to assist her. Once she was outside, the wind picked at her short cap of curls, and Amanda was exceedingly grateful for the shimmering black and gold wrap about her shoulders. It wasn't cold exactly, but the wind, this close to the ocean, was definitely brisk.

Nicholas wrapped her arm through the nook of his, and asked, "Are you ready, ma'am?"

She smiled at him. A happy, flowering smile that bloomed in her eyes and cheeks. Never would she forget him. If she lived to be more than one hundred years old, she would always, always remember the name Nicholas Champagne. And always would she remember the man with love. She swallowed. *Love? God help her.*

"Ready," she said.

And together, they walked across the wooden planks, and down a short flight of stairs to a waiting bay runner. The man at the controls of the little boat grinned at them and tipped his hat.

"Evening, sir. Evening, miss."

He handed them both life jackets, and Nicholas slipped his on and then turned to help Amanda with hers. He tightened the strap across her lower back, and double-looped it at her side.

"Nice and snug you are now," he said, smiling down at her.

Amanda sat in one of the bucket seats, and gazed out at the wide expanse of dark blue ocean. It was just beginning to dawn on her that they were in fact heading out to sea, toward the twinkling lights she could see in the distance.

Nicholas draped an arm about her, and asked in a husky undertone, "Cold?"

Amanda shivered, but not because she was cold. "I'll never be warmer than I am tonight," she said, and she pressed hot lips to the side of his face.

His rubbed the length of her arm as the boat picked up speed, and they literally skipped across the water, leaving a trail of foaming white behind.

"Is this how you treat all of your girls?" *Was this how he had charmed Sheila?* The wind blew the black curls about his face, and there was a simmering and completely indecipherable expression in his eyes.

"You're my only girl," he said.

And his answer pleased her. Pleased her so much that Amanda found she couldn't look at him for a good long stretch, for fear that he might recognize the beginnings of whatever madness now had her in thrall.

The wind blew her eyes dry, and she snuggled against his broad, warm chest, and gave herself up to the evening. Time and space ceased to have any meaning at all, as she rested with her head against him, listening in full-blown contentment to the solid beating of his heart beneath her ear. She could stay exactly this way forever. *She could stay with him forever, if he but wanted her; needed her.*

But forever was so short, and before very long they were bobbing on the water, just portside of a sleekly magnificent yacht. Amanda was speechless. Completely speechless.

Mechanical stairs were being lowered, and there was a flurry of activity on the yacht. And in no time at all, she was being helped on deck by what seemed like a dozen hands at the very least.

"Welcome aboard, Mr. Champagne." A smartly dressed man in a blue blazer and cap smiled. "Welcome, Miss Drake."

Nicholas extended a hand, and shook heartily. "Captain Tolbert."

The yacht was simply massive, and Amanda's eyes darted hither and yon as she walked beside Nicholas.

He looked down at her with dark pensive eyes. "We'll have dinner first and then I'll show you around . . . OK?"

She nodded, for her grip on intelligible conversation had not yet returned. He brought her hand to his lips and pressed a kiss to her knuckles, and dark turbid emotion rose in Amanda at the feel of him.

Captain Tolbert walked with them to an intimate little cherry-wood-paneled dining room where a table for two stood waiting. On the table, a heart-shaped box of specially imported chocolate truffles. The captain saw them seated, and then took his leave with the promise that "Dinner will soon be served."

As soon as they were completely alone, Amanda

said with sparkling eyes, "I can't believe you did all this for me."

Nicholas opened the heart-shaped box, and selected a strawberry-colored confection. He offered her the chocolate, and she accepted half of it, and then fed him the remaining half. He ate it slowly, pulling each one of her fingers into his mouth in a painstaking and extremely thorough manner.

Amanda closed her eyes and absorbed the feeling: the rough velvet stroke of his tongue, the soft silky walls of his mouth, the hot, aching burn. . . . This was like nothing else. Never had she known that such purity of sensation could be so profane.

He kissed the center of her palm, and she felt tears prick her eyes. *How was she going to do without him now?* How could she live for the rest of her life with any other man, knowing fully well that Nicholas Champagne was the only one she wanted? Needed?

They rose, almost as one being, and went to each other, her hands lifting to cradle the strong, muscular back.

"Nicky." And his name was as much prayer as it was affirmation.

He kissed her masterfully with eyes closed, arms about her in a manner that seemed infinitely right. "Are you hungry?"

She stroked the side of his dear face. "Not for food."

"Mandy," he said with glittering, shiny eyes. "What is this thing between us?"

She looked into his eyes and saw herself, behind the flesh, behind the bone, behind the masculinity; she saw that strange essence that was her very self, looking back at her. And it was like staring into a mirror and realizing for the very first time that there was another soul on this earth that was the perfect complement to hers; that no longer would she take this journey alone.

"I . . . I don't know." How could she say what she really believed it to be? Was it love? That strange recognition of complementary souls?

He stroked a slow finger across her lips. "I've never felt like this before. Not for anyone."

She looked up at him and with the glimmer of a smile said, "At least you'll remember me then . . . when I'm gone."

His brows lifted. "Gone? I thought you'd decided to stay in Jamaica with me."

"I meant . . . in years from now. When you're old . . . when I'm old."

He threw back his head and laughed, a warm sound that traced its way down the curve of her spine.

"Have no doubt about that, Mandy, my love . . . I'll remember you, all right."

She smiled at him and said, "Let's dance."

He went across to the built-in stereo, flipped a switch, and music flooded the room. He held out his arms, and she went to him. It was a steamy love song, and she moved slowly with him, dreamily pretending that they would last forever, just as the song said.

Nicholas looked down on the shiny cap of hair, and a troubled frown creased the skin between his eyes for just a moment. It was true what he had told her. Never before had he felt such a bond with a woman. His normal manner of doing things would have been to bed her as quickly as possible, repeat the process a couple of times just for posterity, and then rid himself of her with all possible speed. But the thought of following that very course now left him with a hollow feeling. He felt something else for Amanda Drake, and he wasn't clear on what that thing was exactly. He liked her, yes. He enjoyed spending time with her, talking to her. But what he felt was somehow more, more than just that. . . .

She looked up at him, and he lowered his head to rub his nose gently against hers. And for the first time, the word *love* flitted into his brain. And he recoiled from it sharply. *Love? Ridiculous!* He just needed a solid night with a woman, that was all; a solid night spent with her and her feathers, with her soft legs wrapped around that sweet spot about his waist. His brain was backed up, fogged out; anyone could see that. He didn't *love* her.

She traced the curve of his upper lip with a tentative finger as the song changed to another, and asked, "What's the matter?"

He kissed the finger and said, "Just thinking."

"About our dinner?"

She got a chuckle out of him with that, and she was glad. "Put on some Bob Marley," she said.

He raised an eyebrow. "You like reggae?"

She moved her waist from side to side in a very suggestive manner and said, "Of course, ma-an." She stretched out the syllable in a very Jamaican manner.

"Summer's been teaching you how to speak like a Jamaican?"

She nodded and twisted her waist again. "Yeah, ma-an."

Nicholas grinned at her. "You'd better not keep that up, girl . . . or you mightn't make it through dinner."

He switched CDs quickly, and turned back to her. "Know this one?" And he began to sing: "Roots, rock, reggae . . . dis'a reggae music."

He held her by the waist and moved his hips in

time to the throbbing rhythms. And Amanda matched him twist for twist.

"You move pretty good, Mr. Champagne," she said as they continued to dance completely in synch.

He winked at her. "You ain't seen nothing yet."

Amanda laughed. *God, what a man he was. What an absolutely lovely man.*

He pulled her in close, and they slow danced to the reggae, their hips moving perfectly together.

The knock on the door was soft, and they were both so engrossed in each other that they very nearly didn't hear it.

"I think dinner's here," Nicholas said after the second knock.

"Send them away," Amanda said with a wicked giggle.

Nicholas smiled. "Whatever you want, darling." And he moved toward the phone.

But Amanda stopped him with a hand. "I was just kidding . . . don't do that."

They sat at the table again, and Nicholas picked up the white wall phone and said, "Come in."

And three waiters wearing white tunics entered, before them a trolley laden with a virtual cornucopia of food.

Nicholas leaned forward to unfurl her white linen napkin, as the headwaiter busied himself with the unveiling of various silver-domed niceties. The two remaining men removed violins from beneath the trolley and began to play a sweet windy melody.

The lights were dimmed, and the candles sitting on the table lit. The tears were back in Amanda's eyes, and she bent her head to hide them. He was right. She would never forget. Never forget this night. And him. Never.

Plates of succulent roast beef smothered in warm

brown gravy, along with creamy white scoops of mashed potato, with sprigs of parsley sitting on top. Crackers already spread with Beluga caviar. Hot, soft rolls, split and oozing golden butter. Thick and spicy black-eyed-pea soup with shavings of cheese melting in the middle. These things Amanda saw through the blur of water in her eyes. She felt his gaze on her, but could not look up at him.

Nicholas motioned to the three men, and quietly, unobtrusively, they left the room.

His finger went beneath her chin, and as he lifted, a solitary tear ran down the flat of her face.

"Darling," he said, "why are you crying?"

Amanda blinked spiky lashes and shook her head. And after a moment of struggling, she managed: "It's . . . it's nothing. Really. I'm just being silly."

"Tell me," he said softly.

"I can't . . . I just can't believe you did all of this, went to all this trouble for me. No one before ever . . ."

Nicholas smiled in a manner that very nearly caused fresh tears to spill from her eyes.

"I care for you, Mandy," he said. "Why wouldn't I want to make you happy?"

She didn't have an answer for that. It was just so unreal, so completely unbelievable. Men like Nicholas Champagne did not exist. She knew this to be true. She had met her share of men, and she knew.

Nicholas carved a slice of meat and offered it to her, and she took it, holding his hand as he moved the fork to her mouth. She met his eyes, and almost as though pulled by some magnetic force, she leaned forward to offer him her mouth. And he took the offering slowly, sweetly, lingering over the sampling of it with infinite care.

"Mandy . . . can we go to bed?"

TWENTY-THREE

In the luxuriously furnished master bedroom, the large four-poster bed was definitely the center of attraction. Standing at least two feet off the ground, and requiring the assistance of polished wooden stairs to ascend to the down-filled mattress, it was without question the bed of a tycoon, a wealthy man, a man well used to the finer comforts of life. And as Amanda undressed slowly for him, molten jealousies rose to shimmer in her eyes. Just how many women had he brought to this very bed? To these very sheets? And how many after her would lie with him here, waking sleepily in his arms, satiated and content after a night of pleasure?

He lay on the bed now, bare from the waist up, watching the unveiling with those sinful black eyes that promised so much, and revealed so little. She tugged on the little zipper in the back, and obligingly it yawned to the mouth of her panty hose. The music playing softly in the background made her suddenly feel as wicked as he now looked. And with a little twist of a smooth rounded shoulder, the dress was down about her waist, and then drifting like a black cloud to puddle around her ankles. She still wore her heels and panty hose. And she walked to her bag now, with a deliberate sway in her hips. Fur gloves. Peacock feathers. Oils that warmed to the touch. Yes, he would remember this night. And her.

She turned, treasure trove in hand; he laughed at the sight of it, and the love that had been hiding like a wild thing in her breast came forth.

"Mandy, you delicious slip of a girl. Come to me."

And she went. She went with the heat of new love bubbling in her eyes.

He lifted her to the flat of the bed without effort, and she bent to sample his lips. *Oh, like nectar he was. Sweet. Hot. Indescribable.*

Hands pressed to the small of her back, fingers moving in a manner that defied all description. Breaths intermingling, soft flesh mating in that supremely satisfying way.

She straddled him, slipped into her fur-covered gloves. He lay back with trusting eyes, and another time flashed before her eyes, and she was deeply regretful.

"Nicky."

"Darling. . . ."

"I'm sorry. . . ." She had not said it before. Had not apologized for what she had so stupidly done. So wrongfully done. But now she needed to say it. Needed him to know that she would never hurt him, never let anyone, anyone at all hurt him.

He touched her face with a gentle hand, and she turned her lips to his palm. He knew her meaning. No further words were needed. Softly, softly, she moved her hands across the wonderful expanse of brown skin, and he closed his eyes. She closed hers, too, moving in a dream, in a moment of suspended time. Her fingers, skilled by years of tutelage, peeled the remaining layers of clothing from him. She lifted his hands, to kiss each warm finger. And he turned her, smoothly, expertly. His hands moving to peel the delicate gauze from her waist, down the length of each leg, then drifting up again to the frill of cloth about her bosom. He lowered his head to savor the texture of each brown pink nub. And she bit her bottom lip with the soul-searing pleasure of it, his name stumbling from her lips in broken entreaty.

He raised his head to look down at her, and in that moment, with gazes interlocked, she could believe, could really believe that he loved her. He left her for just a moment to slide on adequate protection, and when he returned, instinctively, her legs climbed to that exact spot about his waist, into that perfect groove required for sublime synergy. And his hands dipped beneath, to hold her, position her, and she waited trembling, fiercely impatient.

His lips on hers again, hot, needful, and then that for which she had waited, maybe an entire lifetime: He entered her, achingly slow, achingly sweet. And she cried salty tears with each deep, long languorous stroke, clinging to him like a limpet, rising to meet him, arching to match his rhythm. Never. Never had she known this. In all the times before, in all the times to come, this would be what she would judge all others against.

He kissed her tears, and whispered her name, over and over. And her nails curved like talons into the flesh of his back, urging him on. Pleading. Pleading with him not to stop. Never to stop. Never.

"Mandy." Her name a broken thing on his lips.

Head thrown back, cheeks wet, she could hardly think enough to breathe. Her legs tightened about him, and he bent his head against the side of her face and moaned with the supreme satisfaction of it. And she felt all the more deeply because he did, too. *Oh, how could she live without him now? How could*

*she go on as though her entire world and everything that
she believed had not been shattered all asunder?*

Shuddering breaths. His? Hers? Time softened
and spread around them like lace. She held him
with tender fingers, nameless joy in her eyes. And
strangely, there was the reflection of the very same
in his.

Nicholas kissed her mouth softly, and in the dark
room, with the boat listing gently this way and that,
nothing else but satisfying her mattered. He lowered
his head to begin again, and he knew, as he felt her
fingers gather in his hair, that he was very close to
losing his soul to this woman, his woman, his pocket
Venus. . . .

Morning broke with stealthy quiet, and Amanda
awoke to it softly, her eyes blinking open to behold
golden shards of dancing sunlight. Her limbs were
heavy, but her mind was as clear as a patch of blue
sky after a violent storm. In her arms he slept, arms
and legs entwined with her own. She was full, full
to the very brim with every possible offshoot of that
inconsistent emotion the world described as happiness.

She felt him stir, and she bent her head to kiss
the sleek black curls. He stretched, sighed, and then
opened sleepy eyes.

"So . . ." he said, and his voice rasped a little on
the early morning breeze. "You're really here with
me. It wasn't another one of my dreams."

She stroked the hair back from his face with a
smile. "What a dream that would've been."

A flash of devilry came and went in his eyes. "Did
I do good?"

"Umm." She nodded.

And she clambered atop him with hot flashing eyes. It was time for more of the same. And Nicholas lay back in absolute contentment, his hands moving to span her tiny waist as, again, the mind-numbing pleasure began.

It was almost midday before they could even think to tear themselves away from each other. By then, the sun was high overhead, and beating down on the gleaming white boat. Outside, the raucous chorus of wild parrots drew Amanda from the bed to stand out on the little veranda. She shielded her eyes against the white sun. They were anchored somewhere just offshore, bobbing gently in a wonderful blue green cove with nothing to see but coconut palms and white sandy beach for miles in either direction.

Nicholas had fallen back to sleep after a very satisfying several hours, but with Amanda absent from beside him, his slumber grew choppy and discontented. Still more asleep than awake, he muttered her name, groped around blindly for her, and got nothing but empty space. Complete awareness came upon him sharply then, and his eyes opened to search for her.

"Mandy?"

He sat up, saw her out on the veranda, and his breathing slowed. Panic. It had been panic he had felt upon waking to find her gone. But she had left him before, so why not again? Even if they were in a boat, in the middle of the ocean, she was such a magician, his pocket Venus, that she might actually find a way to do it.

She turned her head toward him now, as if drawn by his thoughts, and he smiled at her. She beckoned him with a hand, and he paused to pull on a robe, and then went to her in his bare feet.

He wrapped long arms about her, and bent to nuzzle her neck.

"Where are we?" Amanda asked.

A gust of salty wind whispered a reply, stirring the leafy heads of a multitude of nodding coconut trees. Nicholas kissed the side of her neck. "Negril," he said. "Just off the coast of the Royal Palm Reserve."

Amanda's heart beat thickly. "Are we spending the day here then?"

He turned her to face him. "That was the plan . . . unless you have somewhere else in mind?"

She gave him a wicked grin. "Let's go across to Miami . . . I'd love to do some shopping there."

Nicholas chuckled. "Maybe next time, my sweet. Today, I want to have you all to myself. We're going to go swimming . . . and then . . ."

She raised an eyebrow at him. "And then?"

"And then . . . we'll just have to do whatever it is that comes naturally."

And so the remainder of the day was spent. They frolicked like young seals in the warm blue, kissing, touching . . . holding. Later in the afternoon, when most of the heat had burnt off, they partook of a picnic lunch on the white sandy beach, feeding each other, and laughing at nothing and everything. The day passed as quickly as a fickle lover, and when the last remnants of light bled from the sky in a blaze of scarlet glory, Amanda leaned back in his arms, too filled with the wonders of the day to speak.

Nicholas cradled her cheek against his and said, "This has been the best day I've spent in years. Maybe even . . . ever spent."

Amanda played with the thick band of his watch, and wondered what he would say if she told him that somehow, somewhere along the way, she had developed deep feelings for him. Had developed love for him. Would he laugh at her in that wonderful way of his? Or would he run screaming into the sea, as Summer had so rightly described?

He threaded his fingers so that they lay smoothly against the round of her scalp, and then turned her head so that he could look directly at her. "Didn't you have a good time?"

She smiled at him. *How could he be unsure of this?* "I'll remember this time with you for the rest of my life."

He cuddled her close and breathed a sigh across the top of her head. "I wish we could stay here for at least another day. . . . But we'll have to get back soon. Amber will be missing me."

"Yes," Amanda said. "She loves you, that little girl. And I don't wonder why, even for a second."

He grinned at her. "No?"

She stroked his face with a tender hand. "No."

And the playful grin on his face turned into a smile that flickered for an instant around his lips, and then went to rest softly in his eyes.

Summer was waiting for them out on the wrap-around veranda when they returned late that night. Nicholas helped Amanda from the car, and his eyes went immediately to his sister-in-law.

"What're you doing out here at this time of night?" he shouted up at her. Summer shushed him with a hand, and came galloping down the stairs at high speed.

"I was waiting for you . . . both," she said as soon as she was at the bottom. "There's someone inside. . . . waiting. She came early this morning, and insisted on staying until you'd returned."

Nicholas lifted Amanda's overnight bag to his shoulder. "Who is it?" he asked.

Summer bit her bottom lip, and the light of worry came and went in her eyes. "Amber's mother."

If Amanda had not been standing directly before Nicholas, she surely would have fallen. A cold flush ran the entire length of her body, and for a full minute she could not draw breath. *Oh, God. Oh, God. Oh, God. Not Sheila. Not now.*

Her thinking became fractured, desperate. *Maybe there was some truth to the legend she'd been told at Rose Hall about the Rolling Calf bringing bad luck.*

Amanda felt Nicholas's eyes upon her, and Summer's, too, but she could not rouse herself from the thick suffocating panic. Knowing Sheila as she did, she knew that it would be mere minutes before all was divulged. Not only would it come to light that she and Amanda were both long-time acquaintances, but the reason that Amanda had come to Jamaica in the first place would also be made clear.

"Amanda?" Summer's worried voice. And then Nicholas talking to her, too, telling her not to worry, that he would handle things inside. She accepted limply the warm hand reaching down to hold hers, and she followed him, her mind churning. How could he know? How could he possibly know that once he got inside, once he saw Sheila, everything, everything would be at an end? He would despise her. And Summer, his champion, would hate her, too. Amanda would be asked to leave immediately. It wouldn't matter at all that she had not yet completed the many paintings she had been hired to do. Nothing would matter more than getting her out of the house with all possible speed.

She saw the screen door open, saw Gavin come to stand on the lip of it with Amber in his arms, and Amanda trembled inside at the scene she knew without question awaited.

"Where is she?" Nicholas asked his brother, and his voice was as hard and as uncompromising as Amanda had ever heard it.

"Waiting out by the pool. She's quite a drinker, that one," Gavin said.

"Dada." Amber stretched her arms for him, and Nicholas took her, taking a moment to fuss over her. Then he looked down at Amanda, and with eyes that had lost all of their customary warmth, said: "This shouldn't take too long." And he left her standing there with dry fearful eyes.

"This should be interesting," Summer whispered to Amanda. "Let's go out to the kitchen . . . maybe we'll be able to hear some of it from there."

Amanda smiled numbly at Rob, who was sprawled on the ground with a laptop computer at his side.

"It's not hooked up to the Internet," Summer said when they were out of earshot.

Amanda gave her a completely blank look. "What?"

"Rob's computer . . . we made sure he couldn't do any more mischief on the Internet for a while."

Amanda sat and looked at her hands. What a way this was to have everything end. How long would it be now before they all realized what kind of person they'd invited into their home, into their lives? Five minutes? Ten maybe?

She bit the edge of her nail, and almost jumped out of her skin at the feel of Summer's warm hand on hers.

"You're icy cold," she said, rubbing her palm down the flat of Amanda's arm. And her voice was suddenly concerned. "Did you . . . you and Nicky have a fight or something?"

"What? No. Nothing like that."

Summer sat beside her. "Then what? You look terrible. Like you're about to keel over or something. Are you sick?"

Amanda looked at her. This woman whom she loved like a sister, could she tell her? Would she understand?

"I . . . it's something, something I did."

Summer held her hand. "You can tell me. Believe me, I'll understand, whatever it is. And who knows . . . maybe I'll be able to help."

Amanda shook her head. "No," she said. "On this one, no one can help. No one. He'll never understand. . . ."

"Nicky'll never understand?"

She nodded, almost tearful. "I can't explain."

Summer gave her a little hug. "Amanda," she said. "I think there's something I should tell you."

Amanda's heart gave a painful thump in her chest. Did she already know? Had Sheila already told them then?

Summer was still speaking, and she tried her best to listen to what she was saying.

"That gallery you worked for in Ocho Rios . . ."

"Yes?" Amanda nodded. Was she to be blackballed now with the entire artistic community in Jamaica? Would they put the word out that she was not to be trusted? Not to be allowed into the homes of any decent self-respecting folk?

"Didn't you think it strange that you got an invitation to my wedding?"

Amanda blinked. "Strange? No. Not really. Most

of Ocho Rios was invited. And the invitation was for the artists who worked at the gallery. Not for just me."

Summer smiled at her. "The invitation was for just you."

"No. Really, it wasn't. How could it have been? You didn't even know me then." *But what was this conversation about? What did it really matter if the invitation to the wedding had been personally addressed to her or not?*

"Gavin invited you. But he sent it to the gallery and made sure you would come."

Amanda sucked in her lip. "Why? Why would he even do that?" *It made no sense, what she was saying.*

"He brought you here to Jamaica," Summer said slowly, and then waited for a moment for the words to sink in. "Yes," she said, nodding. "And not even I knew about it."

Amanda was beyond understanding, so she just let Summer talk, and with each word, her heart lifted a little more.

"He brought you to Jamaica for Nicky."

"Nicky?" Amanda whispered stupidly.

"He got the gallery to make you a great offer." Summer lifted her eyebrows. "You'd be surprised at how agreeable people can be when a little money changes hands."

"But he didn't know me . . . before I came here."

"He knows all about you . . . and Sheila."

Amanda's heart tightened in her chest. *So, this was it. They knew, and this was Summer's way of telling her that it was all over.*

"Yes," was all she had the strength to say.

"No," Summer said, and her eyes were very kind. "You don't understand. Gavin knows that you and Sheila are friends. That's how he knew about you

in the first place. Through Sheila . . . when she was
here in Jamaica. Don't you see? Sheila had a picture
of both of you that she kept on her dresser."

"When . . . when she lived here . . . at the
house?"

Summer nodded. "When she and Nicholas had
their brief fling."

Amanda's brain was moving like quicksilver now.
"Nicky . . . does he know all this too?"

"Nicky doesn't know . . . and won't ever know
that Gavin brought you here, unless you tell him."

"But . . . why? Why me? How could Gavin just
choose me like that?"

Summer shook her head. "There's one thing you
have to figure out really quickly with this family of
men. They love each other. More than siblings in
any other family I have ever run into. It's one for
all, and all for one. You know?"

Amanda let the trace of a smile curve her lips.
Yes, that was the truth. These Champagne men were
like no others.

"Nicky did the exact same thing with me . . .
don't you remember me telling you that he chose
me, too?"

Amanda nodded. "Yes." And there was a trace of
thickness in her voice. "I remember."

"And my husband is a very good judge of character. He doesn't miss a trick, if you know what I
mean. So, if he selected you for whatever reason . . .
I for one trust his choice."

Amanda took a breath, and then released it in a
long sigh. "It's almost too much to be believed. But
God, I was so worried that you . . . Gavin would hate
me. Want me out. I came here to Jamaica with different intentions, you see. Sheila . . . and I . . ."
And she told the story that had she had kept secret

for so very long. When she was through, she sat back, determined to weather whatever recriminations might be forthcoming. She deserved it, she knew.

But Summer just pressed her hand and said, "The very first time I met Nicky Champagne, I was completely convinced that he was one of the good guys. He was a bit flirty, flirty . . . but I loved him right away. There's much more to him than meets the eye . . . as you probably already know."

She knew that. Oh, God, how she knew that. "But . . . I don't think he'll understand about everything, do you?" Her eyes hunted Summer's face for confirmation that what she'd just said was not true

Summer stood and went to the window to peer out at the pool deck. "I wouldn't tell him all this just yet, if you know what I mean? Let the arrival of Sheila settle for a bit. Let's see what she wants first."

Amanda stood, and took a turn about the kitchen. "I know what she wants. She wants to pay Nicky back for not marrying her . . . for taking Amber from her—"

Summer turned with raised eyebrows. "Taking Amber from her? I was at the hospital when that child was born, let me tell you. I was right there. And Sheila absolutely did not want the baby. She wouldn't even hold her. Told me, she did, to take the child away."

Amanda's mouth opened and closed soundlessly. "Didn't want Amber?"

"That's it in a nutshell. I don't know what she's up to now. But trust me, whatever it is, it's definitely not about Amber."

Amanda sank back on the stool. God Almighty, what had she gotten herself involved in? She had completely trusted Sheila's version of things. Over the months of knowing Nicholas Champagne she had of course come to question many of the things she'd been told. But never, never once did she suspect that Sheila had fabricated the entire thing.

"They're coming in," Summer said now, and she dropped the window shutter back into place. "Behave as naturally as you can." She held up a finger. "And remember, don't mention anything I just told you."

Amanda stood, and prepared herself. Her heart was thrashing around in her chest. This was it. The moment of truth.

Gavin was in first. Then Nicholas. Then Sheila. And they saw each other instantly. Sheila, not as tall as Summer, but tall enough and as lithe as ever with that dancer's body Amanda had often wished she herself possessed.

Sheila was all smiles, holding out her arms. "Amanda, can you believe I'm actually here?"

Amanda's eyes widened a fraction as they went immediately to Nicholas, standing so stiffly in the middle of the room. His face was blank. Completely blank. She moved toward her friend only because it would appear strange if she didn't.

"Sheila." And they were hugging each other, but inside Amanda was dying, for Nicholas was looking at her now as though he had never seen her before. Her eyes followed him as he walked from the kitchen, and a fine shudder went through her at the sound of the front door slamming shut.

Sheila held her face and said, "Let me look at you. Well, you look just great. Put on a couple pounds here and there maybe . . . but all in the right places."

Amanda took Sheila's hand in hers and said stupidly, since Summer had of course already met

Sheila: "Summer . . . this is Sheila. A friend of mine. A very good friend."

Summer, who had been leaning against one of the counters watching the entire scene unravel, came forward now. "So, did you get things sorted out with Nicky?" she asked Sheila.

Sheila smiled and held on to Amanda's hand with tight fingers. "I'm going to stay . . . for a while."

Summer nodded. "I see. Well, I'll leave you and Amanda to catch up. We're throwing a little party tomorrow, and I have to go see about things."

TWENTY-FOUR

It had been a difficult night. Sheila had finally divulged the complete details of her plan for Nicholas Champagne, sitting on the edge of Amanda's bed and glowing like a lit-up Christmas tree.

"I'm going to marry that man," she had told Amanda. "He would've married me four years ago when Amber was born, but that older brother of his put a stop to things. But that won't happen again, not this time. This time, I'm going to get him."

Amanda stood by the window now, looking down on the bustling activity beneath. Sheila was her friend, had been her only friend for years. But there was no way on God's green earth that she was going to let her get her hands on Nicholas. What she had to do was figure out very carefully how to stop her without ruining their friendship forever. Things were already over with Nicholas. But she had always known that there was no future in it for them. Undoubtedly, he despised her now. She had seen his eyes, and how he had looked at her last night. Had understood the betrayal he must have felt. If she hadn't been so filled with sorrow now, she might have found the room to cry. But she was somehow strangely beyond tears. Almost beyond feeling.

A shudder rippled across her skin. Gavin should never have chosen her for his brother. She was rot-ten to the core. Bad to the bone. Not worthy of a man like Nicholas Champagne. Not worthy at all.

There was a knock on the door, and Amanda turned from the window to call, "Come in."

Summer's head popped around, noise spilled in, and Amanda gave her a halfhearted "Hello."

Summer closed and locked the door behind her, and stood looking at Amanda with flashing golden eyes. "And why are you hiding up here?" she said after a moment. "Have you given Nicky up to this . . . Sheila? Is that it?"

Amanda swallowed away the dryness in her throat. "Nicky was . . . was never mine. Not really."

"Not yours?" And Summer laughed. "He's been yours from the start. If you only had the eyes to see it. Listen, I know Sheila's your friend and all that. But you're crazy if you give up on Nicky without a fight. You love him, don't you?"

Amanda let the question wash over her for a moment. *Yes, she loved him. Of course she loved him.*

"Sheila's my friend."

Summer's eyes widened. "That doesn't answer the question. If you don't really care about Nicky, and you were just having a bit of fun with him then . . ."

"I care," Amanda interrupted. Then more calmly: "I care. I care about him very much. Very, very much. And, I'm not going to let Sheila hurt him."

Summer sat. "Hurt him? What do you mean?"

Amanda struggled with the words. "She . . . she intends to trick him into bed with her. . . . Somehow. Maybe by . . . by getting him drunk . . . then force him to marry her because of it."

"She what?"

Someone else pounded on the door, and Summer called out irritably: "We're talking in here."

"It's Janet," the voice said.

Summer stood. She had quite forgotten that Janet Carr had also been invited to the party. During their marathon day of shopping, her attitude toward Janet had softened, and it had seemed like the thing to do at the time. Now, she wasn't sure whether she regretted proffering the invitation or not.

"Janet," Summer said, opening the door. "You're a bit early."

Janet's eyes flickered between Amanda and Summer. "Thought I'd come early, in case you needed help with anything. But I can come back if I'm interrupting. . . ."

"No. Come in," Amanda said before Summer could respond. "We were just talking about Nicky."

The door was closed again and locked, and Amanda came across to the bed, and motioned to Janet to do the same. All three women sat, and in a very clear and dispassionate manner, Amanda explained the dilemma at hand.

In a bedroom on the other side of the house, Sheila Bonaparte was just coming awake. She stretched beneath the pristine white sheets, and released a very contented sigh. *Now, this was more like it.* She was so tired of struggling to make a living. Tired of dancing her heart out in smoky little bars, and filthy basement places. It was way past time that she started living at the level she deserved. She had been a fool to let Nicholas Champagne slip through her fingers four years before. She had really thought then that she had what it took to make it as an actress in Hollywood. But the years had shown her firsthand what a very rough business it was. Her agent had gotten her a few small parts in even smaller movies, but even those had dried up after a while. And the older she got, the less of a chance, she knew, she had of making it. Youth and beauty mattered in the movie industry, and she was quickly running out of the former if not the latter. So, she had been forced to make a hard decision. Return to Jamaica and live like a queen. Or continue to take her chances. She had decided that it made much better sense to return to Jamaica, marry Nicholas Champagne, and live, live, live.

She would hire a nanny to look after Amber, and as soon as the child was old enough she would be sent off to a good boarding school. The plan was perfect. Amanda, in her legendary way, would set Nicholas up, and then she would be there to knock him right down the aisle. Amanda had only agreed to help her, of course, because she'd believed all of the stories she had been told about how badly Nicholas had treated her. But it had been the only way, the only way to get back into the man's good graces. And Amanda had been the best person to send to do the job, since there was no chance at all that she would ever be interested in Nicholas Champagne herself. It was a well-established fact that she would have nothing whatsoever to do with a good-looking man.

A smile sloped across her face as Sheila got out of bed and padded on bare feet to the window. The breeze immediately caught at her hair, sending it in a swirling halo about her head. *This place, this place was beautiful. There was no doubt about that.* And maybe with the Champagne money and influence, she'd be able to become a star of sorts in Jamaica, and then who knows where?

She combed long slender fingers through her hair, and went to the bathroom to begin the long and diligent process of creaming and toning her skin. She spent careful minutes patting on a layer of ice-cold cream, paying particular attention to the skin just beneath and above her eyes. That was where the signs of aging would begin to show first. And she would have no lines or crow's-feet on her face.

"You're ugly," a little voice behind her suddenly said, and Sheila spun around with a half-creamed face.

Amber. "How did you get in here?" she asked. She had no motherly feelings whatsoever for the child. Amber was a Champagne through and through. There was absolutely nothing of Sheila in the little face, or in the huge black eyes. It was all Nicholas. All Champagne.

"Dada says you're my mommy."

Sheila turned back to the mirror and continued her careful creaming. "Yes, I am," she said. "What else does your daddy say about me?"

"He says you want to take me away with you."

Sheila turned again, her face completely covered with cream now.

"Wouldn't you like to come and live with me for a while?"

"No," Amber said with no hesitation whatsoever. "I'll always stay with my Dada. Not with you. I don't like you. You're bad."

"Well," Sheila said, turning back to her busywork, "that's just too bad, isn't it? Because if I decide to take you away with me, there's nothing that your daddy can do to stop me."

Cotton balls in hand, Sheila paid no further attention to the child, and was therefore caught completely unawares by the sensation of a mouthful of very sharp teeth closing on the fleshy part of her leg.

The cotton balls fell from her hand, and she shrieked, "Oh, you horrible, horrible child. Let go. Let go of my leg this minute."

But Amber held on for dear life, sinking her teeth solidly into the soft skin of Sheila's calf.

Down the corridor, Gavin heard the raised voice, and came running. He burst through the door without bothering to knock.

"What in the name of heaven is going on here? Amber! Stop it this instant!"

The child let go of the leg immediately, and Sheila sank back against the bowl of the sink.

"Look at what that . . . that creature you have raised has done. . . ." And she turned her leg to reveal the raised bite mark on her leg.

Gavin picked the little girl up. "Amber," he said, "why did you do this?"

The black eyes looking back at him were solemn and surprisingly adult. "She said she was going to take me away from Dada."

"I said no such thing," Sheila said with flashing eyes. "You . . . and Nicholas have raised a liar."

Gavin put Amber down, and with a little pat on her behind said, "Go and find your Aunty Sumsum. We'll have a talk about biting later."

After the child had left the room, he closed the bedroom door and looked at Sheila. His eyes were cold, dark, dangerous, and for just a moment, a shiver of fear ran through Sheila.

"You're staying in my house," Gavin grated, "against my better judgment, and as such, I will treat you as I would any other invited guest. But let's get one thing straight right now, lady. You will not be taking Amber from us, *ever*. Do I make myself clear?"

"The child misunderstood my meaning." But she found herself talking to his back.

Sheila watched him walk from the room, and she turned back to the mirror and began wiping the cream from her face in smooth strokes. *Mr. High and Mighty Gavin Champagne didn't scare her. He didn't scare her one bit.*

Nicholas scooped Amber into his arms, and squeezed her. "Where have you been hiding, cherub?"

"Dada," Amber said, taking her father's face between her two little hands. "You won't let me go away from you, will you?"

Nicholas kissed his daughter on both cheeks. "No one's taking you anywhere. OK? You believe me?"

And the little head nodded.

"OK then," he said, putting her down. "Go down to the kitchen and ask Mrs. Carydice to make you a snack."

He watched her charge down the stairs, and then made a beeline for Amanda's closed door. He stood there for a moment with his head bent. *There was little point in fighting his feelings for her any longer. No matter what she had done or set out to do, he still wanted her. Still needed her. Would still fight to keep her.*

The three women seated on the bed turned as one at the knock on the door.

"Who?" Summer asked.

Nicholas rattled the handle. "Me."

Amanda closed her eyes. *Here it was. This was it. The horrible breakup scene.* Janet uncurled from the bed, and offered a hand to help Summer up.

"So," Summer said, "we need to talk about this some more, maybe after the party. Agreed? And don't do anything silly."

Amanda gave a stiff nod. "OK." She had never felt more utterly hopeless in her entire life. Not even when she was being bounced around from relative to relative had she felt like this.

Summer opened the door. "Harry here yet?" she asked.

A smile curved Nicholas's mouth. "Well . . . well. What is this I see? Janet Carr and Summer Champagne in the same room? Am I in the twilight zone?"

Summer winked at Janet and then pinched him in the side. "You'd better be nice to Amanda," she whispered, "or I'll put you in the hurting zone."

Nicholas chuckled. "Harry's over at the main house getting settled. Mik too. They'll be over soon enough, I expect."

"Good," Summer said, smiling. And with that, both she and Janet disappeared down the stairs.

Nicholas closed the door after them and stood looking at Amanda with hooded eyes. "I took your advice and went to see my mom this morning," he said.

Amanda swallowed. "You did?" Her brain was so numb and cold that, for a good couple of seconds, she'd had no idea what advice he'd been referring to at all.

He came forward with that stealthy catlike grace she had come to know so well, and Amanda watched him warily. *Why didn't he just get it over and done with? Why prolong the torture? Why not tell her what he thought of her? Tell her what an underhanded and utterly despicable person she was? She could take it. She could take just about anything at all now.*

He stood over the bed looking down at her, and
Amanda felt compelled to stand and face him. His
eyes met hers directly, and for the life of her,
Amanda could not read them.

"Didn't you sleep well?"

"What?" Amanda blinked.

He reached out to touch the tender skin beneath
her eyes. "You've dark shadows. . . ."

"Look," Amanda said, and she trembled a bit inside before the words actually came out. "Why don't
you just say what it is you're going to say, and get
it over and done with?"

"All right. I will." And he sat at the foot of the
bed.

Amanda tilted her chin and waited. *It didn't matter.
It didn't matter that he no longer wanted her. They'd had
a good time together. A good time. And she would cherish
those memories of him for the remainder of her life. And
no one, no one at all, not even he himself, could ever take
that away.*

"I want you to live with me."

The world tilted for a second, and Amanda stared
at him with dark, confused eyes.

"You what?" *Was he crazy? Completely out of his
mind? What was he saying? What was he talking about,
living together?*

He took her stiff fingers in his and pulled her
to sit on his knee. "Are you saying you don't want
to?"

Amanda struggled to free herself. "I don't understand what it is you're saying to me. Sheila . . ."

His arms wrapped about her and very effectively
put an end to her squirming. "I don't want Sheila.
I never did. What happened between us should
never have happened . . . but I have Amber, and
for that I'm glad."

"But . . . but . . . what about me . . . her? Don't you care?"

He shrugged. "She told me all about it last night, about your coming here to Jamaica . . . to exact some sort of revenge. But she must have lied to you . . . about me. I know you well enough to know that you would never agree to something like that out of malice." He gave a short, hoarse laugh. "At least now I know you're not loopy. She put you up to the whole handcuffing scene. . . . Am I right?"

She nodded, still not really understanding. "You're not mad at me then?"

He lifted an eyebrow. "Darling. . . ." But what he'd been about to say was interrupted by a knock on the door and a very cheery voice saying, "Amanda? Are you awake yet?"

"It's Sheila," she whispered, and slid off of his knee. Nicholas held her hand.

"Send her away," he said.

She looked at him with tortured eyes. "I can't. And she can't find you in here either."

He gave her a look of complete unconcern. "What do you want me to do, climb over the veranda and jump to the ground?"

"You've got to hide." And she looked about her with wild eyes. "The bathroom . . . the shower. She won't go in there."

Nicholas lay back on the bed. "What are you so worried about? There is nothing, absolutely nothing between that woman and myself."

"Please, Nicky."

The knock came again, and Amanda pulled at his hand. "Please. Do it for me."

Nicholas came slowly to his feet. "The things I do for you . . . and you haven't even given me an answer yet. . . ."

Amanda shushed him and pushed him into the bathroom. "Stand in the cubicle," she said. Then she smoothed her clothes, and went to open the door.

Sheila breezed in on a wave of perfume. She looked well-rested and fresh.

"Were you in the shower?" she asked. "I thought I heard you talking to someone."

Amanda gave her a brilliant smile. "Talking to someone? How could I be talking to anyone when I'm in here completely alone?"

Sheila went to the window to have a look out. "They're bringing in pigs. Can you believe it? Tell me this family isn't completely crazy."

"Oh, they're for the party this afternoon," Amanda said, and she went to have a look out the window. Down below, she caught sight of a familiar face and waved. *Harry Britton*. It seemed like years since she'd last seen him.

"Where's Nick?" he shouted up at her. Then he caught sight of Sheila, gave an exaggerated wolf whistle, and tossed up: "Who's your friend?"

Sheila beamed, well pleased with the frank appreciation in the eyes of the man just below.

She gave Amanda a pat on the arm. "I'll be back in a moment."

A sudden crash from the vicinity of the bathroom forestalled any possible response, and Amanda spun around. *God Almighty. What was happening now?*

In the bathtub, Nicholas lay sprawled on his back, somewhere beneath his right leg a rather large piece of soap. He sat up gingerly, a frown wrinkling the smooth skin of his forehead. *Hell and damnation, what was he doing cowering like a criminal in a wet shower stall? Amanda Drake had him so mixed up that he didn't know whether he was coming or going. And he*

*had a sneaking suspicion that should she ask him to dance
the hula hoop stark naked in the middle of downtown
Kingston, he'd be more than willing to do that too.*

"Nicky. Are you OK?" Amanda pulled back the
glass door and peered down at him.

Nicholas gave her a heavy frown and said, "No.
I am most certainly not OK. I think I've broken my
spine, and a few other parts I don't think I'd better
mention right now."

Amanda pressed her hand to her mouth, and did
her darnedest not to smile, but the struggle was over
before it had even begun.

"Come on, get up," she said, giggling. And she
extended a hand to help. He wrapped long fingers
about her wrist, and before Amanda knew what was
happening, she was lying atop him in the tub.

"Laughing at me, are you?" he growled.

She struggled to right herself, chuckling still. "Let
me up," she whispered. "Sheila's gone for the moment. But she could be back at any second."

"Sheila, Sheila, Sheila. That's all I get from you.
Aren't you going to kiss me and make the hurt all
better?"

"You're not hurt."

"So you say." And his eyes roamed her face mood-
ily, finally settling on her pert rosebud mouth.

"OK. Just one then." And Amanda lowered her
head to give him a quick kiss. But his hand came
up to cradle the back of her head, and very effectively turned what she had meant as only a playful
little peck into a very protracted caress.

They broke apart, breathless, fingers intertwined
and trembling.

"I've got to have you again," Nicholas said against
her ear.

Amanda buried her face against his neck. "Maybe later," she said. "After the party."

"No. Now. Right now."

She lifted her head. "We can't."

"We can. The door's locked, isn't it?"

She nodded. "But what if someone knocks? Harry's here. And there're so many people all over the house right now."

"No one will come by for a while. Trust me. And if they do, you can just tell them that you were in the shower."

He smiled at her in that very wicked way, and Amanda felt a deep sense of illicit excitement thicken in her blood. Just a few hours before, she'd been so desperately hopeless about everything, and now here was the man she loved, in her arms, again. *What a miracle. What a sensual benediction.*

She returned his smile with equally wicked eyes. "OK," she said. "But you'll have to be quick about it."

Nicholas turned her gently, and Amanda closed her eyes. *What had she done to deserve this? To deserve him?*

At the feel of his hands sliding beneath her skirt, she uttered a deep throaty purr for she knew instinctively, there would be nothing quick about this. . . .

TWENTY-FIVE

The party was in full swing by three o'clock that afternoon. A little area behind the manor house had been cordoned off and filled with thick, slippery mud. Into this makeshift pen had been placed a bevy of spotted pink porkers. Mik and Rob sat atop the wooden rails of the pen now, cowboy hats perched jauntily on their heads.

"Come on, Harry," Rob bellowed as Harry Britton attempted unsuccessfully to hold on to one of the squealing pigs.

The remainder of the crowd was firmly in the Champagne camp, as both Gavin and Nicholas charged this way, and that, throwing themselves into the capture of the pigs with reckless abandon.

Amanda, Summer, and Janet stood at the ready with buckets of water, shrieking with laughter as the men slithered and fell in the muddy enclosure.

"Time. Time," Mik shouted gleefully after more than ten minutes had gone by without a successful capture. "No one wins."

The three mud-splattered men doubled over, panting. And Nicholas lifted a hand to say, "OK, Mik. Let's see if you and Rob can do any better." And he slithered over to the lip of the pit to be doused with a bucket of water.

And so it continued for the remainder of the afternoon. The women, with the exception of Summer and Sheila, also got into the spirit of things, and tried their hand at the muddy pit, much to the amusement of all the men. It was a rowdy, happy afternoon with much laughter and joking back and forth. And Amanda had never known such utterly unrestrained joy. The only dark cloud hovering very persistently on the horizon was Sheila. Sheila and the predatory manner in which she watched Nicholas. Sheila and the dastardly plans she had in store for the man Amanda loved.

At one point during the later afternoon, Summer pulled Amanda aside to whisper, "You know, I've been thinking. Why don't we just tell Nicky what Sheila's up to? That should nip her little scenario in the bud, don't you think?"

Amanda's brow wrinkled. "But if I tell him, she'll know I did, and then . . . I know she probably doesn't deserve it . . . but I still feel. . . ."

"Loyal?"

Amanda nodded. "I know it's twisted. It doesn't even make sense. . . . But we've been through a lot of stuff together, you know?"

Summer sighed and wrapped an arm about Amanda's shoulders. "You're a crazy chick, do you know that?"

Amanda chuckled, and was still smiling when Harry came over and flopped down on the grass beside them both. He fanned himself with his battered-looking cowboy hat, and said, "Looks like I'm going to win that wager after all."

Summer poked at him with a foot. "Are you gambling again, Harry Britton?"

He grinned at her. "So, have you and Janet Carr kissed and made up then?"

Summer cast a glance over at where Janet stood

by the pigpen. "As long as she stays away from Gavin, I don't have a problem with her."

The black eyes regarded her steadily. "So, you've given her her marching orders then?"

Summer gave the round of her stomach a little pat. "She's always known the deal. The moment she steps outta line . . ." And she made a tossing gesture with her thumb.

"Besides," Amanda added, "I don't think she was really interested in Gavin anyway. Seems to me she was lonely for friends or something, and didn't know how to make them."

"Such a generous woman you are," Harry said. "Pity you prefer Mr. Champagne."

"Oh shut up, Harry," Amanda said, grinning. "You would run . . . what is it, Summer?"

"Screaming into the sea," Summer supplied helpfully.

Amanda nodded. "That's right. You would run screaming into the sea if I ever transferred my attentions to you."

They all laughed at that, and when Mrs. Carydice came out to announce, "Food's ready," they all traipsed onto the pool deck and settled down at the long redwood table. When the entire gathering was seated, Gavin went across to retrieve a bottle of the sparkling bubbly from a bucket of crushed ice. He went about the table, filling each proffered glass. With that done, he held up his glass. "A toast . . . to my wife. May she have a blissful and completely comfortable pregnancy."

Drinks were raised all around, and beneath the table, Sheila placed a hand on the bulging muscle of Nicholas's left thigh.

Harry made the next toast: "To a dozen more children."

Everyone laughed, and Gavin slapped Harry on the back. "Take it easy there, Britton. Are you trying to scare my wife?"

Out of view, beneath the table, Nicholas very firmly removed Sheila's soft hand from his thigh, and shifted his daughter to sit in the space between.

"Dada," Amber said now, "I want to say somethin'."

And the table waited, as she raised her glass of apple juice and sweetly said, "God bless Uncle Gavin, and Aunty Sumsum."

They all had a go at offering up a toast, and then Nicholas stood to say, "We've a gift for you, Summer."

Summer, who had until now been watching Sheila with a hawk's eye, beamed at Nicholas. "A gift for me?"

"That's right."

Summer exchanged a glance with Amanda, and said, "I hope he remembered to get me diamonds."

Nicholas winked at her. "This, my love, is way better than any diamond. Mrs. Stevens . . . Mr. Stevens?"

And Summer's parents emerged from within, their faces wreathed in smiles. Amanda reached a hand to grip Summer's. "What a lovely surprise," she whispered. But Summer had not heard her; she was already up from her chair, and running across the deck to embrace her mother and father.

"Mom . . . Dad," she said, gripping them tightly and smothering them both with kisses. "I can't believe it . . . you're here?" Then she turned to give Nicholas a fond look. "How did you manage to hide them from me?"

Nicholas pulled up two more chairs, and when everyone was again seated, he said: "Having your parents here, Summer, was not the surprise." He turned to Mavis and Henry Stevens. "We wanted everyone together when we gave you the news."

Summer's brow crinkled. "News?"

Henry Stevens smiled. "Is my daughter having twins?"

Nicholas took a breath. "No," he said. "But we have found your missing daughter, Catherine."

Stunned silence greeted the pronouncement. Amanda poured some water from the pitcher and pressed the glass into Summer's hand. "Drink," she said.

Summer's parents turned to each other, and the collective expression on their faces was one of weary acceptance.

Henry Stevens gripped his wife's hand tightly and said in a voice that broke only once, "She's . . . dead then? Her body's been found finally?"

Nicholas came across. With one hand on Summer's shoulder, and the other on her father's, he said as clearly and as simply as he could: "She's here."

Summer turned in her seat, eyes spitting fire. "She's here? What do you mean she's here? Buried beneath the property, you mean?"

Nicholas turned her head so that she was forced to look directly at Janet Carr, who until now had been observing the proceedings with lively interest.

"Summer . . . Mr. and Mrs. Stevens, this is going to come as a bit of a shock, but here it is. Your daughter is seated at this very table." And he turned to look at his sister-in-law. "Summer, my love, Janet is your sister. Janet is Catherine."

For the next several minutes, things were very confused indeed. Summer sprang from her seat, called everyone at the table a pack of liars, and then rushed into the house in a flood of tears with Gavin on her heels. Mavis Stevens fainted. Henry Stevens and Janet Carr sat rooted to their chairs like pieces of petrified wood.

Amanda left Nicholas to tend to things at the table, and rushed into the house after Summer. She found Gavin standing outside their bedroom door, and could clearly hear the sounds of sobbing coming from within.

Gavin gave her a helpless look. "She won't open the door."

Amanda pressed his hand. "Let me try," she said. And she went to the door and knocked softly. "Summer? It's Amanda. Let me in."

After a moment more of knocking and softly coaxing, the door was suddenly pulled back, and Summer stood there on the threshold with red-rimmed, streaming eyes. Amanda gave Gavin an apologetic little smile, said, "We'll be out in a little while," and then closed the door directly in his face.

They emerged hours later. Summer was calmer now, and Amanda was satisfied that she was well over the initial shock of things.

"It's not so bad," Amanda kept repeating over and over as they walked down the stairs. "It's really not so bad. Think of it. You have a sister now. A sister. Think how happy your parents are going to be about this. I mean, it's just incredible. Can you imagine? After all these years of searching, to finally find her. And the trouble Nicky and Gavin must have gone to, to actually pull this off. It's a wonderful thing really. A miracle, no less."

Amanda kept talking softly as they made their way down the long corridor. Summer drew a great hiccupping breath and said bravely: "Well, we are getting along a bit better of late. And you did say that you didn't think she was interested in Gavin, didn't you?"

Amanda nodded and gave her a consoling pat on the back. "I really think that she's much nicer than she appears. Just give her a chance."

Gavin met them halfway down the stairs, and Summer wrapped her arms about him and said, "I'm sorry I said all of those awful things to you a little while ago."

Amanda left them in each other's arms, and went in search of Nicholas. She found him standing in the kitchen talking to Harry.

"Here she is now." Harry smiled. He clapped Nicholas on the back. "I think the wager is officially won," he said, and he gave Amanda a very peculiar look, which she didn't understand at all, and within very short order, disappeared from the kitchen.

"Were you talking about me?" Amanda asked.

"Yes." And Nicholas came to stand right before her, hands stuffed into his pockets.

"No more surprises, I hope?" she said.

Nicholas gave her a rueful smile and rubbed a hand across his jaw. "Yeah, maybe we shouldn't have told them exactly like that. But I really didn't expect screaming hysterics and fainting."

Amanda looked at him with soft affectionate eyes. "Summer's OK now. It was just the shock of it all. How're her parents and Janet doing?"

Nicholas flipped up a window shade and peered out at the deck. "Well," he said after a moment, "everyone's still talking and still conscious as far as I can tell."

"And Sheila?"

Nicholas leaned back against the counter. "Harry's

taking her across to the Sans Souci resort hotel. I don't think it a good idea that she stays with us any longer. She seems to have designs on me, and I know how uncomfortable you'd be with that."

Amanda gave him a very direct look. "Harry's not going to play around with her, is he?"

Glinting black eyes met hers. "Do you have designs on Harry, too?"

She chuckled. "Silly. It's Sheila I'm concerned about. Harry is a bit of a rogue, you know. And Sheila . . . she's not really a bad person, but she's lost, I think . . . and likely to do anything because of it."

Nicholas took her hand in his. "Let's go for a walk on the beach, and I'll tell you what we've decided to do about Sheila."

TWENTY-SIX

"Well, I'm all through with the paintings," Amanda said, walking into the sitting room and giving Summer a great big smile.

Summer looked up with a set of pins in her mouth. "Just a minute," she said.

Amanda stood watching her pin and gather fabric to the foot of the settee, and let her mind wander for a bit. It had been a month since Gavin had packed Sheila very happily off to work as a showgirl in a big Las Vegas production. And a month since Nicholas had made the startling revelation that Janet Carr was Summer's long-lost sister. And for the most part, things had settled back into a relatively normal routine. Summer's parents, after recovering from the initial shock, had been simply beside themselves with joy. And Janet overnight had become almost a completely different person. She had apologized repeatedly to Summer for causing her past distress, and had assured her that just as Amanda had guessed, she had never had a serious interest in Gavin at all. She had been lonely, she'd said. And the Champagne house had always been filled with family, laughter, and love, something she had always longed for, and never thought she'd ever have.

It was still unclear to Amanda, though, exactly

how Janet had been taken, and as she stood watching Summer fasten the frilly scallop to the base of the settee, she asked, "Is anyone ever going to fill me in on what exactly happened with Janet?"

Summer looked up now, all pins safely in the thick fabric. "Nicky would've told you, but you've been locked away in that room of yours painting from morning till night."

Amanda knelt beside her to adjust a frill of fabric. It was true; there was no denying it. She had been essentially locked away for the past four weeks. She'd allowed herself only a few precious moments with Nicholas in the evenings, and then had gone right back to work afterward.

"I wanted to have the paintings all done before Janet's shower."

"Hmm," Summer said. "Well, I'll give you the long and short of it. The housekeeper took Janet off with her. She was having trouble with her husband, and couldn't have kids of her own, so she figured Janet would do just fine since she was so attached to her."

"So, how'd she end up here, in Jamaica?"

"My mom and dad wouldn't give up looking for her, so the woman figured that she had to leave the country. She changed Catherine to Janet, and gave them both new last names."

"And the husband, what happened to him?"

"Oh, he was always a ne'er-do-well. He became a drunkard and just faded out of the picture."

"Wow," Amanda said. "It's really amazing, you know. If you hadn't lost your job four years ago . . . you'd never have come to Jamaica . . . never have married Gavin, and if you hadn't married him, your parents would never have found Janet. It's incredible how everything just fits together sometimes."

Summer's eyes became suddenly solemn. "I can't even imagine what my life would've been like if I hadn't met Gavin."

Amanda gave Summer a considering glance. "Well, you wouldn't have that baby, for one. You know, you're beginning to get really huge now."

Summer gave her stomach a rub. "This is my first and maybe last time. I don't think I could go through all this discomfort again."

"Well, I'm going to have lots of babies," Amanda said, rolling to her feet.

"With Nicky?" Summer asked with a sly little look.

Amanda chuckled. "What makes you think Nicky wants to have any kids with me?"

Summer held up a hand and said, "Please. You know the man is crazy about you. Help me to my feet, would you?"

Amanda helped her stand, and then bent to rest her ear against Summer's stomach. "I can tell you now, girl . . . this baby is definitely a boy," she said.

Summer waddled over to a chair and sat. "No way," she said, "I'm having a girl. Definitely a girl."

The front door swung open and closed noisily, and Nicholas came in, stomping his feet on the mat before the door.

"Nicholas Champagne, do not bring that sand in here," Summer called out.

Amanda went to the front door to kiss him hello, and he grinned down at her. "What did that shrew just say to me?"

"I heard that," Summer bellowed.

Amanda took him by the hand and led him back outside. "It's best not to mess around with pregnant women. They can be dangerous when provoked."

"I know," he said, and he took her in his arms.

"When are you going to give me an answer, Amanda Drake? Are you going to live with me or not?"

Amanda stroked the side of his face. "I can answer you now. Now that everything has calmed down a little."

He kissed her hand. "OK. I'm ready."

She took a breath, and then let it out again in a tight little sigh. "If you had asked me this two years ago, I might have said yes. But I have too much respect for you . . . for your family to do anything like that."

"Umm," he said, and he nodded at her in a very sage and understanding manner. "I thought you might say something like that."

She looked up at him. "You did?"

"I did. And that's why I took the precaution of getting you one of these." And he pulled something smooth and velvet and black from his inside jacket pocket.

Amanda looked down at the square box with a trembling soul. Nicholas lifted a hand, snapped his fingers, and suddenly there was an entire horde of people out on the veranda. Amanda's eyes darted from one to the next: *Gavin. Rob. Mik. Summer. All smiling. Could she dare to hope?*

Summer grinned. "He's been planning this for weeks." She presented Amanda with a solitary white rose, and then together they all said, "We the Champagnes speak for our brother Nicholas when we ask, 'Will you join our family?' "

Nicholas bent his head and said in a husky rumble, "They mean to say, will you marry me?"

Amanda bit her lip and fought against the prickling of tears at the backs of her eyes.

"Yes," she said simply. *Yes. Yes. Yes. A thousand times yes.*

"And now," Nicholas said, hugging her to him, a hint of mischief in his voice, "you'll have to ask my mother for my hand in marriage."

Amanda squeezed him tightly, and looked up at him with shining eyes. "Nicholas Champagne, you've had everyone fooled all along. You're no ladies' man."

He looked down at her with gleaming black eyes. "On the contrary, my sweet . . . I've been one lady's man from the very beginning. I fought a losing battle from the very first time I saw you. I love every feather and handcuff in your arsenal . . . but most of all, I love you."

EPILOGUE

Five Months Later

Ester Champagne sat in her favorite chair facing the ocean. It was a bright blue day, and a dappling of golden sunlight rippled across her legs as her fingers flashed expertly over the knitting in her lap. Nicholas sat at his mother's side, a large ball of wool in his hands. In the kitchen, a sweet voice hummed over the clinking of plates. Ester looked down at her son now, her eyes bright.

"You're going to marry that girl, aren't you, Nicholas?"

A flash of deep emotion in the black eyes came and went, and then he answered, "Yes, Mom. You like her, don't you?"

Ester Champagne nodded. "This one can cook, not like the other, cat-eyed one your brother married."

Amanda popped her head out of the kitchen for a minute to ask, "Everything all right out here?"

Nicholas smiled. "We were just having a little talk about you."

"Yes," Ester agreed, and she gave Amanda an extended perusal, and then demanded, "Come here, girl."

Amanda came forward, wiping her hands on the dishcloth that hung from about her waist.

"Turn around, let me look at you."

Amanda obliged her, spinning with a little flourish.

"Um-hmm," Ester said with satisfaction. "You're a little one, but you've got good childbearing hips. How many grandchildren are you thinking of giving me?"

"Mom . . ." Nicholas began, but a grinning Amanda shushed him.

"As many as you'd like me to have, Mom."

Ester Champagne beamed, a flowering from ear to ear that gave a quick glimpse of the woman she must have been at one time.

"You, girl . . . are my kind of people." She held Amanda's hand and looked up at her with the magnetic black Champagne eyes, which all of her sons had inherited. "Amanda Champagne . . . I like the sound of that."

Nurse Robbins came bustling into the room just then. "Gavin called," she said, and her eyes gleamed with excitement. "Summer's gone into labor."

Amanda and Nicholas looked at each other, a mixture of fear and exuberance on their faces.

Amanda squeezed Nicholas's hand. "She's going to be all right. Don't worry."

Ester Champagne very calmly folded up her knitting, and said, "Well, come on, come on. Why are you two standing about like lampposts? Let's get moving."

An hour later, the entire Champagne clan, Ruggles included, was seated in a shiny waiting area in the Ocho Rios birthing center. Nicholas sat with his hands between his legs, head bent, eyes closed. Beside him, Amanda cradled Amber on her lap, and every so often she would be forced to bend her head and softly request, "Amber, sweetheart, leave poor Ruggles' whiskers alone. He doesn't like it when you pull at them like that."

Mik, Rob, and Ester Champagne were hard at a game of cards at a small table in the corner of the room, but it was clear that their minds were elsewhere.

A door opened, and every eye in the room darted toward it. A nurse in a pristine white uniform appeared, smiling. Nicholas was up from his seat to demand, "Is everything OK in there? Why's it taking so long?"

The nurse gave him a very tolerant look. "Her cervix isn't fully dilated yet. But it shouldn't be too much longer now."

Nicholas sank back into his chair. Christ Almighty, but he hated all of this talk about cervixes and dilation. It was enough to drive any sane man completely out of his mind.

The nurse looked at Amanda now, smiling. "She'd like you to go in. Think you can handle it?"

Amanda was up immediately. "Yes. Of course."

The nurse led her to a little anteroom and she suited up quickly. Her heart throbbed in her chest as she put her feet into the little white paper booties and said, "I'm ready."

She was led into the birthing room, and the thing that struck Amanda first was the absolute immensity of Summer's abdomen as she lay propped up in the bed. It seemed to stick straight up from her slender body, like a huge distended melon. Gavin sat by the side of the bed, and he appeared to be in more pain than Summer.

Amanda went over, and Summer, whose eyes had been all but glazed over until then, focused on her with some difficulty.

"Mandy," she said through tight lips. "I hate men."

Amanda stroked the back of her hand and said to Gavin, "She doesn't know what she's saying."

"Where's my mother?" Summer yelled now. "I want my mother."

Amanda rubbed a bit of ice across her lips, and said softly, "Your mom and dad are on the way. Janet, too."

Summer absorbed this bit of information, and then turned eyes beady with pain toward her husband.

"Why did you do this to me?" she asked, her eyes blazing fire.

"But, darling . . . it was your. . . ."

"Don't talk to me," Summer bellowed. "Just don't even talk to me." Then she turned and gave one of the attending nurses a malevolent glare. "I want drugs, do you hear me? Forget about this natural childbirth mess. Give me drugs. Everything. Whatever you've got, I want it."

Another hour, and Mavis Stevens was with her daughter, bending over the bed and speaking to her in a very firm manner.

"Summer, women have been going through this very experience since the beginning of time. We're built for it. So, stop all this crying and carrying on and push."

"I don't want to," Summer wailed.

Her mother grabbed her hand. "Did you hear me? I said push."

Amanda pressed a tissue into Gavin's hand, for a lone tear had slipped from his eye, and wound its way down his face. He wiped roughly at it, and said, "I can't stand this. She's hurting . . . and I can't help her."

Amanda held his hand and said, "It'll be over soon. It'll be over soon."

Just outside the door, Nicholas paced, sat, and rose to pace again. The other men huddled around the small table, their game of cards abandoned, everyone waiting anxiously for word from within.

The door opened again, and Amanda peered out. "Janet," she said, "she wants you."

Adam Nicholas Champagne came into the world screaming, maybe just a decibel louder than his mother herself. With eyes squeezed tightly shut, and fingers curled, he exploded into life. Amanda watched with joyful eyes as Gavin bent forward to give his wife a kiss, and smiled when she heard him whisper, "We've a boy, my love. A big, beautiful boy."

Janet was on hand to help with the cutting of the umbilical, and was heard to exclaim, "Summer, his eyes are just like yours."

The baby's eyes were open now, and it was true. His head was a mass of thick black curls, his face his father's very own, but his eyes—his eyes were the color of gilded champagne.

"He's beautiful." Amanda sighed, going across to kiss Summer, too. And Summer reached hungry arms for the sturdy wiggling body and, smiling down at him now, said, "Yes. He is at that."

Suddenly, the room was filled to capacity with a crush of bodies and a babble of voices. Nicholas went directly to bedside to demand, "Where's my niece? Let me see my niece."

Summer grinned at Amanda and Janet, and offered him a peek at the bundle. "Meet your nephew," she said. "Adam Nicholas, meet your Uncle Nicky . . . the man responsible for bringing me here to Jamaica."

All of the Champagnes crowded in to have a look, and there was much exclamation on the baby's size and poundage. Somewhere in the thick of the crowd, Ester Champagne was heard to remark, "Jesus, God, the baby has his mother's cat eyes. . . ."

And Nicholas held onto Amanda's hand and smiled down at his mother. "Yes, Mom," he said, "beautiful Champagne eyes."

ABOUT THE AUTHOR

Niqui Stanhope was born in Jamaica, West Indies, but grew up in a small town in Guyana, South America. Because her parents traveled quite a bit and always took the entire family along, the summers of her childhood were spent exploring the rich cultures of the Caribbean, South America, and North America. Niqui emigrated to the United States in 1984. She now lives in California.

Niqui admits that novel writing never occurred to her until after she had graduated from the University of Southern California with a degree in chemistry. She is now the author of NIGHT TO REMEMBER and DISTANT MEMORIES. And in the Champagne family series: MADE FOR EACH OTHER (Book One), WEDDING BELLS (Book Two), and SWEET TEMPTATION (Book Three).

Niqui would love to hear from you, so please contact her at: PO Box 6105, Burbank, CA 91510, or e-mail her at Niquij@aol.com.

COMING IN DECEMBER 2001 FROM
ARABESQUE ROMANCES

__WITH A SONG IN MY HEART
 by Jacquelin Thomas   1-58314-132-4 $5.99US/$7.99CAN
When millionaire Brennan Cunningham III proposes to Elle Ransom, she feels like the luckiest woman alive. Then she discovers that Brennan doesn't believe in romance and wants a wife strictly for companionship. Now Elle is determined to show him a passion he'll never forget—and set his soul on fire with a love that will join them forever.

__PRELUDE TO A KISS
 by Bettye Griffin   1-58314-139-1 $5.99US/$7.99CAN
From freak injuries to fainting spells, Vivian St. James's dates always seem to need a doctor. But what she needs is a husband. Whenever her paramours land in the ER, gorgeous Dr. Zachary Warner is on duty—and their mutual attraction is unmistakable. Could he be Mr. Right?

__THE POWER OF LOVE
 by Marcella Sanders   1-58314-167-7 $5.99US/$7.99CAN
Riva Dae Cain retreats to a luxury spa, hoping some pampering will take her mind off the turmoil in her life. The relaxing atmosphere gives her just the breather she needs—until she meets sensual private investigator Lance Caine, a man who inspires her deepest desires.

__LOVE LOST, LOVE FOUND
 by Viveca Carlysle   1-58314-171-5 $5.99US/$7.99CAN
Nia Sebastian puts all of her energy into her career. Then Brett Faulkner walks back into her world. Five years ago, their conflicting ambitions drove them apart. That breakup, plus a bad marriage, left Nia determined to steer clear of relationships. But time seems to have mellowed Brett into a man who could easily steal her heart and derail her life . . . again.

Call toll free **1-888-345-BOOK** to order by phone or use this coupon to order by mail. ALL BOOKS AVAILABLE DECEMBER 1, 2001.

Name_____

Address_____

City_____ State_____ Zip_____

Please send me the books that I checked above.

I am enclosing	$_____
Plus postage and handling*	$_____
Sales tax (in NY, TN, and DC)	$_____
Total amount enclosed	$_____

*Add $2.50 for the first book and $.50 for each additional book. Send check or money order (no cash or CODs) to: **Arabesque Romances, Dept. C.O., 850 Third Avenue 16th Floor, New York, NY 10022**
Prices and numbers subject to change without notice. Valid only in the U.S. All orders subject to availability. NO ADVANCE ORDERS.
Visit our website at **www.arabesquebooks.com.**

More Sizzling Romance from *Jacquelin Thomas*

More Arabesque Romances by
Monica Jackson

More Sizzling Romance from
Candice Poarch